STONE FISH

STONE FISH
•
Olivia Ferrell

AVALON BOOKS
NEW YORK

Published by Thomas Bouregy & Co., Inc.
160 Madison Avenue, New York, NY 10016

PRINTED IN THE UNITED STATES OF AMERICA
ON ACID-FREE PAPER
BY HADDON CRAFTSMEN, BLOOMSBURG, PENNSYLVANIA

STONE FISH

Chapter One

The wind was like sandpaper on my skin and the sun was merciless. Gripping the window post as the jeep lurched across a cut in the sand, I squinted at the sky, hoping for sign of the rain that had been promised. We'd been driving for hours, the three of us, and the border was almost within sight. It was then I heard the intermittent drone in the distance.

"Faster—faster—"

The buzzing sound grew louder, more persistent. The dream melted away like fog, just as it had before—

Buzzing. The sound was grating in its regularity. The phone. I tried to tell myself it would go away, but it didn't. Whoever was calling was stubborn. Keeping my eyes tightly closed, I fumbled for the receiver and finally managed to get the right end of it to my ear.

"Hummm."

"Margaret?"

Only one person ever called me Margaret. I squinted one eye at the clock. The green number three mocked me.

"I'm hanging up, Gary."

"I—we—need your help."

"Goodbye, Gary."

"It's about Susan!"

1

There was something in his voice—

"Susan?" Exhaustion made the mental wheels move slowly. I was so tired my bones ached. "I thought she was in college . . . somewhere."

"She—she's dead."

Shock washed over me like a flood of cold water. Pushing away the pillow, I rolled over and sat up, pulling the covers with me.

"What happened?" My voice was rusty, like half the desert still coated my throat.

"The police say suicide. It happened last night."

Pushing tangles of hair from my face, I tried to absorb what he was saying. Suicide and Susan didn't match up. Of course, it had been a long time since I'd seen her.

"Suicide?" That didn't sound right. "How? Why?"

"No obvious injuries. No weapons. No one knows. They're doing an autopsy. We won't know anything until—"

"I don't know what to say. I'm so sorry. If there's anything—"

"There is. The authorities in that hick town aren't telling us anything. You know people. People who can help us find out what happened."

Though I had long ago told myself I had put away any grievance against Gary, automatic resentment welled up inside at his tone. That's the way it always with the Bradys; everything reduced to who you knew and what they could do for you.

"Where did it happen?"

"A little town outside Fayetteville, Arkansas. She was a first semester sophomore at the university there."

"I don't know anyone in Arkansas."

"Nobody does. But you know who to call. Someone who knows someone. Nearly every time we went out you ran into somebody from some place no one ever heard of."

"Gary—"

"Look, all I'm asking for is a little help in finding out

what happened to my sister. Is that too much? I thought you cared about her."

Obviously he wasn't above a little emotional blackmail, and it worked. I drew a long, deep breath and released it slowly, trying not to let him make me angry.

Strangely, from somewhere behind doors long ago locked and bolted, a memory floated up. A memory that stubbornly attached itself to the present. A memory of hope that had been smothered by expectations too heavy for any new marriage already overburdened. A memory that stubbornly reminded me there was still some garbage stuck in the corners of my past that was long overdue for a digging out and throwing away. I felt defeated. I wasn't ready for this, but then, would I ever be? Besides, I owed this to Susan, if not to myself.

"Okay. Let me see what I can do. I'll call you tomorrow— today. Give me your number."

"I'm at LAX. I'll be in New York in a few hours. Thanks, Margaret. This means a lot to me."

After Gary hung up, I relaxed back against the pillows, his news racing around in my mind, bumping into questions that had no answers. Tears stung my eyes as I remembered Susan Brady. Young, happy, untroubled Susan. Dead. Why? The girl I'd known wouldn't have considered suicide, no matter what the police thought. But that left murder, which was just as absurd.

Susan had been a quiet, unassuming teenager, a member of the literary club, and an honors student who would certainly have had her choice of scholarships. Her life was just getting started and now she was dead. What could have happened?

Dawn had pinked the sky before I fell asleep again, but I was wide awake only a few hours later. While sipping at a cup of instant coffee that had little more effect than to wash a bad taste out of my mouth, I pulled on jeans and an oxford shirt and then stuffed my feet into low-top boots.

With a last glance around the loft to which I'd come home to only a few hours before, I grabbed my camera bag and ran down the stairs to the street. It had snowed again during the night and traffic had melted it enough to make the slush almost curb deep. I hunched my shoulders deeper in my parka. Cold November days made me long again for southern California; sometimes, but not often. When I'd left the west coast I'd left a lot behind, stuff that I didn't want to drag with me to a new life.

The problem was that Gary was sure to bring some of the past with him, and I wasn't sure how I was going to deal with that.

My first stop was the newspaper stand on the next block. There was nothing in the Times about Susan, but I hadn't expected there to be. The suspicious death of a college girl in a small Arkansas town wouldn't warrant mention in a New York paper. Not unless it was connected to a larger event.

But then, perhaps it was. I'd been kicking around a story idea for a while—ruminating, I called it—keeping an idea on a back burner to simmer until it boiled down to nothing or jelled into a story. Perhaps now there was something to work on. It at least gave me something to start digging with.

Flagging a cab, I gave the cabby the address for Front Page Magazine.

"Ain't you Maggie Rome?"

"Yes."

"You been over there at the war?"

"Yes. Just got back yesterday."

He glanced at me in his rearview mirror. "Just like the Gulf War, 'cept we're whippin' butt this time. 'Course, guess we did then too. Just quit too early." He shook his head.

I didn't need to respond. He entertained himself. I hadn't been in the Gulf ten years earlier, but this time I'd heard all the whines and whumps of the Tomahawk and Skud missiles, as Dan Rather had so poetically described the sounds of battle. My adrenaline had never been higher, and I'd never taken better photos; I'd also never wanted to leave any place more. Racing across the desert where there were no landmarks, holding to the jeep with one hand, to my camera with the other, my shirt wet and plastered to me under a flack jacket, my skin caked with sand dust, my lips so dry they were splitting no matter how much water I tried to remember to drink, was not an experience I wanted to repeat.

"Tough, huh?"

"Pretty tough."

"How long you worked for Front Page?"

"Five years."

"Like it?"

"I can't imagine doing anything else."

Though since coming back I'd begun to wonder if I wanted this nomadic existence for the rest of my life. But then, I didn't know anything else and I liked seeing the result of my hard work as a Front Page exclusive. I guess one asks a lot of questions when the possibility of dying is more real than you thought possible at thirty years old.

"Guess you travel a lot."

"Almost all the time."

"Married?"

"Nope."

"Too bad. Kids are great."

I smiled. In his mind, marriage meant kids. In mine, it meant—what? I didn't know. I hadn't thought about it before. Maybe I'd stopped thinking about it since the divorce.

Front Page had been my salvation. It had given my life purpose and meaning and I gave it everything inside me in return. And it had paid off. Even cabbies knew me by sight. It signified a certain kind of 'success', but I wasn't sure how I felt about that part of it. Success, for me, was a good story, not recognition on the street.

Front Page offices occupy a building that managed to meet the criteria laid down by the conservative publisher as well as the upscale image needed for a magazine covering current news events. The bottom three floors of the granite building housed the working staff and middle management.

The other three floors were the corporate offices, including the legal staff.

When I'd been offered the job with the fledgling news magazine it had been a dream come true. Ever since I could remember I'd wanted to be a journalist. I'd gotten my first taste of writing and photography on the staff of the school newspaper. College had only sharpened my appetite for needing to know the how and why of things.

During my four years at UC, I'd worked as a gofer on the staff of a small newspaper in southern California. I'd been lucky enough to have an editor who was willing to teach me, and I'd soaked up everything like a thirsty sponge. He'd taught me to use my camera as a third eye, an extension of my arm and mind. I'd learned so well that I looked at everything as the camera would see it. I had learned the peculiar talent of seeing everything in a square, the extraneous bleeding out to nothing.

It was there, too, that I'd begun to develop an intuition for a different angle on a story and be able to support it with the stark photos that had now become my trademark.

By the end of the year my confidence had taken great strides. I was soon handling all the photography and writing some feature stories. Two years later, with his blessing, I moved to a larger paper.

Then I'd met Gary.

Usually I did not think about my marriage and what had happened, but Gary's call, combined with my introspective mood the last few days, had resurrected it all again.

We'd met when I covered a break-in at his men's clothing store. Someone had smashed the windows and sprayed graffiti on the outside of the building and a whole wall of expensive men's suits. Though the store was in a fashionable area, and none of the other stores had been affected, the police had to assume it was a random gang incident. Gary had been furious and frustrated.

I'd been sent to shoot photos and get a story for the county paper. He was uncooperative at first, but then, after I bought him a cup of coffee and listened to his angry tirades, he cooled off and gave me the information I needed. Before the afternoon was over, he asked for a date and I accepted.

Soon we were dating seriously. By the end of two months we knew we were in love. And now, looking back, perhaps we were—at least as 'in love' as we could understand at the time. I don't know what Gary thought, but I was in for the long haul.

A psychologist would have had a field day with that one. *Patient is a product of a* conventional *dysfunctional family. Patient appears set on overcompensating for lack of consistency by trying too hard to succeed at relationships.*

I stared out the window at the grayness. The clouds still hung low, threatening more snow. Pedestrians hurried along the sidewalk, their heads bent against a brisk, cold wind. Passing cars threw gray slush against the window of the cab. Gray and cold. How appropriate for the day I'd see Gary for the first time since the divorce.

I had looked forward to marriage with a kind of Cinderella complex, I suppose. Prince Charming and all that. Far too soon the glass slipper had cracked.

He complained that we didn't have enough time together because I worked at night most of the time and was on call twenty-four hours a day. I thought his grousing every time I left the apartment, or called to say I was late, was a sign that we were 'in love', and I liked his possessiveness.

It wasn't until much later that I realized the only attraction between us had been our differences. He was conservative, I was spontaneously liberal. He was suits and ties, I was jeans and t-shirts. But our only serious arguments had been over my erratic work schedule.

Using all the usual cliché reasoning, like being together would be easier once we were married, I'd set a wedding date for February first.

When we'd decided on a wedding date, Gary's parents invited us to dinner, I thought, to discuss plans. I'd been so excited about meeting them. I'd never had a family not a real family, and I hoped to be close with Edward and Pauline Brady, and Susan.

The night we were to meet, I'd been sent to San Diego at the last minute to cover a story and was running late, as usual. I'd called Gary from a pay phone halfway between San Diego and Los Angeles to tell him I'd meet him at his parent's home. He wasn't happy but finally agreed.

I'd arrived at the Bradys' forty-five minutes late, still dressed in my work clothes, no makeup, and my hair pulled back in a sloppy ponytail. I had hoped to have a few minutes to wash up before meeting his parents.

When Gary opened the door I began to apologize, but stopped when I saw all the people in the room behind him. Until that moment I hadn't realized that the Bradys entertained with a formal dinner party every Friday night.

I stood there in that large foyer, one nearly as large as my entire apartment, in my rumpled jeans and dusty boots, my canvas camera bag over my shoulder, and stared at the dark suits and long dresses of the other guests like a gardener at a coronation.

It was months later before I realized that that instant had been an omen of sorts. In any event, it had set the pattern for my relationship with the senior Bradys.

Edward and Pauline hadn't been able to cover their dismay at my rumpled appearance. They'd introduced me carefully to the other guests, apologetically explaining the reason for my attire. Only my own talent for assuming a certain persona when necessary had filled the awkward moments. It was all I could do to keep from running from the house, but I'd told myself that the Bradys' disapproval didn't really mean anything, not if Gary loved me.

Later, hindsight being twenty-twenty; I realized the marriage had been a mistake from the first. From the moment the engagement was announced, the senior Bradys assumed they would plan everything, including the wedding, the honeymoon, and our future.

My parents were more than happy to agree. Money was tight, as usual, and I'd refused to bend to their desire to have an 'at home' wedding in Missouri. I didn't know anyone there any more; besides, I couldn't take the time off work to fly back and plan everything. My parents came to the wedding on plane tickets I bought and were duly impressed by the Bradys and everything they represented—especially mother. I flew home a month later to attend daddy's funeral. I hadn't been back since.

We'd been married two months when Edward and Pauline began to ask when I planned to resign my job at the paper. When I blurted out that I wasn't about to, their calm facade slipped a bit. Until then, Gary had been fairly tolerant of my work schedule, but that tolerance began to fade quickly.

Our differences grew more obvious, and a great deal less interesting—formal dining vs. impromptu spaghetti and wine, my being on-call vs. his nine-to-five job. To give myself credit, I tried to be flexible but somehow things just kept getting more and more complicated.

It had taken me two years to realize I was only being a coward by trying to cope. By then all efforts to work things out between us were strained beyond recall and the decision to divorce had been a relief, at least for me.

I still thought it was the best decision I'd ever made. Mother, of course, still thinks I somehow lost my mind. She frequently reminds me of it via phone calls and melancholy letters. It is more a case of what 'should be' rather than 'what was'. In any event, mother is faithful to her mission to make me believe I made the biggest mistake of my life by divorcing Gary.

"Here it is."

After paying the cabbie I dashed up the cement steps, waving to Fred, the doorman, who tipped his hat in a courtesy that was peculiar to his old world nature.

I picked up two weeks worth of phone messages at the reception desk and threaded my way through the reporter's bull pen toward my office. When I stopped at the crudely made CONDEMNED sign tacked to the door, cat calls and whoops made my return ceremony complete.

I tossed the sign into a waste basket that was empty only because the cleaning staff persevered and flicked on the overhead light.

"Welcome home," I greeted the room that was crammed full of my working life and kicked the door shut.

In the center of my desk was yet another official looking note from the building's cleaning service, to the effect that they could not possibly clean the office in the state it was in. I wadded the note and it joined the condemned sign in the wastebasket.

I glanced around the crowded space. In my absence, the 'ambiance' of my office had deteriorated even more. Shelves overflowed with reference books, held semi-upright by awards or plaques of commendations I hadn't found time to hang. Stacks of files covered every available space in a chaotic organization that had probably instigated the condemned sign and others like it. It might look like chaos, but I knew exactly where everything was. As soon as I put something in a file drawer it was lost forever.

Dumping my camera bag in a corner, I reached for the phone and punched out a familiar number.

"Evans."

"Charlie, it's Maggie."

I pictured the slightly balding, fortyish detective leaning back in his chair, tie loosened, balancing a cup of coffee on his knee. All the medical reports in the world couldn't convince Charlie that twenty cups of coffee a day weren't necessary to 'keep his motor running'.

Charlie Evans had been my contact in the police department since we'd worked a homicide together three years earlier. His attitude toward reporters then, especially female reporters, had been barely tolerant.

But when he found I knew my business, kept out of the homicide team's way and did my homework, he at least talked to me. When one of my photos had picked up an interesting piece of evidence which I'd carried directly to him, our pact of friendship had been sealed.

"Hey, Maggie. Thought you weren't due back until next week."

"Had to get out now or stay, and I had my story."

I had been lucky in getting an interview with the leader of a small resistance group. In fact, Ben was going to be very happy with what I'd come back with.

"I'm doing a little snooping around, Charlie."

"What's up?"

"Have you got anything on a suspicious death in Arkansas yesterday?"

"The only thing I know about Arkansas is what I see on the news."

"Come on, Charlie. A college student. Susan Brady. Suspected homicide." At least it was in my mind.

"I'll see what I can find out."

"Thanks. I'm at the office."

He called back fifteen minutes later.

"Not much on the Brady kid."

"Give me what you've got."

I reached for a legal pad and dumped the stack of phone messages.

"Armen, a small town outside of Fayetteville. University of Arkansas college student found near death in her apartment. A couple of girls who lived in the building found her and called an ambulance. She died a short time after reaching the hospital. That the one?"

Hearing the words in a dispassionate voice made Susan seem such a nonperson.

"Uh, any possibility of it being another of that string of co-ed murders on college campuses in the last two years?"

"Not that I can see. Not the same MO. This one looks like a clean suicide."

"What makes you say that?"

"Poison. That's a woman's weapon."

Poison? I traced a large P on the pad with my pen as my mind raced.

"What kind?"

"No word yet. Autopsy's scheduled."

"Let me know if something else turns up, will you?"

"What's your connection?"

"Just something I'm looking into."

"Uh-huh, keeping secrets. Well, I know a guy down there. Used to work with him but he went to the sticks after a shooting. Good cop. Maybe he would know something."

"His name?"

"Neal Conrad. He's the sheriff or something down there."

Neal Conrad. The name didn't ring a bell so he'd been on the force before my time. Probably went to the woods to retire in the sheriff's office of a nowhere town where nothing happened . . . until now. Made me wonder what kind of investigation he'd conduct. I just hoped he hadn't mucked around in it so much there was nothing left to look at.

"Thanks, Charlie."

"Sure thing. Keep in touch."

My hand was still on the receiver when Ben Wood shoved the door open with his foot.

"Thought you'd take today off."

He handed me a cup of coffee which I accepted with gratitude. My first dose of caffeine had already worn off and the rigors of the last few weeks were catching up with me.

Ben shifted a stack of files from a dusty upholstered chair to the floor before sitting down.

"When are you going to clean up this place? An untidy desk, an untidy story."

"Show me a reporter with a tidy desk and I'll show you a boring reporter."

With our standard opening volley past, I lifted my cup in a salute of thanks and sipped it carefully before answering Ben's original question. The coffee machine didn't make the best coffee, but it was guaranteed to be boiling hot. More than once I'd suffered through the day with a scorched tongue.

"What are you doing here?"

"There's a couple of things I want to check into."

"New story?"

"One we discussed a few months ago. The co–ed murders."

Ben rescued a stack of snapshots in peril of falling from the corner of my desk. "Thought that was old news." He shook his head as he flipped through the photos. "In spite of everything you've tried to teach her, Mrs. P still can't get the heads and arms in her pictures."

"At least those are in focus."

I had met Mrs. Pine the day I moved into the loft. The plump, white haired lady had intercepted me at the front door of the apartment building, clucking over the state of my plants and suggesting remedies for their sad condition. Within minutes she'd snipped off half the yellowing leaves, leaving them practically bare. I was ready to pitch them out, but she'd assured me they'd come back healthy.

Certain she was wrong, I was resigned to buying new ones to kill, but they'd miraculously recovered. Of course, her persistence in reminding me to water them regularly, and doing it herself in my absence, had been a contributing factor. The woman was an Irish grandmother to the tenants in the building and immediately took me under her ample wing to issue reprimands and cajoling and sympathetic phrases in the same robust tone.

Anyway, after I'd dragged in the few pieces of furniture I'd owned, and after I'd trudged up the two flights of stairs with all my darkroom equipment, Mrs. P had offered a welcome cup of coffee and cake.

In short time I discovered the sprightly eighty-year-old kept tabs on everyone's comings and goings. In self-defense, I hired Mrs. P to come in weekly to dust, accept dry cleaning, water plants, and pick up mail while I was away on assignments.

Unfortunately, Mrs. P's hobby was photography, but while she wielded a dust cloth with exceptional skill, she was absolutely dangerous with a camera in her hands.

Our friendship had grown more when she'd showed me her scrapbooks, each filled with hundreds of pictures of her husband, long deceased, her four children and their spouses and her grandchildren, pictures of people with heads cut off, or half bodies, or faces out of focus. I'd given her numerous tips on proper focus and framing since then, but she couldn't seem to grasp the idea of handling a camera.

Ben tossed the photos back on my desk.

"Back to your story. I thought we'd decided the co-ed murders weren't connected."

"I've got something new and I'd like to spend a few days checking it out."

"Oh? What?" Ben sipped his coffee, a skeptical look on his face.

I pushed back in my chair and propped my feet on the edge of the desk while balancing my coffee on my belt buckle.

"I, uh, got a call early this morning."

"An informant?"

"Not exactly."

The phone rang and I sent Ben a look of apology as I picked up the receiver. Charlie had a few more things, but not much, on Susan. I hung up the phone and finished my notes before picking up my coffee cup again and looking at Ben.

"What's going on?"

"I, um, that call I got this morning."

"Um hum," Ben prompted.

"It was from Gary."

His left eyebrow shot up in surprise.

"Oh? What did he want?"

"I probably never mentioned that he had a sister."

"No, you didn't."

I turned the Styrofoam cup round and round between my hands, trying to find a way to tell Ben the story without sounding totally maudlin.

"Susan was in junior high school when Gary and I married. She was quiet, sweet, gentle. A typical enough teenager, I suppose, though she didn't talk on the phone as much as I had. She always reminded me of Snow White, or Cinderella. A little unreal, always looking for her prince. She was very special."

Tears stung my eyes and I focused on the coffee cup to fight them.

"What happened?"

"She's dead."

"I'm sorry."

There was a long moment of silence. Ben was a sensitive man, and our relationship went far beyond managing editor and journalist. He was the man who made the rules, but after hours he'd often been my father figure, my sounding board. I appreciated his objectivity, but even more I appreciated his honesty and support for my sometimes wild ideas.

More than once he'd countered my stubbornness with wisdom I didn't want to recognize. And more often than that he'd listened to my rantings and ravings about the injustices of the world. When I let myself get too emotional over what I'd experienced, he'd be the one to tell me that when the emotion was gone, I would be dead as a reporter.

With his guidance I'd learned to use my emotion, pouring it out on paper, then coming back and sorting out the waste to create the kinds of stories that had won me the big awards.

Yes, I had some talent. But even more than that I had a bulldog tenacity that made me dig until I had all the answers. And I had an editor who would let me dig until I got ridiculous about it. As a result, we had a very special relationship that worked well for us both.

Suddenly I realized I'd been staring at my cup for several minutes.

"Gary wants me to find out what happened to her."

"And what did happen to her?"

"The authorities don't know for certain. Poison, they think, which spells suicide for them. But the Susan I knew wouldn't do that. But neither would she have had any enemies."

"What did Charlie have to say?"

"Not much. A college student found dead in 'Ar-kan-saw' means nothing to New York cops. It doesn't matter that she was young and vital and had so much promise—"

I scooted down in the chair and stared at the stained ceiling, almost wishing I was slogging around Europe somewhere.

"There's just so many, Maggie."

I drew a deep breath. "I know. It's just that . . . I knew this one. And I knew what potential she had. How special she was. I know she wouldn't have killed herself."

I was going to ask for a big favor, and he would probably turn me down, but I had to do it.

"I want to go to Arkansas, Ben. I have to know what happened to Susan."

"I know she was your ex-sister-in-law, but this isn't your problem now."

"Gary asked me to help."

"Let the authorities do their job, Mag."

"I will, and they'll have an official opinion, but they won't give me the answers I need."

"Why do you have to do it?"

I mulled that over for a minute.

"For me, Ben. I feel—I feel like I abandoned her."

His eyebrows jumped halfway up his forehead. "You're feeling guilty?"

"Yeah, in a sense. But more than that, I just can't let her be dead without a reason. Not just for Gary, or his family, but for me. And I need the backing that working on a story can give me."

"I can't authorize it."

I sat up. "What if I worked at it from the angle of the coed murders, eight over the past two years."

"That's a pretty long reach."

"There could be a connection."

"You're personally involved. It's not good journalism."

"Ben—"

"You're going whether I okay it or not, aren't you?"

"I've got some time due."

Ben pinched his lower lip between his thumb and forefinger as he considered the alternatives. Ben always considered all the options.

"Okay. Five days. Then I want you back on the Bridger indictment."

Relief flooded through me. "Thanks, Ben."

"You check in every day."

"I will, I promise."

"Fat chance," he said, getting to his feet. "By the way, Connie's been wanting to see you."

Oh, great. "I don't have time for overzealous accountants."

Ben smiled knowingly. Constantine, or 'Connie,' as everyone called him would be lurking around every corner for me once he knew I was in the building. Our confrontations were becoming historic.

"Be careful."

Chapter Two

During the next few hours I went through the file into which I'd stuffed information on the college campus murders, including the individual assaults and the front-page headlines in Florida. But there wasn't enough there to begin a serious investigation. I'd just started dialing the research department when the door pushed open with a brief knock.

"Gary."

The knot of tension in my stomach curled tighter. Suddenly I was more acutely aware of the clutter of my office and the dust motes floating in the air.

Gary looked around the small room uncertainly. "How can you work in here?"

The comment was so typical I laughed, and the knot of tension uncurled a little.

"I rarely do. This is where I camp out between assignments. Sit down."

At least the chair Ben had occupied earlier was still empty.

Gary sat down gingerly, carefully straightening the creases in his trousers. The irritation felt good; it kept my feet on the floor.

He'd changed little—still tanned, his blond hair sun-streaked, his smile still as automatically wide and toothy as if he posed for a photo. The carefully maintained look of aristocratic arrogance bred into him was securely in place. Not even sorrow could budge it.

"Coffee?"

"Um, no. I had a dozen cups on the plane. What have you found out?"

"Very little, so far. There seem to be few clues."

"They've got to know something."

He sat forward in the chair, resting elbows on knees, his hands clasped. His red eyes made it obvious he'd been up all night, but I saw, too, that he was freshly shaved.

"It's only been twenty-four hours. The sheriff's waiting for the autopsy."

He paced to the window and stared out, a muscle in his jaw jumping with tension.

"Pull some strings, Margaret. Find out what happened."

"Gary, this isn't a situation where I can demand anything. The sheriff—"

"To hell with the sheriff. I'm on a flight to Fayetteville," he glanced at his watch, "in four hours. I'll ask my own questions."

I drew a long breath of resignation. "I'm on that same flight."

He spun around. "You're going to Arkansas?"

I shrugged. "I thought I'd work on an angle for another story."

"Perfect! Between us we'll find out what happened to Susan. I'll make hotel reservations."

A little alarm rang in my mind. "Gary, I work alone. And I'll make my own reservations. Besides, won't you be staying with your parents?"

His tilted slightly to the right; he looked almost pleased. "You're afraid to be with me."

The shift caught me by surprise. Was he right? Was my reluctance to spend any time with him because I didn't want

to be reminded of my failures? No. I'd faced all that. In any event, it wasn't something I wanted to dig into now.

"Don't get in my way."

"I'll see you at the airport."

After Gary left, I phoned Mrs. P to tell her I'd be gone for a few days.

"But you've just got home. You're not taking care a–yerself."

The Irish lilt softened the chastisement.

"I'm fine. I'll see you when I get back."

"You've got another shut-off notice on your utilities, child. You can't leave before writing them a check."

I groaned aloud. I hated the tedious details of paying bills, keeping records. To get it out of the way I paid everything on the first of the month, no matter when the bills were due. The utility company didn't particularly like my schedule and frequently threatened to retaliate.

"I'll do it before I leave."

Before leaving the office, I phoned research to request every scrap of information they could find on the co–ed murders, telling them I'd phone later with an address so the info could be sent to me. After dropping by the apartment to pack, and write the utility company a check, I caught a cab to the airport.

Gary was waiting at the ticket counter, but I was relieved to discover that, true to form, he was traveling first class. I was not. As soon as the plane was in the air I feigned sleep, hoping to dissuade Gary from coming back. While I felt an obligation, to Susan, to do what I could to find out what had happened to her, I wasn't ready to talk to him—at least not about anything but Susan.

But, as the plane settled into flight, I gave up trying to push aside the memories that seeing him had dredged up.

When I'd met Gary, his father, Dr. Edward James Brady, had been a prominent west coast plastic surgeon. A very busy man, both with his practice and himself, Dr. Brady spent long hours at the hospital and his office. Pauline was the pampered wife whose sole responsibility was to take care of her family and keep their social obligations current.

They were a family who enjoyed their wealth and used its influence as their due. I'd recognized right away that Edward Brady was the autocratic patriarch of the household. Pauline never questioned her husband's decisions, something I couldn't understand even in my semi pre-rebel days.

But I decided that how the senior Bradys ran their lives wasn't my business, except where Gary was concerned. I soon discovered how wrong I was. That, of course, was another subject and one still too tender to explore. There were, I had to admit, a number of unresolved things in my life. Most of them related to my marriage with Gary.

The Bradys had always been anomalous to me. Perhaps that was why when I heard they had moved to Arkansas I hadn't questioned it. It didn't have anything to do with me. But now I had to wonder about a decision that was so out of character.

Refusing the stewardess' offer of a refreshment, I scrunched down, balancing the heel of my boot against the edge of the seat, and stared at the layer of clouds just outside my window. The thing about the Bradys' move still bothered me. Retirement? Dr. Brady was in his mid-fifties. He'd lived for his practice. I couldn't imagine him giving it up so early.

Besides, what attraction was there in a rural community in Arkansas for the prominent family? My mother thrived on the intricacies of small town life. The koffee klatches, morning gossip, shopping, constant speculation about others' private lives, though the word 'sex' never crossed her lips, and 'affair' was only whispered. Everyone was 'god-fearin' folk, no matter what they did behind closed doors, or with whom.

My speculations were interrupted by the fasten seat belts sign. When the plane landed, I waited until the cabin was nearly empty before retrieving my camera bag from the overhead compartment and exiting.

The weather in Arkansas was little different from what we'd left in New York. Piles of dirty snow marked the ends of the runway. The wind was bitter, stinging my face and snatching my breath momentarily when I stepped outside.

The minute I exited the plane, Gary was there.

"I'll get our bags," Gary said. "You get a cab, or something."

He looked as if he expected a horse and buggy to appear to transport us to a boarding house.

I handed him my claim tickets and went to pick up the rental car I'd arranged for before leaving New York. He was waiting at the curb with our bags when I drove up.

"What's this?"

"I like my own transportation. Armen has no facilities, so the clerk suggested a motel not far from here."

"I hope there's valet service. My suits will need pressing."

My foot pressed the accelerator and I whipped the economy sedan from the curb with a screech of rubber, skidding slightly in the slush. Childish, yes, but I felt better.

"Margaret, slow down. The police in this kick town are probably just waiting for tourists."

"But we aren't tourists, are we?" I could feel his irritation with me and decided to enjoy it a bit. It was definitely going to be a long week.

"That's right. You grew up around here somewhere, didn't you?"

"No." I forced my jaw to relax. "I'm from Missouri."

"Well, that's not far. I saw it on the map."

"You should have noticed then that Mountain Grove, Missouri, and Fayetteville, Arkansas, are some distance apart."

"Touchy. Touchy." He was silent for about half a minute. "Where is this Armen? Couldn't find it on the map."

"About twenty miles, the clerk said. A kind of crossroads community. Haven't you visited your folks since they moved?"

"No."

The way he said it made me almost believe he regretted it.

The Holiday Motel sat in white stucco splendor on a main street with old oak trees, now bare, lining the driveway. An effort had been made to create an old southern ambiance in the entry, but it managed to only look like the foyer of the movie theaters I remembered from my childhood. Palms were prominent in every available corner and maple antique furniture crouched solidly on large area rugs. The wood floor boards that creaked with every step were stained dark, but traffic had lightened them over the years.

The green plastic name tag pinned to the lapel of the gaunt man behind the counter had S. Patrick carved in white letters. He wore a suit uncomfortably. I envisioned him driving home in an old pick-up with a gun rack mounted in the back window.

"What can I do for you?"

"Two rooms, please." After fishing out my credit card, I dropped my camera bag at my feet.

"Adjoining." Gary interjected.

The manager peered at us over his glasses and pushed the registration book across the counter.

"None ajoinin'. But I got two right next door. Continental breakfast at eight—juice, coffee and rolls." He glanced at the home address I had written after my name. "This is a quiet place. Folks usually settle down by ten."

"No problem." I managed to keep a straight face. S. Patrick reminded me of Jimmy Stewart in *Mr. Smith Goes To Washington.*

When he read Gary's address his eyebrows spiked up over his glasses.

"Don't get too many California folks here. Don't get many New York ones either."

"I'm with Front Page magazine, here to do some research."

I handed him my magazine credit card.

"And what story would that be?"

"Just some research on midwest colleges and why students from the coast choose them."

Mr. Patrick nodded sagely. "Can't say many of 'um come in here." He handed me a room key and another to Gary. "Up the stairs and on the right, halfway down the hall. The Magnolia opens at 10:30 and closes at 9. The menu might not be what you're used to, but the food's good. Then there's the Gold Road out on the highway. Has your seafood and steaks. They tell me it's good. That bunch outside 'a town runs it."

"What group is that?"

"The Glorious Church. They got some kind of school out there."

My curiosity was captured. "I don't think I've ever heard of them."

"Surprised you didn't see some of the students at the airport. I saw the airline tags on your luggage."

"Some young men dressed in baggy khaki, close cropped hair?"

"Yep. Always two by two, like on the ark. 'Cept men stick with men and women with women."

"What are they doing at the airport?"

"Handing out tracts, asking for contributions to the cause. That television program they got goes all across the country and, from what I hear, they make a lot 'a money. Wouldn't know it from the looks of the place though. Looks like an old army barracks. Real strange folk," he repeated. "But, they don't cause no trouble."

Causing no trouble seemed to be one of Mr. Patrick's main concerns.

"Um, thanks."

I picked up my suitcase and started for the stairs, my camera bag over my shoulder. Gary followed, carrying his two bags and a carry-on, complaining about the decor as we climbed the stairs. The Holiday was sure to lack his high standards for comfort.

"I'll dump my stuff and be over in a minute," he said as we exited the stairwell.

I only nodded, knowing Gary would have to hang all his suits in the closet, put his underwear in a drawer, and set out his shaving gear first.

The room was nice, if you ignored the jungle print of the drapes and matching bedspread and the dull brown of the carpet. I'd been in a hundred that were much worse. By now I hardly noticed them except to be grateful when the water in the shower was hot.

Flipping open the suitcase, I dialed Front Page on my cell phone. After giving the research department the hotel address from a notepad on the small desk, I made a second call to Charlie.

"Anything new on the Brady death?"

"Autopsy incomplete, but prelim confirms poisoning. A search of the apartment didn't turn up a glass, or any trace of the poison. They want to say suicide, but the case isn't closed yet. Doesn't seem logical she'd drink the stuff then wash her glass and put it away."

I wasn't so sure about that. If Susan was anything like Pauline she would have.

"So, for right now it's a possible homicide with no clues and no suspects." A part of me wanted to hear that someone had killed Susan. I didn't want to believe she'd killed herself. Nothing, in my opinion, could ever be that bad.

"Looks like it."

"I don't suppose there's any way she could have gotten poison accidentally. Pesticide or something?"

"Not likely."

"Okay. Thanks, Charlie. Is there anyone you can call who can smooth the way for me down here? I'll want to talk to the officer in charge of the investigation. Maybe that one you used to know."

"I'll see if I can track down Neal."

"Thanks, Charlie. I owe you."

"I'll add it to your tab. Keep in touch."

Just as I was ending the call, Gary knocked at the door and I swung it open automatically. I had to smile. He was impeccably dressed in slacks with a razor sharp crease, a white broadcloth shirt and a blue v-neck sweater. As he stepped inside, his critical gaze swept over my worn jeans and untucked oxford shirt with the sleeves rolled back, ending at my stocking feet.

"I thought perhaps you'd change."

"I'm comfortable. I just called New York. The autopsy prelims are in."

He looked more apprehensive than concerned, but perhaps I was trying too hard to read him. After all, it had been five years since we'd been close enough to know what the other was thinking.

"And?"

"Can you think of any reason Susan would have come into contact with poison?"

"No." Gary frowned thoughtfully. "How could such a thing happen?"

"The question is, why would she drink poison?"

Gary paced the room. "Suicide." He tested the word again. "Suicide." He released a long breath. "Maybe being here is a mistake."

"You want to drop it?"

"Perhaps we should."

I studied him thoughtfully. "Why wasn't Susan living at home?"

He shrugged. "Independence, I suppose. When she entered college in California she lived in the dorm, over Mom and Dad's protest. They wanted her to stay at home."

"When did she transfer to the university here?"

"Last year. She dropped out for six months when they moved here, then started again about a year ago."

"What was her major?"

"I don't know."

That surprised me. "You don't know?"

"We weren't close. Just exchanged notes occasionally, spoke on the phone every two or three months." He shrugged. "She was hard to talk to. You know how much age difference there was between us. And, after we divorced—" He shrugged again, "there was some distance between us. She was very attached to you."

"I'm sorry."

"Well, then they moved here."

He looked as if that was enough explanation of why he had lost contact with his family. Perhaps that was why he was so intent on finding out what had happened to his sister now.

"Why did they move?"

"Dad decided to retire. Relax. Learn to fish." He stared out the window, but I doubted he was really seeing anything. "I haven't even seen Mom and Dad since they moved." He turned around. "What happens next?"

"Well, I'm going to get something to eat, then wait for an e-mail from Front Page. They're looking up some information to support my reason for being here."

"Which is?"

"I'm following an angle on coed murders."

"You think Susan—"

"No, I don't. Not really. But there's enough connections to give me a reason for being here. The police and others will be more cooperative if they don't know I have a personal reason for asking questions about Susan."

"I see. Well, I guess we can try The Magnolia Room."

"You try The Magnolia Room. I'm going to do a little exploring."

"Then I'll come with you."

"Absolutely not. I can find out more just by listening. The fewer people who know I'm connected with the family the better. Besides, you won't blend in."

"And you will?"

I looked down at my jeans, blue oxford shirt and boots,

then back at Gary's GQ casual. "Better than you. Besides, S. Patrick down there has probably already spread the word that New York and California have invaded the peaceful town of Fay–ette–ville, Ar–kan–saw. People are going to be cautious about talking to strangers. I can get further by blending in and listening."

"I can be discreet."

I laughed. "Your idea of discreet is demanding that the cook be grilled for incompetence when your steak is over-done . . . while remaining seated at your table."

"You're letting your personal feelings—"

"Save it, Gary." I slipped the strap of my camera bag over my shoulder. "I'll be back later. See if you can stay out of trouble while I'm gone."

I ignored the angry set to his mouth and walked out, slamming the door just a little harder than necessary. He hated it when I talked to him like a child, and I had to admit I did it on purpose when he had irritated me beyond my brief patience.

After walking off my temper, I found the Parakeet Café a few blocks down the street from the hotel. I stepped inside and a half dozen patrons looked up curiously at the ring of the bell over the door. I glanced around the room as I shrugged off my parka and hung it on one of the line of pegs fastened to the wall near the door.

The large rectangle room was lined with booths, the center populated with well-worn wooden chairs and tables covered with red and white oil cloth.

It was a contrast of colors and styles—black and green floor tile, chrome and red vinyl counter stools, yellowed woodwork and unremarkable wall color, where it was visible around cross stitched adages. Decorating touches were principally silk and straw flowers attached to cane mats, and pictures that must have hung in the same spot since World War II, or before.

I chose one of the dozen or so stools at the counter.

"What can I getcha?"

The woman behind the counter was a bleached blond, her age as indecisive as the cafe decor. Her uniform had survived breakfast and lunch, if the blotches on the apron were any accounting, and the fire engine red polish on her long nails was chipped.

"Coffee. How are your burgers?"

"Grilled. Cheese and bacon extra. Tomata, lettuce an' onion on the side."

She chewed her gum with determination.

"I'll take a cheeseburger and some fries."

"Fresh apple pie?"

"Homemade?"

"Made 'em myself this mornin'."

My mouth watered. "Vanilla ice cream?"

"Ala mode it is. I'm Ida Belle. You're new."

It wasn't a question.

"Umhum." I sipped the hot coffee and let my tongue adjust. It was strong enough to have walked alone. "Staying at The Holiday for a few days."

"Vacation?"

"Working. Maggie Rome. Front Page magazine."

"Here about the girl?"

"What girl?"

I'd honed my approach on countless assignments. It was better to let the information come of its own, when it would.

"That girl they found dead over in Armen. Susan somethin'."

"What happened? Maybe it's something my magazine would want to look into."

"Suicide, they say. Neal Conrad, the county sheriff, eats in here all the time. Not married, you know." She rested one hip against the counter. "Poison he said. Kinda strange, don't you think? I mean, who poisons themself?"

So, Charlie's friend *was* the sheriff here.

"Not something I'd choose. But who knows about college kids."

"Yeah. Got two teenagers myself. Never know what they're gonna do."

Just then the bell over the door jingled again and Ida glanced up with a wide smile. "Neal. We was just talkin' 'bout 'cha."

The uniformed man was definitely not the paunchy retiree I'd expected. Close to forty, maybe thirty-seven, thirty-eight, one could never tell on men who had a solid strength like his. He was big and solid, like a football player, brown hair cut close, pleasantly weathered face. He started toward us with a slow rolling gait, automatically adjusting the holster on his hip as he slid onto a stool next to me, blowing on his cold hands. I could imagine him walking a beat, swinging a night stick, but not sitting behind a desk.

When he glanced at me I noted Sheriff Conrad had the kind of eyes that saw and catalogued everything in a glance, but revealed nothing. In other words, a younger version of Charlie. No wonder they'd kept in touch all this time.

"Well, what more could a man want than to have two handsome ladies talking about him?"

I'd never thought of myself as 'handsome'. As a kid I'd been called 'carrot top'. Fortunately my hair had darkened to a deep red by the time I reached high school; just in time for me to become overly conscious about the freckles that peppered across my nose and cheeks.

"This here's Maggie Rome. Works for Front Page magazine. We was just talkin' about that girl over at the college, poor thing. Maggie thought her magazine might be interested in the story."

A bell rang back in the kitchen and Ida disappeared through a set of swinging doors.

"I've seen your name. You've covered some pretty big stories. What's your interest in Susan Brady?"

His blue-gray eyes were keen and assessing. Perhaps

there was interest there, but I suspected it was more from force of habit than anything else. From my side, I was still shucking preconceptions about this county mountie.

"Just wondering if her death fits in with a string of other murders on college campuses over the past couple of years."

"I hear the guy you came with is named Brady."

Information traveled fast in Fayetteville. "Susan's brother."

"How come you're with him?"

"We . . . knew one another a long time ago. He called to let me know about Susan. Since I was working on this story, I thought I'd check into this myself."

"Umhum. Gonna stick with that story?"

Chalk one up for the sheriff. I circled ketchup on my hamburger and drenched the French fries, nodding when Ida offered a refill on coffee.

"New York cops say you're okay."

"You work fast."

"Sam Patrick fancies himself a keeper of the peace. He gave me a call when he saw Brady's name and that you worked for Front Page. I made a couple of calls. Charlie Evans said to keep an eye on you."

"We go back a long way, like you and him."

"Also said you'd helped him out a couple of times."

"Think there could be a connection?" I bit into the hamburger and signaled my satisfaction with a thumbs-up to Ida. "With the other murders? Have a fry." I shoved the basket toward the sheriff.

After eyeing me speculatively for a long moment, he found the temptation too much.

"Don't know too much about the others, but this one looks like a suicide."

"You're sure?"

The sheriff spoke with the same soft drawl I'd heard in Sam Patrick's voice. The kind that made y'all sound comfortable and inclusive. His, though, evidenced a tone of lazy authority that told me that Neal Conrad was a man at ease with his role as a rural law enforcement officer. Comfortable enough to make me wonder whether he'd originally been from the mid-west, and temporarily transplanted to New York.

Either way, he'd apparently made the transition well. Arkansas, I knew, had enjoyed it's share of front page notoriety because of the criminals who'd chosen the rough terrain to hide out in. And there were the survivalists who had chosen the mountainous and heavily wooded areas to practice their tactics. Keeping the law wasn't an easy job, but Neal Conrad struck me as a man who knew his business. Obviously he'd left New York, and whatever had happened there, far behind.

"No wounds. No weapons. No disturbance. Just like a lot of young folks," he shrugged. "She couldn't cope and took the easy way out."

"Guess I never thought of poison as being 'easy'."

"It's not. But there's no other conclusion."

"The autopsy confirm what kind of poison?"

"Sure did. Just came from there. Strychnine. You know the family?"

"Not lately. I knew Dr. and Mrs. Brady when they lived in California. I don't understand why they moved here to retire."

"Me, neither. But, they keep to themselves. Stay behind the fence at that big ole place they own outside town. Have to talk into a box at the gate if you want in."

Well, that was interesting. The Bradys hadn't been so security conscious when I'd known them. Only pretentious.

"What were they like in California?"

"Very proper." I snagged another french fry. "Very, very proper."

"Humph!" Neal snorted. "You know 'em."

"The coroner's sure about Strychnine?"

"He's good at his job."

"Anything else?"

"Said she wasn't pregnant. Girls said she didn't have a steady boyfriend. Dated around some, but not a lot and not lately."

That interested me. Perhaps a bad relationship, or one the Bradys didn't approve of, had been the reason they'd left California. A little drastic, but they'd been very protective of her.

"Any possibility of accidental poisoning? Isn't Strychnine used in rat poison, that sort of thing? Or was she taking cold tablets or something that could have been tampered with?"

"Didn't find anything like that. Besides, she'd ingested enough to do the job twice."

"Doesn't Strychnine work pretty quickly?"

"Yep. Course, it depends on what she had to eat recently. That kind of thing. But she'd have had to work fast to wash a glass and put it away, considering how much she downed. The girls found her on the floor in the living room."

"You say the apartment wasn't broken into?"

"That's right. If it was murder, she let them in."

"Who found her?"

"For your story?"

"Maybe. Any problem with that?"

He shrugged, making his shirt stretch alarmingly across his big shoulders. "Most of it will be in the papers tomorrow. I'd appreciate you clearing anything you run across with me before you send it to your magazine."

"Sure thing. Who found Susan?"

"Two girls who live in the apartment under hers. Seems they'd all three planned to go to breakfast and when Susan didn't show they went up to get her. Found the door open. They called out, got no answer, went in. They called an ambulance and the dispatcher called me. I was just coming on duty."

"You were the first officer on the scene?"

"Nope. Bill Moore was in a car just half a mile from the place. He got there first."

"You said she was conscious. Did she say anything?"

The sheriff contemplated another french fry for several moments. "She was unconscious when he got there but one of the girls said she kept saying 'I'm sorry. I'm sorry.' Over an' over. No one seems to know what she was sorry for."

I thought about what Susan could have meant by those words. Sorry for something she'd done? Or for something that could have made someone want to kill her.

"Then what happened?"

"Well, the ambulance took her to the hospital. She was convulsing and they tried artificial respiration, but she died just minutes after arrival. There was nothing they could do."

I swallowed the wave of emotion that made me want to cry out, 'why not! why wasn't there anything that could be done!' and concentrated on my questions.

"What did she do the night she died? Who did she see?"

"I checked that. She had a horse at Greenleaf Stables. Went out there that afternoon late, rode a while, then went back to her apartment. Some friends picked her up and they drove into town. Spent time at Jonathan's." He munched another fry.

"Jonathan's?"

"A little bar where the kids hang out here in Fayetteville." I noticed he pronounced it Fayettevul. "After a beer or two they went on to three other campus 'watering holes', looking for friends, playing pool and pinball. Then a bunch of 'em went for pizza and beer. They dropped Susan off at her apartment about 1:30 in the morning."

"No chance the poison could have been in the beer?"

"Pitchers. And the Brady girl wasn't a drinker. I'm told she had only one mug, at the pizza place. She ordered a Coke at the other places. Besides, like I said, it was too big a dose, according to the doc."

"Umhum." It was all pretty pat, few loose ends. Murder was sometimes neat and tidy, but suicides always left things unfinished, even if there was preparation.

"Where's the apartment?"

"On the edge of Armen. That's why I got the case instead of the police. It's in a three-story house somebody cut up twenty years ago. Used to be an estate of some kind. The Brady girl was on the second floor."

"Okay. There was no forced entry. How about sexual assault?"

"Nope. The coroner checked that. She wasn't a virgin, but—" He let the sentence drop with another shrug of his beefy shoulders.

"Did she talk to anyone outside her group of friends that night?"

"Nope. Real quiet girl, I hear. The kids I talked to said she was friendly, well liked," he shrugged, "but they didn't know much about her, other than she was a good student. I talked to everyone in a six block radius of the apartment, had everybody in the house fingerprinted. No unidentified fingerprints in the apartment. Nothing. No one knows anything. In fact, it seems her closest friends didn't even know she had family nearby."

That was strange. Why did Susan feel secrecy was necessary?

"What was she wearing when she was found?"

"One of those Mickey Mouse t-shirt kind of things. Bed wasn't slept in though."

"Isn't that strange? Considering the hour?"

"Not if she didn't go to bed. Looked like she was studying."

"That would make suicide a little impulsive, wouldn't it? Susan wasn't an impulsive girl."

"Wasn't she? Well, whatever. I'm not having much luck in closing this case. I'd like to have found a glass or something, or a motive, to tidy it all up."

"Could I see the apartment?"

"Why?" His face was half covered by the hand holding the thick crockery coffee mug as he sipped at a fresh refill.

"Maybe I could help? I did know her once."

"The case is still open. Don't need reporters poking around."

How far could I push him? "Sometimes we can find out things, get people to talk when they won't talk to the authorities. Besides," I shrugged, "I've got an in with the family. I'll clear everything through you."

"See that you do," he growled. "See that you do." He fished a dollar bill out of his pocket and shoved it across the counter. "See you later, Ida," he called toward the kitchen. Then he tapped me on the shoulder with his index finger. "And see that you watch your step. Obstruction of justice could keep you here a day or two longer than you'd like."

"I'll remember that."

I watched the sheriff stride out. He brought the movie *Walking Tall* to mind. I had the impression that he missed very little and, what was that phrase? Cast a long shadow? That could be a help, and a hindrance.

"Good lookin' man, ain't he? I can tell you he sets tongues waggin' when he first got here."

"Yeah?"

Ida Belle wiped down the counter again. "Umhum. Man lookin' like that, unmarried, from the city. More than one wanted to find out what made him tick, if you know what I mean."

I did. I'd wondered myself what was the story behind Neal Conrad's exit from New York and why he'd chosen to hide himself in the Ozark mountains. What was it Charlie had said? Something about a shooting?

I paid for my lunch and with a wave to Ida Belle, shrugged into my parka. Next stop, Susan's apartment.

Chapter Three

I asked directions at a service station and then drove to Armen where Susan had lived. Armen was like a thousand small communities in the midwest. A main street with a market, a hardware store, a flower and gift shop, a tiny bank branch, a couple of antique shops. The houses were small, well kept. Many had Christmas lights already lining the eaves.

The apartment house sat a mile beyond the end of the street. I sat in the car at the curb for several minutes, trying to see the Civil War era house through objective eyes. But Susan's image kept intruding. It didn't seem the sort of place the Bradys would have chosen for their daughter, nor Susan for herself. She was, after all, a child of affluence.

Melting snow marked empty flower beds, with brown stems spiking through. An overgrown climbing rose bush lifted a riot of dead-looking, twining strands up the side and over a wide front porch that stretched across the front of the square house. Stairs going up the outside met, I assumed, the fire code requirements but destroyed the original clean lines.

"Well, I can't put this off any longer."

The slam of the car door echoed loudly in the quiet of the winter countryside.

The ornate front door with leaded glass in the top panel, swung open easily. Security was obviously not a major concern even now. Anyone could walk in. I couldn't help wondering if that was what had happened the night Susan died.

It was obvious from the foyer that the house had once been a showplace. An elegant dark oak staircase with an ornately carved rail curved up on the right. The door to the left had probably opened into what had been a receiving room, and the hall leading toward the back might have lead to the original family living quarters. According to what the sheriff had said, the girls who had found Susan lived in those rooms now.

I climbed the stairs slowly, not looking forward to confronting the rooms where Susan had lived. Just as I rounded the corner at the top of the stairs a figure stepped out of the late afternoon shadows. I swallowed a squeak of surprise.

"Miss Rome."

My heart leaped into my throat, then I sank against the wall. "Sheriff. You scared me."

"Sorry. Thought you might come directly out here."

"I hate being so predictable."

His laugh was a short, low rumble from deep in his chest. I was struck, suddenly, by how comfortable this man was in his own skin. A woman would be lucky to have this man.

"I thought I'd walk through the apartment again, so I decided to wait a while to see if you'd show up."

His sudden cooperative attitude made me suspicious, but the key he twirled on the end of his finger was an invitation I couldn't resist.

"Well, let's do it."

He loosened one end of the yellow banner blocking the crime scene and unlocked the heavy, carved door. It swung open with a faint squeal that raised bumps on my arms.

He stepped back, but I couldn't make myself walk into the apartment.

"Miss Rome."

I glanced up at him. "I feel a little strange going in there."

"Not quite so easy being objective in this case, is it?"

"No."

I made myself step into a large room that was darkened by pulled drapes. Shivering slightly, I pulled my parka close.

"The heat's been turned off," he drawled, raising a shade then moving on through the apartment.

I stopped in the middle of the living room and turned slowly. This was where Susan had lived for over a year, where she'd studied, brought boys, laughed with girlfriends over pizza and Cokes, griped about professors and term papers. What else had happened here? What had gone wrong?

The apartment was what I might have expected, had I thought about it. The walls were painted an off-white, contrasting starkly with the dark stained floor. A tobacco brown couch and two cinnamon colored upholstered chairs sat at the edge of a large area rug that was patterned with browns and blues in a floral pattern.

There was the mustiness of a closed space, the lingering tang of cigarette smoke, and something else so subtle I couldn't name it. Maybe it was only emptiness.

Two tall bookcases overflowing with textbooks and notebooks covered one wall. Susan's purse was still tucked in a corner of the couch. A pair of jeans and a shirt were roped over the back of a ladder-back chair. Papers, a ballpoint pen, and pads of sticky-notes in various colors were scattered across a small table. Curious, I leaned over to read the top sheet.

"Term paper. Maybe she was working on it that night."

Suddenly a wave of emotion washed over me and tears stung my eyes.

"This is so . . . so sad," I whispered, the sound seeming loud in the room. "She was so gentle. So . . . unthreatening. Who could have—"

"You're sure someone did?"

"Yes. I wasn't, entirely, earlier, but I am now. I just can't imagine anything that would make her—"

He waited while I regained some composure.

"See anything out of the ordinary?"

"I wouldn't know." I shrugged deeper into my coat. The cold seemed to seep into my bones.

I walked into the kitchen. It had no personality. The cabinets were painted white, the sink was white, the refrigerator, stove, the floor. I opened the cabinets, looked under the sink. The sheriff waited patiently while I opened drawers and doors, poked around in the few canned goods.

"Beer and soup."

"Yeah."

The bedroom was next. Again there was the white woodwork, white walls. Several drawers of a battered dresser were hanging open with underwear and sweaters trailing out.

"You searched the place?"

"Umhum."

The closet door stood open but the clothes still hung neatly on hangers. The family had obviously not been allowed inside to retrieve belongings or do any packing. The bed, as Neal had said, was still made. I sank onto the edge of it and stared at the room. The corded spread was rough beneath my fingers.

"This is strange, knowing she lived here, and won't ever come back. She was . . . so special. I found her once, in her room, reading a volume of the encyclopedia."

I remembered the day as if it had been yesterday. Somehow every experience with Susan had become clearer in the last twelve hours.

"I asked if she had a paper to do, but she didn't. She'd heard something on television that caught her attention and she'd wanted to find out more about it. She ended up reading the whole volume. M, I think it was."

"You know the family a long time?"

"Not too long, I guess, in the whole scheme of things."

I met his gaze and we each weighed the moment. He had the kind of face that inspired confidence; square features well-defined and blue eyes that could appear open and friendly but could quickly turn frosty. His hair was not regulation trim, like New York would have demanded. A piece of it fell over his forehead. Squint lines fanned out from the corners of his eyes. How old was he? Thirty-five? Thirty-seven?

"Gary Brady is my ex-husband."

His eyebrows lifted a notch. "How ex?"

"Very ex. We were married . . . a little too long. Been divorced five."

"Must be some residual stuff there, for you to come down here—"

"I'm here for Susan. Not Gary, or his parents. Maybe a little bit of guilt involved here, because I didn't stay in touch with her. And now this—"

I wrapped my coat close and lay back on the bed, staring up at the ceiling. Memories echoed with Susan's laughter, with the wide-eyed innocence of the fifteen-year-old girl I'd known. Neal Conrad was leaning against the door frame watching me. I got up. I was glad he was there. He seemed to give the room some definition. I didn't want to be alone in this sterile place. It was almost as if Susan hadn't really lived there; as if it had been a sham.

"Could someone have made the bed after killing Susan?"

"Doesn't seem likely."

I stretched to touch the wilting leaf of a philodendra plant that hung from a planter in front of the window. It looked ignored.

I pushed off the bed and rifled through the clothes hanging in the closet. Jeans, shirts, a few jackets, a heavy coat, a couple of dresses, shirts. All school clothes. None of the dresses Susan would have worn had the family stayed in California. There were no name brand clothes, no evening dresses, no furs. I glanced around the bedroom again.

"Does anything about this room strike you as strange?"

He glanced around. "It did. What are you thinking?"

"Susan was a nineteen-year-old college student. There are no stuffed animals, no posters. In fact, no pictures at all."

"Maybe she didn't—"

"The Susan I knew loved stuffed animals. Her room at home was full of them. And it was a very feminine room. All eyelet lace and pastel. Pillows on the bed in bursts of color. This is so sparse."

I turned in a slow circle.

"I wonder—"

"What?"

I finished the circle. "I wonder why the Bradys moved to Arkansas."

It was dark when I parked the rental in the motel lot. I was checking for messages at the desk when Gary came down the stairs.

"Where have you been?"

"Checking out the town."

"I thought we agreed to work together."

With a glance at S. Patrick, Gary took my arm and pulled me away from the reception desk.

"I agreed to be on the same flight with you," I reminded him. "That's all. Why aren't you with your parents?"

"I called them earlier. They just want to be alone for a while."

That didn't make sense to me, but then, people handled grief in a variety of ways. Besides, the Brady family hadn't been all that close. I'd been disappointed in discovering that.

"I was going into The Magnolia Room for dinner. It's too cold to go out to find someplace decent."

"Looks fine to me."

The desk clerk was watching us curiously and had probably heard every word, and would, I was certain, duly report it to anyone who would listen. It was that kind of town.

The Magnolia's decor mirrored that of the motel reception

area. White ceiling fans stirred the dry, warm air lazily. White wicker chairs with jungle print cushions squatted beside tables trimmed in wicker, a strange contrast with the wide windows looking out on cold blue-white snow.

The few patrons hardly acknowledged our entrance, and it took a few moments to catch the attention of the hostess.

"Sit anywhere ya' like," she drawled, picking up two plastic coated menus with gold tassels. Her green plastic name tag said GINA.

We chose a corner table, well away from the other guests.

"Dogpatch," Gary intoned, glancing at the menu, deriding the girl's accent and tight uniform.

I hadn't seen the cartoon strip in years, and probably no one else had. It had been popular once, portraying the life of a fictional hillbilly family in the Ozarks. I'd never liked the cartoon, disliking its stereotypes.

"What can I bring y'all to drink?"

"Coffee, black, and water," I ordered, scanning the specials.

"I don't suppose you have wine?"

"The drink selection's listed there." She pointed to a corner of the menu with the eraser end of her pencil.

"Coffee and iced tea for me," Gary said without looking up.

"Back in a jif."

"Quaint," he murmured.

"I don't want to draw attention to us," I warned him. "If you can't keep quiet, then go home, or out to your parent's house."

His look was so like Edward, his father, that I was stunned. Wasn't the daughter supposed to grow up to be irritatingly like her mother? But then, Edward Brady had been the dominant person in the family. His word was law.

"What have you been doing? I expected you back long ago."

"I talked to the sheriff." I studied his face. "And went out to Susan's apartment."

He frowned. "You went out there? Why?"

"I just wanted to see the place. Aren't you curious?"

"That's morbid. Of course, you always did have a peculiar sense of propriety. Did you find out anything?"

"Not much." I ignored his dig. "The coroner confirmed that death was caused by a large dose of Strychnine."

"Strychnine? Where would she have gotten that?"

"That's the question, isn't it?"

After Gina brought our coffee and took our order, Gary asked the question I'd been hoping to avoid.

"How are you doing, Margaret?"

I turned the cup on the saucer.

"Fine," I replied after a long moment.

"I've read your work in Front Page. Impressive, for what it is. I've never found political or news reporting very . . . creative. How can you go to those places; those places where there's nothing but filth and poverty? Couldn't you do stories in the states?"

"There's filth and poverty everywhere, Gary. It isn't solely a third world problem. I've been at riots, police brutality hearings in L.A. and I wasn't impressed by the civility exhibited there."

The inability to understand anything of what I did was stamped on his face. Whatever Gary Brady didn't want to touch him, didn't. It was as simple as that.

"You were in L.A. and you didn't call me?"

"It wasn't a social visit. Besides, I sent in my photos and story and took the next flight to Somalia."

"Surely there are other things you could do. I've seen your stories on the national parks and the pictures were incredible."

"Explain to me why I should do just pretty pictures and stories."

He shrugged. "It's not something I can, or should, explain. I'm just concerned for you."

I sipped my coffee. "No reason you should be."

A muscle jumped in his jaw. "You always were very single-minded."

"I prefer to call it focused."

"In any event, there was never room for anything else in your life. Just work."

The knot tightened in my stomach. "There was always room, it just didn't fit your schedule."

"You call working day and night, dropping everything to run out and take a picture of some dead body 'making room' for a husband and family?"

The knot tightened. "It was my job, Gary. I was building a career. That was important to me."

"Your 'career' superseded everything else. Your 'career' kept guests waiting, embarrassed my parents."

I heard once again the echoes of past arguments. I resented that he made me feel like I had to explain; even more that he could still make me feel guilty. I pushed it aside, refusing to bend to it again.

"More to the point, I embarrassed you by not being what you thought I would be, or should be."

"You could have been a top photographer, Margaret. Your pictures could have hung in the best galleries."

"But I'm not a gallery photographer. I'm a news photographer. And I like what I do."

"Bottom line, our life together wasn't important enough for you to try anything else."

"My job was—is—a big part of me. Rejecting that was rejecting me."

"Okay, okay. You wouldn't quit your job, but why move across the country? If you'd stayed in California maybe we could have worked something out."

"Knowing that wouldn't happen, that it shouldn't happen, is why I left. Besides, moving to New York was a good change, personally and professionally."

"You're saying that because our marriage failed, your career flourished?"

"No. Not because of it. In spite of it." I waited until his gaze met mine. "I've worked hard during the past few years.

At first I filled every minute because I didn't want to think about having failed at something that had been so important to me." It was hard to say that even now. "I was a cripple trying to find a way to recover."

"And now?"

"I work because I love it. And for right now that's enough."

Anger flushed his face and his lips thinned. His gaze flicked around the room as if he was afraid someone could have overheard. Appearances were everything to the Bradys.

"It appears to have been a good exchange. Marriage, a comfortable lifestyle, family, for traveling at the drop of a hat, living out of a suitcase and questionable hotels in dangerous places. How could I question that?"

"Being bitter isn't a luxury I can afford, or want."

I didn't tell him about the sleepless nights, the hours I'd paced the floor worrying whether I was doing the right thing, whether moving to New York and starting a new life was a positive move forward or escape for a coward. Was it, I kept asking myself, a way to keep from seeing Gary again, being reminded of the failure of my marriage, of my own failures? Or was it a way to shut the door on the past so I could begin fresh?

"Why should you be bitter? The divorce was your idea. You apparently got exactly what you wanted."

What I'd wanted was a home and family as well as my career. Had I wanted too much? Was I paying the price of wanting to be 'super woman' like so many had before? Or did the fault lay deeper than that?

I'd reached the conclusion that I'd been blinded by the idea of love and marriage, refusing to see the reality of trying to be a part of a family so far out of my realm of experience that my love didn't have a prayer of surviving. But listening to Gary again prodded those doubts to life again, and I didn't like the way it made me feel.

"It was either that or give in and become something I couldn't live with."

"How can you say that? All I wanted was for you to be my wife. You can't tell me that was difficult." His gaze met mine in challenge. "We had some good times together."

I wouldn't let him do this to me. I refused to carry all the guilt. He hadn't wanted to talk about it before, so why bother now? If he had any illusions about patching things up, then I wanted to smother them now. I didn't need, or want, this kind of complication.

"Gary, being your wife meant becoming just another thing you owned, like becoming a pet on a leash. Come. Go. Fetch. Heel. I tried, but I couldn't do that."

He sat back in his chair and shook his head slightly as if I spoke a foreign language.

He flicked open his napkin and studied a slightly raveled hem briefly before spreading it on his lap. I let resentment feed my courage. I'd never been good at baring my soul. Perhaps that had been part of the problem. Maybe I expected him to read my mind, as I thought he should do mine.

"You're being childish."

I could almost smile at the predictability of his response. That withdrawal into an archaic formality had always gotten to me. It had made simple arguments explode into something totally out of proportion more than once.

"That's what it felt like. Show up at six, formal dress. No, green isn't a good color, blue is better. Say hello to George because he's daddy's associate, and be nice to Claudia because she's president of the business women's chapter of the Chamber of Commerce, and it's important to talk to Julia because she's on the merchant's committee, and Anne owns a large retail business so—"

"Was that so hard? Was it so hard to help me in my business?"

I rested my elbows on the table and leaned toward him.

"Gary, talking to them was like talking to a wall. I don't do small talk. We had nothing in common. When you get down to the nitty gritty, you and I had nothing in common."

"Small talk. What's wrong with small talk? Smile, nod, and make a comment. That's all you had to do. Was it so hard?"

"I don't know how to talk for two hours and say nothing that I can remember, and not care. It was like putting my brain on hold and my face on automatic. Smile here. Smile there. Nod and say 'umhum' in the right places. Care whether or not Joanne's housekeeper quit just before the biggest sit-down dinner of the year. Be genuinely concerned when veined shrimp arrived instead of deveined. I couldn't do it."

"You should have tried, for me."

"I did. That's when I discovered there had to be more. I had to live for me, Gary."

"I don't understand. My parents didn't understand."

"I'm sorry that you didn't. It wasn't important for them to."

"Well." He stirred his tea unnecessarily. "You criticize me for being manipulative, but you're callous."

I shrugged. We would never agree on the reasons why our marriage hadn't, couldn't, work.

"Perhaps."

Fortunately our dinners arrived just then. I picked up my fork, then watched Gary study the steak he'd ordered. He poked at it gingerly with his fork as if expecting it to rise up off the plate.

This was familiar and I relaxed to watch the process, hiding a smile as he picked up the edge of the steak with a single tine of his fork and peered beneath it.

I leaned forward and whispered. "Is something hiding under there?"

He didn't appreciate my humor.

"I asked for medium rare to well. This thing could have walked out here."

"I'm sure you won't hesitate to send it back."

"Not a moment."

He snapped his fingers as if expecting the waitress to appear like a genie out of a bottle. When it didn't happen, he looked around, his displeasure obvious in his face.

I caught Gina's attention and smiled at the knowing look on her face as she sauntered across the room. I suspected the hostess had heard Gary's earlier comments and a conspiracy had been cooked up in the kitchen.

"Somethin' wrong?"

"This steak is bloody rare. I asked for at least medium. Please have another prepared."

"Most folks 'round here like it that way."

"I'm not 'most folks'. I like my steak medium. That's just pink, not bloody, not charred. Medium. Can you take care of that?"

"I'll have th' cook put it back on th' grill."

"No," Gary lifted his fork for emphasis, "you're not listening. Putting it back on the grill will make it tough; tougher than it already is. I want a fresh steak."

The plate disappeared, but not without leaving a blotch on the placemat when the waitress snatched it away.

"No wonder the guests avoid eating in here. The steak will probably be inedible."

No, the steak didn't have a chance. Not once Gary Brady set his mind to finding fault.

The second steak was at least less rare, more acceptable though Gary studied it at length.

"I swear, if you send that back I'm going to walk out of here and catch the first plane back home."

"You won't," he said, sure that I was totally hooked on finding what happened to Susan.

To my relief he began cutting his steak, avoiding the middle and most rare portion.

We ate in silence and went to our rooms the same way. I felt bad about that, in a way. I'd come to help, not rake him over the coals for something that had been as much my fault as his.

After a shower, I pulled an oversized t-shirt over my head and got into bed, but not to sleep. I lay, staring up into the darkness, sorting through the few facts I had on Susan's death. It was my impression that though the medical examiner said Susan had committed suicide, Neal Conrad hadn't fully accepted that statement.

Neal Conrad. Charlie's word that Conrad had been a good cop was enough to make him all right in my book. Charlie wasn't quick to give praise and for him to have kept in touch with the former detective was high recommendation indeed. Now, if I could get the sheriff to work with me, and not against me, I might be able to pick his brain a bit and add to my small store of information. Besides, I was growing more curious about the New York drop–out who seemed to have embraced the Arkansas lifestyle, drawl and all. What had made him leave the city? And once he decided to leave, why had he chosen Arkansas?

I sorted through the e-mail of articles about coed murders while eating my complimentary continental breakfast, noting similarities in columns on a legal pad. There weren't many. Each murder remained unsolved, the suspects having been eliminated one by one for lack of evidence, or because of a solid alibi.

The only correlation to Susan's death was that all the victims were young college women. But my gut feeling said there was a correlation somehow to what had happened to Susan.

Two of the five young woman had been kidnapped off campus then left in a remote location to be found hours after their death. It occurred to me that the bodies were put where they would be found in just hours, not days. I made a note to myself in my spiral notebook to think about that.

Every lead, the police stated, had been followed; every possible connection between the murders explored. Even a cult angle had been investigated since a group had organized near where the last murder had occurred. Like Susan's, none of the murders had been solved, but none of them had been death by poison either.

Returning to my room to work, I found a second e-mail with a note from research:

Mag—These aren't related to the coed murders, but co-ed related. Thought they might be of interest. Cathy

I began reading, a frown growing deeper the further I went. The articles dealt with coed kidnappings that were assumed to be fraternity pranks that had gotten out of hand. I straightened and reread each article. Not only were the girls kidnapped in vans, but the prank, if it had been that, had taken a turn toward the sadistic when the culprits bound and gagged the girls, assaulted them, then shaved their heads and dumped them in a remote area.

The campus fraternities had been investigated and all denied being involved. No concrete link could be established and everyone was cleared. Reason said that this was a dead end, but the journalist part of me demanded I follow this thread to the end.

Was Susan murdered by someone she knew? Or was this just another case of a bad college prank gone wrong? No, something inside me said there was a link. I just had to find it.

I sipped the cup of coffee I'd brought upstairs and grimaced at its cold bitterness. Glancing at my watch, I decided to get out of the hotel before Gary got up and insisted on accompanying me, but first I called Cathy.

"Hi, Mag. Get the clippings?"

"First thing this morning. Thanks for the quick work. I need you to look up something else for me. Anything you can find on a group called The Glorious Church."

"Who are they? Some kind of religious cult?"

"Yeah. Find out who's the founder, where they come from, what they do, how they're financed. That sort of thing."

"Some connection with the murders?"

"It's probably nothing, but one of the murder articles

mentioned that the police had talked to some cult members during the investigation, and there's a group here. Probably no connection, but I want to satisfy my curiosity."

"I know. Get it out of your way so you can get on with something else. I'll e-mail what I find."

Fifteen minutes later I was on my way to the local newspaper office to do a little research on my own. Since The Glorious Church had a television show, perhaps there had been something about them in the local papers.

The newspaper office could hardly warrant the name. The old building housed a hardware store, leaving a tunnel down one side for the newspaper—The Armen Reporter.

I pushed open the heavy door of the office and winced when a bell jangled over my head. A front desk was empty, dusty. File cabinets lining the wall to the right were wood and probably almost impossible to open, judging by the overflowing stacks of files on top.

"Need to place an ad?"

The tall man was gaunt, his cheeks sunken, shoulders stooped. All he needed was the green eye shade to be someone out of an old Jimmy Stewart movie.

"No, I'd like to see—"

"You're that city gal."

I stuck out my hand. "Maggie Rome."

"Frank Hawkins, publisher, editor, reporter, ad manager. His handshake was limp fish. "What can I do for you?"

"I need to do some research, see some back issues."

"Don't have any of that computer stuff."

Hope faded. "You've got back issues—"

"Sure. They're back there," he thumbed over his shoulder, "in date order. You can read what ya want, long as you're careful. Don't want no torn pages."

"Okay."

It would be simpler if I could ask him what I wanted to know but I had my doubts that he'd remember dates and detail I needed.

"Don't have anything on that Brady girl, if that's what you're looking for."

"It's not. I came to check out coed murders in general."

"Thought she was a suicide."

I followed him to a dark room at the back of the offices and sighed inwardly when he turned on the light. I'd never seen such a disorganized mess.

"How long have you owned the paper?"

"Twenty-three years this past fall."

A paper a week for twenty-three years and a copy of each hung on a wood dowel in shelves lining the walls. It would take forever to find what I wanted.

"Okay if I stay a while?"

A corner of his mouth twitched in what was as near a smile as Frank Hawkins probably ever managed.

"I make a lousy cup of coffee. Better carry in your own."

"When do you close?"

"Six, seven. Folks come in after work, you know." His thin shoulders shrugged slightly under a faded flannel shirt. Tired khaki pants rode on hipbones, held up by a worn leather belt plus brown suspenders. The heels of scuffed brown wingtips that had seen better days dragged slightly as he left me alone in the musty, paper-lined room.

Armed with two legal pads and two automatic pencils, I settled at the square table in the middle of the room and began skimming editions of Armen's claim to a print media.

Several cups of coffee later, eyes gritty, nose stuffy, I'd learned that Tony and Sophia Belgrade had moved their organization to the Fayetteville area five years earlier, building a school on one hundred acres of previously undeveloped land. An article six months later described the construction of a church on the property, but there was no mention of a ground breaking or announcement of services.

Tony and Sophia Belgrade were the heads of The Glorious Church but I found only one photo of them. I studied the blurred images carefully. Tony wore dark glasses, jeans, and a cowboy hat that obscured most of his features. The diminutive Sophia looked like one of the porcelain dolls often advertised in magazines, with her dark hair piled high atop her head, a flowing dress that covered her from neck to toe. Apparently she was the spokesperson for the group since all articles quoted only Sophia's comments.

I left the newspaper office knowing my next stop had to be the television station where The Glorious Church taped their weekly show.

Presenting my credentials at the front desk, I asked to talk to the account rep handling The Glorious Church.

"That's Brian Parker. I think he's still here."

She punched out an extension number and waited.

"Brian? A Ms. Maggie Rome, with Front Page magazine, is here to see you." She put down the receiver. "He'll be out in a minute."

"Thanks."

I unsnapped my parka and glanced around the reception area. The receptionist returned to watching the huge television screen playing the stations' programs. Other than the large TV, the station reception and office area wasn't much larger than the newspaper offices. Made me wonder what kind of studio they had.

"Ms. Rome?"

A tall young man in a dark suit with a red power tie approached with his hand out.

"Brian Parker. I have admired your work."

His grasp was firm and brief.

"Thank you. That's always nice to hear."

"How can I help you?"

"I'm doing a piece on cults and their impact on college age students. In my research I ran across an article on The Glorious Church. I understand you handle their account and I wondered if you'd talk to me a little about their program."

"They could tell you more—"

"Oh, I intend to talk to the Belgrades, but I wanted to get some background first."

Brian shrugged. "Don't know what I can tell you, but why don't we talk over coffee. I don't guarantee quality, but there's lots of it and it's hot."

I followed him to a small room with four Formica topped tables.

"It's cold out there, isn't it? I've tried to work inside today."

Several candy and snack machines lined one wall. The ash trays overflowed. Brian pushed one aside and wiped the end of one table with a paper towel.

"Sorry for the mess."

"Looks like the break room at Front Page."

He poured two cups of coffee. "Guess they're all alike, more or less. Now, what can I tell you about The Glorious Temple?"

Dropping my bag on the floor, I pulled out my steno pad and pen. "Have you handled the account since the Belgrades moved the church here?"

"Yeah. They'd hardly begun building that compound out there when they came in one day and asked about going on the air. It was my first big account and I wanted it bad. But, management was cautious," he shrugged. "Them being new and all. No credit references. At least, none they would give us. It was a little strange and my boss was real antsy."

"What happened?"

"Well, Jack, the station manager, agreed to put 'em on the air on a week to week basis. Them paying the production costs ahead of airing, then the air time each week. That way we don't get stuck, you know."

Everyone I'd talked to had that same comfortable drawl that made it seem they were in no hurry to do or say anything. I found my nerves winding a little tight with an urge to make them say things more quickly, more precisely. But then, I found Neal's slow drawl comforting somehow. A contrast of feelings I'd dissect later.

"I understand. But they've been on the air nearly five years? Any pay problems?"

"Not a one. Tony marched in here that first week with two of the bodyguards who travel with him all the time, carrying a briefcase full of cash. It was impressive, let me tell you. They tape on Tuesday night, after the late newscast. Every Friday night he's here, even though we told him long ago it wasn't necessary any more."

"Where's the money come from?"

"Donations. You should see Sophia on that show. She's a master at soliciting money. They've got a post office box, and from what I hear, they get sacks of donations. Then there's the students. They work the airports and malls for miles around, handing out tracts, selling flowers, books, taking donations. Whatever works. It's something new every week."

"I wouldn't think little stuff like that would generate the kind of money they need for a continuing program, plus a church and school."

"You'd be surprised. Fifty thousand cash each month for us, on top of whatever it takes to run a fleet of vans and Caddys. And, I hear they've got a shop in Nashville where they sell fancy western clothes. I've never seen it, but they tell me the students earn their pocket money by sewing the fancy jackets and stuff."

"They still pay the station cash?"

"Yep. Their choice." He sipped his coffee again and grimaced. "Worse than usual." He leaned back in his chair. "Tony and his bodyguards show up every Friday at midnight, just like clockwork."

"What's the show like?"

Brian smiled. "They're taping tonight. Want to watch?"

"They wouldn't mind?"

"Why should they? I'd think they'd welcome the publicity."

I wasn't so sure, but I did want to see the taping. "Thanks. I appreciate your help."

"No problem. Besides, I'd like to pick your brain a little, learn a bit about the larger market."

"Don't know what I can tell you."

"Anything will help. I don't intend to stay here much longer. Like to try New York maybe." He tossed his empty cup toward an overflowing waste can and acknowledged his miss with a wide grin. "Be here before the late news ends. I'll have Hank look out for you. He's the director."

When I returned to the motel there was a note from Gary. He'd gone out to see his parents and wouldn't be back until dinner.

I zipped my parka up to the top and shivered as I walked to the car. The wind had come up again and fingers of winter seemed to pluck at my bones. The sky was gray and heavy. I hoped we didn't get more snow. The last thing I wanted was to be snowed in with Gary.

Neal Conrad was sitting in a booth in the back when I entered the café and I flashed him a smile. Ida Belle lifted a coffee pot in salute and I curved my thumb and little finger to form a coffee cup before starting toward a corner booth.

Neal's voice carried easily over the clatter of dishes and conversation.

"Ms. Rome. Care to join me?"

"If you'll call me Maggie."

I slid into the booth opposite him as Ida Belle slid a steaming cup of coffee across the table.

"This is all I need right now, Ida. Thanks."

Neal waited until Ida Belle returned to the kitchen. Once again the measuring quality of his gaze struck me. This was a man who held secrets close while seeming to be open and cooperative. This hinted at many hidden facets of the man; facets that might be interesting to investigate. His gaze slid over me in speculation and I knew he wasn't at all satisfied that I could be trusted, even with Charlie's recommendation. Not yet, anyway.

"I brought something for you to read." He slid a folder toward me.

"The coroner's report."

"Umhum."

"Why give it to me?" I blew on my cold fingers.

"Thought you might see something."

"Homicide?"

"Case isn't closed yet."

I skimmed the report, then read it carefully. Neal had been right. The coroner had done his job well.

Using my laptop, I'd done a little reading on the internet about Strychnine, its properties and effects. When my first thought upon hearing the word had been 'rat poison,' I hadn't been far wrong. As the report outlined, Strychnine was a component of a variety of tonics and cathartic pills and used as a rodenticide. A fatal dose of Strychnine was 15–30 mg with an exposure limit of 0.15 mg/m3. According to the coroner, Susan had ingested twice that.

"This is very thorough."

"Martin watches a lot of TV. He works as if any evidence might be presented in court."

His grin was infectious.

I forced myself to read the entire report. The coroner had noted urine and blood tests, gastric washings, feces, body fat, hair and nail clippings along with detailed notes on the stomach contents, liver, kidney, lung and brain biopsies.

"The, uh, doctor's comments, the one who treated her at the hospital, are attached."

I swallowed, wishing the lump in my throat would go away. This was harder than I'd thought it could be. I'd seen several such reports, but this one was on someone I knew. Having Susan reduced to specimens, having her death coldly outlined in milligrams, was sobering.

"From what I see there," Neal commented, "this isn't a case of long-term poisoning that finally resulted in a death."

"You mean, no one was poisoning her for several weeks before she died. Did you suspect that?"

"Nope. That's pretty rare. But a poisoning homicide's pretty rare, too."

"You still think this is a suicide?"

"I'm keeping an open mind. A suicide would keep it simple."

I closed the file and pushed it away. "But then, nothing's ever simple, is it?"

"Nope." He sipped his coffee. "And it gets more complicated all the time."

Chapter Four

Brian was watching for me when I arrived at the television station at ten fifteen.

"They just got here. Taping will start in about half an hour."

The station had been added on to in recent years. The front offices were in the older part of the building, but some of the studios were new.

I followed Brian into a surprisingly large studio and chose a seat at the back of the room where I could watch and listen unobtrusively.

One corner of the studio was a half dismantled kitchen set, the permanent news set in another. But the current activity was centered in a third, larger space. Two cameramen dollied back, making a tall man with a headset strung around his neck and a clipboard under his arm dodge out of the way.

Just then a group of young men and women, all about Susan's age, entered the studio from the left, marching silently in single file. Each wore a navy suit, white shirt or blouse, dark ties, and black polished shoes like they'd been punched out on some kind of assembly line. The girls wore their hair caught back with combs. The boys' hair was cut so short their scalps showed through. They were eerily quiet, exchanging not one word, turning not to one side or the other, but rather marching solemnly in unison.

A woman I identified from the newspaper photos as Sophia Belgrade was talking to the tall balding man I assumed was the floor director. A tall man dressed in black, wearing dark glasses, appeared suddenly from nowhere. Tony Belgrade. Standing back out of the way, he watched the young people line up on risers. I saw two of the girls almost break rank to look at him, but the slight turn of the head was corrected immediately.

Two bodyguards, wearing dark glasses that matched Tony's, lounged close by. Two others stood beside a door leading into the studio from the back parking lot.

I studied the Belgrades carefully, intrigued by their almost cartoon appearance. Tony, in his dark glasses, black jeans, shirt and ornately studded jean jacket, wore his black hair long in a style brushed back from a wide forehead that reminded me of photos I'd seen of Elvis Presley, especially with the number of large diamond rings prominent on both hands.

Sophia, on the other hand, had to be almost fifteen years older than her husband. Her sooty black hair made her pale skin artificially white under the lights. She seemed to be giving explicit instructions about where she wanted the cameras placed, interrupting herself to indicate that the group of young people should move further to one side. The purple and white robes she wore flowed about her body dramatically whenever she moved. After each motion, her hands slid into the sleeves of her gown as if she was in perpetual prayer.

Several assistants began moving in banks of fake ferns and taller plants behind and to the side of the risers where the students waited patiently. White and purple curtains came down to form a backdrop and a stage hand carried in a clear plastic stand on which was placed a large, gilt-edged Bible. Within a few minutes the barn-like studio conveyed the appearance of a richly decorated stage in a large auditorium.

Sophia waved the director aside then turned to the waiting young people. I wished I could hear what Sophia was saying, but whatever it was the students listened carefully, their eyes intent upon her.

"Quite a show, isn't it?" Brian slid into a folding chair next to me.

"It must be a hundred degrees out there under those lights. You'd think they'd let the students relax until time to tape."

"Nope. They bring 'em here in vans then trot 'em out, tell 'em where to stand, and there's never a word spoken. They stand on those risers until Sophia's satisfied with the take. They usually sing two songs during the show. Did I tell you they record and sell cassette tapes of the group? Actually, they're pretty good. These are the 'elite' of the students. It's just eerie the way they stand and wait, almost without moving a muscle.

"But then, I shouldn't be surprised. Last summer I happened to mention to Tony that I'd bought a house and had to have some landscaping done. Raking, planting grass. That sort of thing. The next morning, before I even got up, two truckloads of the students arrived and unloaded. It couldn't have been much later than six o'clock. Tony had sent them to do the yard work."

My curiosity was really piqued now. Who were these people, and was their school and church legitimate? At the very least, Tony and Sophia and their comic book facade was interesting. There might be a story there after all.

"And?"

"Well, I told them it was okay, that I'd made arrangements for some help, but nothing made any difference. They'd been told to come and work, and they wouldn't be sent away. This was in August, and it must have been a hundred degrees out there, but they worked all day without stopping. I tried to send out lemonade, water, something, but they refused it all. Didn't even stop for lunch.

"The strangest thing was, they never said a word. The

truck driver did all the talking. The rest were like . . . zombies or something. Just like what you see here."

"Ever hear any rumors of drug use?"

"Nope. And I'm pretty tapped into what's going on." He shrugged. "People talk, you know. There's never been anything to suggest it and I've watched 'em. They're just very . . . controlled, I guess is the word. Anyway, they worked at my place until dark, then loaded up in the back of those trucks and left. Everything was done. Weird."

"Sure is." I watched the taping preliminaries. "What's with Tony's dark glasses?"

"Says his eyes are light sensitive. And those bodyguards never leave him. Sophia, on the other hand, has been dying for the last five years."

This caught my attention. "Dying?"

"Here she comes," Brian whispered.

Sophia Belgrade glided across the floor toward them. When she reached out to Brian, I couldn't miss seeing two of the largest diamond rings I'd ever seen on Sophia's right hand. On the left was a ruby and diamond dinner ring that must have cost a fortune.

"Brian, we'll need a crawl on this show. A telephone number for supporters to call in pledges and another for prayer lines."

"No problem, Sophia. I'll have it done when we edit in the morning."

"And who is this?"

Sophia stood with her clasped hands almost hidden in the folds of her gown.

"Maggie Rome, Front Page magazine." She didn't respond to my extended hand so I let it drop. "I'm doing research on some religious splinter groups and when I heard of the success of The Glorious Church I was intrigued. I hope you don't mind if I watch the taping."

"Not at all, as long as you take no pictures, of course. We very closely guard the students from outside influences."

"Oh? I thought part of the work involved reaching the public with pamphlets and tracts."

"Yes, it is. But the work itself precludes opportunity for interrogation."

"Interrogation? Interesting word choice."

Sophia smiled wisely. "Isn't that what it's called when curious people attempt to identify and discredit anything that's different from that which is familiar?"

"I don't know. I usually call it interest, or simply curiosity."

"And you are curious?"

"About The Glorious Church."

"What would you like to know?"

"What is it? Where is it going? I believe I read something about a prophet of The Glorious Church announcing that the world would soon come to an end in a nuclear holocaust, but it didn't happen."

"Yes."

"What happened?"

"I had that vision five years ago. Unfortunately, the media didn't print the rest of the revelation."

"And what was the rest of it?"

"I saw the world in danger of being destroyed, unless some strong intervention occurred, something to change the world direction. Fortunately, France and Germany refused to join the latest conflict, the U.N. adopted a wait-and-see attitude, leaving the U.S. to handle the situation alone and in more control of what would happen. Thus, a change of direction. It was all quite . . . gratifying, really."

What a curious mix of a person she was. Involved in a 'religion' that was very current, perhaps involving mind control—if the student's reactions were any indication—but her demeanor was that of something that reminded me of the movie *Elmer Gantry.* A kind of theatrical flamboyance that 'entertained' television viewers to send money to support the 'mission', but a personal wariness that made my reporter's antennae perk up and set off great clanging alarm bells. The two sides didn't fit.

"Are you suggesting that your prophecy made the easing of world tensions possible?"

"I'm saying the two are linked. Ms. Rome, there are forces at work in the world today that remain unrecognized by most people, even those who claim to be Bible students."

I'd met and interviewed shysters and they all spoke in the most vague of terms, then manipulated the results of circumstances to their own advantage. The word 'spin' was originated with the earliest shysters. Sophia was no different.

"But you understand these forces?"

Sophia smiled indulgently. "You are skeptical."

"Curious. I'd like to learn more about these forces."

Sophia's gaze was direct and held mine for a long moment as if weighing the genuineness of my curiosity.

"Those who have no knowledge, are often the last to seek instruction."

She swept back to the stage area to speak briefly with Tony. I'd have given a week's pay to know what was being said. It was obviously something regarding our short conversation because Tony had the bad grace to look in my direction before nodding briefly. Sophia glided off to talk to the floor director again.

"Well, what do you think?"

"Beneath that elegant, aging facade, is a shrewd and calculating woman."

"She's the brains of the outfit. Absolutely nothing is done without her approval."

"What about her husband?"

"I've never known quite what to think about Tony. I do know that whatever Sophia says, Tony does. And everything out of his mouth is Sophia this and Sophia that."

"What did you mean when you said Sophia was dying?"

"Mostly rumor, but from what I hear she's been diagnosed

as terminally ill more than once. But prayer—the prayers of
the students and the program's supporters—have healed her
each time." He grinned boyishly. "At least that's what they
say."

"Do you believe it?

He lifted one shoulder in a half shrug. "She's still alive."

"But was she ever really sick?"

"That's the question, isn't it?"

Just then the director clapped his hands and the murmur
behind the cameras hushed. "Let's get to it folks. Mrs.
Belgrade, are you ready?"

Sophia turned to the students and held up her hand. Every
eye was on her immediately. Once again I wondered what
kind of training controlled the young people. Whatever it
was, it was very effective.

"You're a witness to the world. Stand up straight. Smile."

She stepped to the edge of the lighted area and raised both
hands. The students stiffened almost imperceptibly. When
music poured through the sound system, they burst into a
rousing hymn that I remembered from Sunday School as a
child. Brian was right. They were very good.

For the next forty-five minutes I listened to Sophia deliver a message that my grandfather would have called a 'hell-
fire-and-brimstone-rouser,' then plead for the support of the
'ministry' through prayer and donations. Throughout the
whole production, the students remained on their risers,
each with a smile securely in place, hardly seeming to move
a muscle. I caught myself wondering how long they could
stand like that without collapsing.

Even as the thought formed there was an almost imper-
ceptible movement on the back row. I sat forward suddenly,
half out of my chair, when one of the girls crumpled and fell
off the back row of the risers. Brian's hand on my arm
stopped me from getting up.

"Don't. They won't appreciate it," he whispered.

"But—"

"Watch."

The girl had fallen like a rag doll, rolling limply off the riser onto the floor with almost no sound. The others remained as they were, as if nothing had happened, except for two girls on either side of the fallen one each took a half step in to fill the space left. The girl on the floor laid there, still as death.

"Someone has to do something."

"When the program is over."

"This has happened before?"

"Oh, yeah. It gets too hot, or one of 'em will forget and lock his knees. She'll wake up in a minute and be real upset that she might have displeased Sophia, but she'll recover as quickly as she can."

"No one helps her? The taping could be stopped and—"

"The first time it happened Hank stopped the taping and a stage hand rushed over with water. You should have seen Sophia. She was livid!" Brian whispered. "Gave everybody in the room a tongue lashing. After that, the few times it's happened, no one's paid any attention. They get up, rejoin the group, and go on."

"Bizarre."

The young woman still lay on the floor. Sophia finished her plea for viewers to 'answer the call to spread the gospel of The Glorious Church' with generous offerings. The students sang a closing hymn.

"Okay, folks, that's it," Hank called out.

"Hank, one moment please."

Instead of releasing the students, Sophia drew the floor director to one side where they conferred for a few minutes.

While Sophia talked with Hank, the young woman began to rouse herself and sat up. I saw her glance anxiously toward Sophia, then toward Tony, who, while looking at her, didn't move. She scrambled to her feet and climbed onto the risers, assuming her original position as if nothing had happened.

"Sarah," Hank signaled to someone out of sight. "Mrs. Belgrade wants to do that last song again."

"What was wrong with it?" I whispered.

"Nothing, probably. But I've seen her make 'em do it over maybe four or five times."

It was nearly two A.M. before Sophia was satisfied with the tape, but the students were still standing ramrod straight and when they filed out the back door not one back slumped in the fatigue I knew had to be there. It was snowing again and the temperature had fallen to the low single digits, but the students wore no coats that I saw.

By the time the last student had disappeared from the studio Tony and Sophia had already departed. I strode quickly to the back door and looked out. A black Cadillac and five vans were lined up on the parking lot, motors running.

"Apparently not all the money goes to buying Bibles," I said aloud.

"Nope," Brian said from behind me. "The Belgrades don't short themselves, but to look at the school you couldn't prove it."

"I'd like to see the school."

"Not likely. No one but the students are allowed inside the compound."

"We'll see about that."

A thin packet from Front Page was waiting for me when I finally got back to The Holiday. A sleepy desk clerk handed it to me with a look that said he thought I was crazy for being out at this hour. I'd noticed that very little was moving on the street after ten.

Still wide awake, I booted up my laptop to review the articles again as I pulled off my boots, tossing the Ropers in a corner. Settling myself on the bed, propped up by thick pillows, I began to read about The Glorious Church, growing more and more intrigued with each article. I don't know when I fell asleep.

A persistent knock at the door dragged me from a deep sleep. Groaning, I flexed my stiff neck and rolled off the bed.

"Just a minute."

I limped toward the door, still rubbing my neck and left shoulder that was cramped from sleeping half on and half off the pillows. One leg felt like a thousand needles were swimming in the veins. Swinging the door open, I started toward the bathroom.

"Come on in."

"I was beginning to think you'd run out on me again," Gary accused. "You look like hell."

"Thanks. I feel like hell." I splashed water over my face and pulled the band out of my hair.

Drying my face, I padded back into the bedroom.

"I knocked when I got back last night, but you were gone. In fact, I checked several times. Where were you?"

"At the television studio watching a taping. How about some breakfast?"

"Want me to call down?"

"Yeah. Lots of hot coffee, and a bagle with strawberry cream cheese. I'm going to take a shower."

Gary made the call while I stood under hot water, hoping to jump-start my brain. I dressed in jeans and a pull-over sweater, then, still drying my hair, returned to the bedroom.

"What's this stuff?"

Gary was reading the articles, frowning at the headlines.

"Some research on a cult group. They've been working in this area the last few years."

"Cults? Thought that went out in the sixties. Love, peace, and all that garbage."

His superior attitude irked me.

"Cults are never completely gone. They sort of ebb and flow, changing colors and purpose, like taking on a disguise. Some mean nothing, but some are strong and dangerous."

A knock at the door announced the arrival of our breakfast and Gary signed for it.

"Here."

I took a sip of the coffee he handed me, then set it aside.

"Have you ever heard anything about The Glorious Church?"

"No. I don't pay much attention to that sort of thing. Why?"

He settled himself in a chair opposite me and buttered a flaky croissant.

"Well, according to this, the church originated not far from where we lived in California. I thought you might have heard something—"

"I never pay any attention to people like those at the airport. That is what we're talking about, isn't it? A bunch of khaki clad, nearly bald kids who look like something out of *The Walking Dead?*"

I had to admit the correlation was appropriate. They all looked thin, pale, almost hollow.

"You've seen them, you just didn't notice. But these seem different from the usual panhandler type of kids. I wonder—"

"I thought you were here to find out what happened to Susan." He threw down the shredded roll. "You're doing what you always do!"

I stared at him, surprised at the edge in his voice and the sudden color in his face.

"What, exactly, is it that I always do?"

"Go off on a tangent. You're not working now, Margaret. You're here to help Susan. I want you to—"

Knowing where this was going I set my coffee cup aside and started pulling on heavy socks.

"What are you doing?"

Jamming my feet into my leather Ropers, I shoved my hair out of my eyes and pulled on my parka.

"I'm going to get some breakfast."

"No! We've got things to do." He caught my arm as I reached for the door knob.

I carefully pulled away from him. "You have things to do, and I have things to do, but not together."

Before he could say anything else, I was out and down the

stairs. Mr. Patrick looked up as I strode across the hotel foyer but I ignored him. Gary Brady was being himself, as usual. Shortsighted, arrogant, demanding. And, as usual, he got to me.

The rental car didn't like cold weather. I waited for it to warm up while watching in my rear view mirror for Gary.

The windows of the Parakeet were fogged over. The number of cars in the tiny lot marked the café as 'the place' even on frigid mornings like this one. The temperatures were hovering near zero and weren't about to improve if the country music radio station could be counted on for accurate weather reporting.

As I waved at Ida Belle behind the counter I saw Neal Conrad in his usual booth. I shrugged off my coat, hung it on a peg that already held three others, and joined him.

"What's good for breakfast?"

"I'm having the Kitchen Sink," he said, his fork indicating a plate full to running over with eggs, ham, hash browns, a side of pancakes, a tall glass of orange juice and coffee.

"I think I'll pass on that."

Ida arrived with a mug and a fresh carafe of coffee.

"Waffles are good," she suggested.

"One, then."

Ida hurried off and I sipped at my coffee, willing my stomach muscles to relax. Neal stacked egg and a square of pancake on his fork and chewed, watching and waiting it seemed.

This country sheriff bothered me a little. He seemed to see inside me and I had the strangest feeling he could read my mind. Even stranger, I wasn't as compelled as usual to protest that everything was just fine. Though I'd never gone for the rough-and-rugged country type, Neal Conrad definitely appealed to me. I tapped the newspaper he'd folded to one side.

"How can you read that?"

A corner of his mouth lifted in a half smile. "You don't like Armen's weekly?"

"I can't imagine anyone even calling it a newspaper."

Neal sipped his coffee. "Are you a newsprint snob?"

"Grammar and layout snob," I admitted.

The warmth of his gaze moving over me made me aware that I hadn't bothered with any makeup and hadn't really done anything with my hair. I never bothered worrying about how I looked. Why start now?

"What's on your mind this morning?"

"Nothing special. Just had a little run in with Gary Brady and needed some air."

"He get under your skin?"

"Always did."

"The past has a way of shadowing the future." He sipped his coffee. "Getting anywhere with your story?"

He knew I wasn't ready to say more about Gary, or our past together. But then, maybe it was just that he wasn't that interested. I didn't like that that thought bothered me.

"Not on Susan. But The Glorious Church sure is interesting."

"Oh?" He finished off the eggs and ham. "What's so interesting about them?"

"Don't you find the whole set-up a little odd?"

"If odd was a crime, half the town would be in jail. Hell, half the world would be suspect and there'd be nobody left to keep things going."

I had to concede he was probably right.

"It just strikes me as strange that they're here, especially when they started out on the west coast."

"Been doing some digging?"

He didn't look disturbed by that. Mildly amused, perhaps.

"What good are sources if you can't use them?"

A rumble of a laugh came out of his chest. I liked the sound of it.

"Heard you were over at Frank's."

"How'd you know?"

"I'm county. I hear most everything that goes on in a

fifty-mile radius. Besides, you made Frank a bit nervous." His gaze slid over me and his lips curved slightly, only momentarily.

"Have you ever gone into that back room? It's like something out of an old movie."

"It's not your big city magazine. It works here."

I poured us both fresh coffee.

"I've worked on a small town weekly. This isn't one. The Armen Reporter is more a neighborhood newsletter."

"Suppose you could do better."

"In a heartbeat, with one hand and a manual typewriter."

He grinned behind his cup, his eyes crinkling at the corners.

"Ever thought of moving to a small town?"

That caught me unaware. "Came from one. Never thought of going back."

His big shoulders moved beneath his uniform shirt.

"Got something against country folk?"

I carefully poured syrup on the waffle Ida Belle slid in front of me, as she bustled past.

"You ever thought of moving back to the city?"

It was his turn to look away.

"Nope."

"Got something against city folk?"

"Only some of 'em. Find what you wanted at Frank's?"

I concentrated on cutting apart the waffle squares, deciding how much Neal could be trusted.

"Curious?"

"Mildly."

"Why?"

"Got my reasons."

"Not willing to share information?"

"When there's something to share."

I weighed the pros and cons and decided it was to my advantage to be cooperative. Besides, the sheriff was an interesting man.

"Well, the church was started by Tony and Sophia

Belgrade in the late sixties. They started out preaching to hippies in Hollywood. Their lives before then are a little hazy, but, Sophia claims to have had a startling Christian experience as a child. Later she had a brief fling in show business, but then turned to full-time evangelism. From what I saw last night, she hasn't left her career in show business very far behind.

"Anyway, she met Tony at a Sunday School thing and they were married just a few months later. Tony was, he says, a successful Hollywood PR man and record promoter."

"What kind of ministry are we talking about? The usual television hoopla?"

"Not then. They claim, though, that they were the beginning of the Jesus Movement when they started handing out tracts and preaching to hippies and drug addicts. Then in the early seventies they moved their growing group to a canyon outside Los Angeles where they took over a failing restaurant. Then they built a school on some acreage nearby. By mid-1985 they'd established The Glorious Church. The building itself was built by the students, I'm told."

"Yeah," the sheriff said, nodding.

"There's a school too?"

"Yeah. It's outside of town, toward Armen."

"I wonder—"

"About what?"

He refilled both our coffee cups.

"Well, things don't fit."

"Don't fit?"

"It's what I do, Sheriff. Keep fitting pieces of a puzzle together until they fit. When they don't, it could mean an interesting story."

I picked up my coffee cup and hid behind it for a minute.

"What about this bothers you?"

"A lot of things. Maybe not as many—I don't know. Maybe it's just that I don't know a lot about this kind of thing and I want to know.

"The ministry seems to differ from some other cults. Their evangelism is pretty high pressure, from what I saw last night. And, the group left California after some people lodged complaints against them."

"What kind of complaints?"

"It seems the church bought a ranch to use as a retreat for some of their more influential, meaning monied, members. When some of them returned from a weekend there, they accused the Belgrades of keeping them virtual prisoners. The curriculum, they said, consisted mostly of badgering them to 'convert'.

"No charges were brought, but when other things began happening, the Belgrades moved the core of their group here. From what I've learned so far, they're doing basically the same things here as they did in California. They built a school, a church, have a restaurant, and a television show that's syndicated across the nation. Speculation is that they've collected millions of dollars, and most of it has gone into the pockets of the Belgrades themselves."

"They were accused of fraud? No charges brought?"

"I'm still digging into that."

"You've managed to find out quite a lot."

"I've got a good research assistant." I allowed myself a smile. "Some of that 'big city' advantage Frank doesn't have."

He acknowledged that with the slight lift of an eyebrow.

"What about Susan?"

"I'm working on that."

"And Mr. Brady. What's he working on?"

My fork hung halfway to my mouth. "What kind of question is that?"

"Sam said he wanted adjoining rooms."

His gaze didn't flicker as I stared at him. "We don't have them."

"Only because there aren't any?"

"Because I'm not interested in starting anything with an ex-husband I haven't seen in five years."

"Is he?"

"Is he what?"

"Interested in starting something."

"Sheriff—"

"Neal."

"Neal, what's this about?"

His gaze flicked over me and his lips curved in a smile. "Just doing a little investigating on my own."

I chewed my waffle slowly. What was happening here? Could it be that the 'interest' was mutual?

"How's your research coming?"

He sipped his coffee then set the mug carefully on the table, keeping his large hand cupped over it.

"Carefully. But that's the way we do things down here. Slow and easy." The way his gaze moved over me convinced me he wasn't totally talking about business. He tossed a tip on the table and slid out of the booth. "Remember what I said. Clear things with me before you go digging around too deep."

I lifted my cup in a salute and watched him speak to several men as he strode toward the door. Neal Conrad was an interesting man. A very interesting man. And I was looking forward to testing out his 'research' skills.

Gary was waiting for me when I returned to my hotel room.

"Ready to talk now?"

"I'm always ready to talk, Gary. I'm just not ready to be bullied."

"But you're wasting time with this church thing."

"I'm exploring whatever comes along. Answering any question that comes to mind." I threw my coat across the bed. "Besides, I'm supposed to be here 'working'. There might be a real story in The Glorious Church. The Belgrades are certainly interesting enough." I combed my fingers through my hair. "How are your folks?"

He drew a deep breath and let it out slowly. It was the first sign, other than anger, that he was deeply affected by Susan's death and the questions about it.

"They're all right. Don't understand what happened to Susan, but I assured them you'd find out something."

"And how did they feel about that?"

I didn't think the senior Bradys would be very receptive to my involvement and hadn't attempted to see them because of it.

"Grateful. The funeral is tomorrow, if the sheriff will . . . if they'll release Susan's body." He paced to the window. "I'll be glad when this is over."

I was beginning to wonder if it would ever be 'over'. In fact, looking into The Glorious Church was a way to avoid brooding about Susan. Her death had strongly affected four lives and I couldn't imagine any of us ever being able to leave it behind—at least, not for a very long time.

I spent a couple of hours making notes on what I'd observed during the taping. Then, shortly after three o'clock, I drove out to the school owned by The Glorious Church.

The complex was enclosed by a chain link fence with a strand of barbed wire running around the top, which made me wonder why such security was necessary. The buildings inside appeared to be unpainted barracks type frame, like World War II leftovers. The church the Belgrades had built, stood just outside.

The church building was a simple structure, with double doors, windows running down both sides, a belfry on top. All in all it would have been a charmingly quaint setting, with thick woods beginning less than thirty yards behind the building, if it hadn't been for the enclosed compound another thirty yards to the right.

Remembering Sophia's comment about pictures, I stopped a short distance down the road. Fitting a close-up lens on my camera, I took a few shots of the somber scene. When I drove up to the gate, a guard came out of a small wooden enclosure.

"I'd like to see either Tony or Sophia Belgrade, please."

"You're not expected."

"I'm Maggie Rome. I met Sophia last night at the television studio. Will you check whether she'll see me please? I'm writing a story and I'd like to talk to her before I send it in."

"It is prayer and meditation time."

"Prayer and meditation?"

I got no response to that.

"Please, you must have some sort of phone in there. Will you tell the Belgrades I'm here and that I'd like to talk to them about The Glorious Church?"

The guard returned to the building reluctantly and I rolled the car window up again, crossing my fingers. The guard returned a few minutes later.

"Park over there," he instructed.

'Over there' was in front of the church on a small white chat lot.

"Follow me, please."

Instead of being led inside the church as I'd expected, he lead me toward one of the barracks buildings. I shivered with the cold, and something else I couldn't name. Dusk was falling fast, casting long shadows, painting the weathered buildings in sooty gray that made the windows seem grimy.

My imagination worked over time. The buildings looked similar to those in the concentration camps I'd seen on television. I frowned, shrugging my shoulders deeper into my insulated parka.

Halfway to the building, I stopped short. Two young men sat on the ground beneath a tree, a chimney lamp between them. They each appeared to be reading a book by the dim light.

I caught the guard's attention. "Wait a minute."

"Yes?"

"Those boys are barefoot!"

"Yes."

I stared at him, amazed at his tone. How could he be so

unaffected by the sight of two young people, barefoot, wearing no coats, sitting on the frozen ground.

"It's ten degrees out here. How can they do that?"

"Physical comfort is unimportant."

"I don't understand."

"Sophia will answer your questions."

"But—"

"Sophia will answer your questions."

From his tone of voice, I knew that no one but Sophia would be talking to me about anything.

He opened the door of the first long, unpainted building. I stepped inside, jumping a little when he shut the door firmly behind us. It was little warmer inside than out, and just as unwelcoming.

The room was barren except for a large painting of Tony and Sophia that hung over a table on which a Bible lay open. Speakers were mounted on the wall near the ceiling, making me wonder what was broadcast over them. There was no sound now. Metal bunk beds with a thin mattress covered by one blanket stood in double rows down both sides of the room. There were no personal effects in evidence, and no lockers in which any could be stored.

Three young men sat on bunks, reading, but they didn't look up when we entered.

"You will wait here. Tony will be along shortly."

I nodded, wondering why I'd been brought to the barracks. Just then my attention was drawn to a door at the opposite end of the room. Two bodyguards stepped inside and unrolled a scarlet cloth across the floor.

Tony entered, walking toward me on the scarlet cloth. He wore the same style of dark clothes he'd worn at the studio—black trousers, loose black silk shirt. A large silver medallion hung around his neck, the circle resting in the graying hair visible in the vee of the neck. His hair was the same dyed sooty black as Sophia's.

Cowboy boots made him seem taller than what I judged to be his real height of perhaps five-feet-nine or ten inches. Without them we would have been eye to eye and I wondered if the extra two inches had been his motivation for wearing them. He seemed the type. The dark glasses were missing, but he'd added a long cape to his ensemble.

Before I could consider the reason for this charade, I heard the sound of flushing in the bathroom. A barefoot young man dressed in loose trousers and an overly large shirt exited. When he saw Tony, he immediately knelt, kissing the large ring on Tony's left hand. He rose and turned away, but as he turned, he stepped on a sharp edge of a nut on a bolt that held a bunk bed to the floor.

When blood spurted from a deep cut, I was horrified to see that he appeared to be totally unaware of injury or pain. He continued walking through the room and out behind me, leaving bloody footprints on the wooden floor.

I forced myself not to react outwardly, but my mind was racing. Were these students on drugs, or was there some kind of mind control involved to make them oblivious to cold and pain?

"Miss Rome. Your visit is a pleasant surprise."

"Uh, thank you for seeing me."

His voice was low, with an intimate quality that made my sexual antennae quiver. Tony Belgrade obviously considered himself very attractive to women. His gaze slid over me, lingering over my breasts, and I fought the urge to step back a pace or two. I did zip my parka. When he held out his hand, I forced myself to shake it, disengaging my fingers when he held it just a little too long.

"How could I refuse such a lovely young woman? Sophia told me how impressed she was with you last evening. She said you were, perhaps, a seeker."

"Seeker?"

"One who wishes to know the truth. I'm sorry to have to

greet you here, but services are being held in the chapel and Sophia is leading study group at the house."

When I'd arrived, the lights at the church had been on but there had been no sound coming from the building, no indication that anyone was inside. Why did Tony find it necessary to lie?

"This is fine. In fact, I much prefer it. Would you mind if I took a few pictures? For my story?"

"Oh, I'm sorry, we don't allow pictures. In fact, Gabriel, will you take Miss Rome's bag? I'm sure you'll be much more comfortable without it."

"That's all right," I began, but found myself relieved of the bag.

"Please, don't be concerned. It will be returned when you're ready to leave."

I suppressed a flicker of apprehension. "I'd like to ask you a few questions about your ministry."

"I'm afraid you will need to speak with Sophia. Perhaps you could come back another time."

"When would be convenient?"

"Perhaps we could call you."

I sensed I wasn't going to get anywhere trying to pick Tony's brain. Sophia was the one everyone talked to.

"I'm at The Holiday, in Fayetteville."

"Yes. I believe you have a friend there with you?"

It was a little disturbing to realize that someone from The Glorious Church had been checking up on me.

"An acquaintance. We both had reason to be here and traveled together."

"And what might those reasons be?"

"I'm on assignment, and there was a death in his family."

"Ah. The young woman connected with the university."

I was glad I'd told the truth. Tony obviously already knew it and my credibility would have been destroyed if I'd told him a 'story'.

"Yes. She was his sister."

"I see. Very sad." Tony began walking me toward the door, his hand firm on my arm. The guards followed. "Perhaps in a few days you and Sophia could talk."

"I'll look forward to it. Again, thank you for seeing me this evening."

"My pleasure. Gabriel, walk Ms. Rome to her car."

As I followed the guard out, I was aware that Tony watched from the doorway of the barracks. Gabriel opened the car door for me, placing my camera bag carefully in the back floorboard, then stepped back, waiting for me to slide inside.

"Thank you."

Without a word, he closed the door solidly, then signaled for another guard to open the main gate which was now locked. I drove back to the motel, more curious than ever about Tony and Sophia, and The Glorious Church.

Chapter Five

Gary stepped out of his room just as I was unlocking my door and followed me inside.

"Where in the hell have you been!"

"Doing a little snooping." I tossed my bag next to the bed, picked up the phone and punched in a long distance number.

"I thought you were going to help me."

"I am."

"You're still playing around with this Glorious Church thing—"

I ignored him.

"Mark, Maggie Rome. I'm fine, how are you? And Sharon?" Great. Look. I need some help on something."

Mark Latham was a newspaper friend I'd worked with in Orange County. We'd maintained contact ever since, trading information and anecdotes on almost a monthly basis.

"Find out everything you can on a cult group called The Glorious Church and Tony and Sophia Belgrade. The Belgrades left there about five years ago, but some of the group stayed behind. I need to know why they left and what's going on with the group there now. Anything you can get me."

When I hung up a few minutes later there was nothing to

do but wait for his return call. I sat on the edge of the bed and began pulling off my boots.

"Why are you still asking questions about this church group?"

"I think I explained that. It made me curious, and I want to find out more about it. There are some strange things going on out there and I think it might make a good story. Did you see your folks this afternoon?"

"Dad has closed himself in the den and mother stays in her sitting room and cries. I don't know how Mom's going to get through the funeral tomorrow."

I stopped writing in the steno pad I used for notes and questions to myself to watch Gary pace to the window and look outside. It was dark outside, making his solemn reflection clear. The slump to his shoulders made me realize that even a family that seemed to lack the most basic of emotions now knew the most terrible of sorrows.

"Losing a child must be the most horrible experience."

"Susan was special to Mom; a late-in-life baby, I guess, does that. I remember when Mother told me about the baby, she mentioned that after I was born and five years passed without another pregnancy, she thought there would never be any more babies. Then, when she suspected she was pregnant with Susan, she didn't tell anyone for a long time, in case of a miscarriage or something."

He stared up into the dark sky and I realized that even during the two years we'd been married, Gary had never talked about how he felt when Susan was born. In fact, conversations generally centered on things, not feelings. In that he was very like his father.

"I remember being a little angry that she hadn't told me she was pregnant. I was in college, away from home, and all of a sudden I got this phone call telling me I had a baby sister. I thought it had to be some joke. I mean, the last time I'd been home no one had said anything. I felt ... betrayed somehow. Like, I'd been shoved out of the house to make room for this new . . . little person."

That intrigued me. I'd always assumed that Gary somehow just tolerated Susan because there were eighteen years between them and because he was self-centered. It had never occurred to me that he'd been hurt when she was born.

"How did you feel later?"

He smiled. "Captivated. She was a charmer. By the time I could get a break from college to get home, she was almost a month old. Lots of black hair, dark eyes, that olive skin. She looked like something out of an Ivory soap ad."

He turned from the window and rested against the sill, his arms crossed.

"I always thought maybe our babies would look like Susan." He shrugged, a musing expression on his face. "But then, with you being a redhead and me being blonde, that was probably silly."

"I didn't know you wanted children."

There were a great many things we hadn't talked about enough, children being only one.

"Of course I did. There are always things one wants to pass on to their children. A heritage, such as it is. My business is doing well, I'm my father's only heir—now."

With his head resting against the window, Gary stared at the ceiling. It was obvious that talking about Susan was emotionally stressful for Gary, and yet, it made me curious. He'd never gone out of his way to talk to Susan, to be interested in her, when we were married. In fact, I'd begun to wonder, toward the end of our marriage, whether he was capable of honest emotion at all. Now it seemed that Gary was aware that time had suddenly run out for him and Susan.

"Did you want children?"

The question jolted me out of my reverie.

"Yes. Not soon, but sometime."

"Got a father in mind?"

"No. It's difficult," I shrugged, wishing he'd not gotten on this topic, "when I travel so much."

"But this is what you wanted." He glanced around the room critically. "Running around all over the world, living in hotel rooms, out of a suitcase."

"It's part of my life, part of what comes with the territory." I ran restless fingers through my hair. "Look, I love my work. I love taking pictures and writing about the people and places that are on everyone's mind but half don't even know where they are, much less know anything about them. I don't expect you to understand, but being a journalist is something I was born to do."

"But we had everything. A great condo, my business was just taking off. My parents would have done anything for us."

"Within certain guidelines," I reminded him. "The first criteria being that I quit my job. Somehow having a daughter-in-law who grubbed around in jeans and boon-dockers with a camera bag slung over her shoulder just didn't fit the 'image'," I made imaginary quotes around the word, "that they had created for your wife."

"It wasn't like that—"

"Yes, it was. You had the same expectations. That's why you didn't see it. Somehow I always just missed being right, about everything. I was too casual, I didn't wear the right clothes, I discussed topics that were too . . . controversial. I insisted upon dragging politics or economics into the conversation, and if that didn't bring a quietus to a dinner party, nothing did."

"I don't—"

"You know it."

He grinned suddenly. "Remember the night you showed up, late as usual, with black smudges all over your face and hands, reeking of rancid smoke?"

Did I ever. The shock on Pauline's face had been so comical that I'd burst into laughter. Edward had been stone-faced, but he was like that much of the time. I'd never been able to put a tag on Gary's father. He was a man determined to be aloof, to hold himself apart, to not let anyone know him. That had always bothered me.

"The night the building supplies company burned down."

"And the night you arrived for a theater party, thirty minutes before we were ready to leave for cocktails, smelling like a garbage dump."

"With shreds of lettuce stuck to my sleeves and pieces of packing material in my hair." She shrugged. "I was doing an exposé on city dump sites and the leeching that was occurring. It wasn't easy to get the pictures I needed to prove my suspicions. But I did it.

"Ninety days later the city passed an ordinance that certain items would no longer be accepted at the landfills. I was very proud of that work." I looked up at him. "I wanted you to be—"

"But I couldn't get past the fact that my parents had been embarrassed." He finished the sentence for me.

"Were they really embarrassed, or just annoyed?"

"I think the words are interchangeable."

"You wouldn't have admitted that then."

"A lot has changed since then."

He looked expectant and I hated to disappoint him, but if he hoped for some kind of reconciliation I didn't want him to hold out hope.

"But I haven't. I still wear jeans, the boondockers are still in place, and I still slog around in the worst places you can imagine. My camera is still a part of me. And I still love seeing my byline every month."

"Then there's no chance we could . . . see whether we made a mistake getting a divorce?"

"Is that why you wanted me to come here with you? To stir the ashes and see if there were a few sparks still alive?"

"You were always good with words, Margaret. I always felt at a disadvantage when we argued."

"And we argued much too frequently for us to ever think

about getting together again. We're both way past that moment, if it was ever there."

I had my doubts about a lot of things, but not this. I'd spent too many long nights raking over those old coals, testing tender feelings to see if there was still any pain, sorting through the possible alternatives and finding none that would have worked.

"That's pretty final."

"Very final." I stood and stretched, more to break the mood than because my muscles were cramped. "It would be a mistake to think we could be together, like that again. Friendship, maybe. But nothing stronger."

"Brutal."

"Quick and deft, that's my strategy. Like a surgeon. It's the only way. That's why I left California immediately after the divorce. There was no use staying and torturing myself with more what-ifs than I already had."

I had started toward the bathroom when his hand on my arm stopped me.

"Do you think about those what-ifs often?"

He was closer than I wanted. I could smell the remnants of his cologne, feel the warmth of his breath against my face, hear the slightly raspy tone of his low voice. Memories stirred ashes long cold. There was no glow, no warmth left.

"Oh, yes, I thought about them. And I answered them."

Why was my throat so thick, squeezing my voice to a whisper? Because saying goodbye again, even though it was right, was always difficult.

"How? How did you answer?"

"By proving to myself I had done everything I could under the circumstances. By learning to live with choices I'd made, knowing I'd made them the only way possible." I turned out of his grasp and stepped back, needing the distance between us. "I loved you. I really, really loved you. At least, as much as I knew how then. If I hadn't, I would have known before we married that we weren't right for one another."

"What is 'right'? What's good for you? What about me?"

"You. Me. What happened to 'us'? That's what happened. There just never was 'us'."

"What are you talking about? There wasn't anyone else."

"I'm not talking about another woman. I'm talking about—" I paced, trying to remember all the reasons I'd listed to myself during those nights after the divorce when I couldn't sleep. "I'm talking about your parents, the image you wanted, no, needed. Your father, Edward, had a plan for you, for me, for our marriage, and when I didn't fit in, he turned his back. I'm talking about all those expectations we had, all those misguided perceptions about what we could be together, what we would have together."

I didn't know whether to continue or not, but if he had any serious thoughts about patching up our marriage, then I had to.

"I'm talking about not being together, about feeling—" I sought the right words. "Feeling less, not more, when we were together."

His face was pale when I turned, and I hated the pain I was causing him.

"You're saying I made you feel . . . less of a person?"

"I'm not explaining it well. I'm sorry. Maybe I don't mean to say less, but I didn't feel more. I needed to feel that I could be more with you than without you, and that wasn't happening." He looked like I'd just slapped him. "I'm sorry," I whispered, not certain whether I was sorry for knowing what had been wrong with the marriage for me, or that he'd forced me to say it. "I'm sorry if you asked for my help hoping to resurrect something between us."

"But if not, why did you agree to come? I mean, if my family—"

"Gary, none of this has anything to do with your family.

Not really. What happened then was between you and me. I'm finished with that. I came because of Susan, and what she meant to me. Because I felt her death deserved to be finalized somehow with you and your parents knowing why she died. I needed to know the why and who of what happened. I felt Susan deserved that."

"I see. Well," he managed, "I guess there's nothing else to say."

"Not on that subject. I think we should stick to what happened to Susan."

"I, uh, think I need a drink."

"Go on down. I want to shower and change, then maybe I'll order something from room service."

He seemed distracted, not certain what to do now. I hated what I'd had to say to him, but I couldn't let him hope for something that was never going to happen.

"Then I'll see you in the morning."

"Fine," I said, starting toward the bathroom again. I heard the door slam behind him. When I felt the prick of tears I blinked them away.

The next morning was cold and overcast. It didn't warm up more than a few degrees before two o'clock. I'd brought one dress in anticipation of the funeral—a dark green wool with long close-fitting sleeves, a full skirt that swirled around my calves when I walked. It was the kind of dress that was always in style and I always took it with me when I traveled in the winter because it packed well and because I always looked good in it.

Gary was subdued and I wondered how much of that was due to our conversation the night before. I knew what it was like to cling to impossible dreams and I hadn't enjoyed making him face the truth about our marriage. Whether he recognized it or not, I'd done him a favor by not encouraging his hopes about my reasons for being in Arkansas with him.

The chapel was quaint, reminiscent of a time long past.

The walls were paneled, matching the mellow hue of the pine seats that were well worn by worshipers searching to know a God that I sometimes questioned.

What kind of God allowed the inhumanity man committed against himself through the destruction of his own world, through the atrocities he committed against another simply because he didn't agree with a philosophy, or the color of his skin, or was jealous of his position?

And what kind of God allowed some nameless, faceless person to snuff out the life of a young woman standing on the brink of discovering her own contribution to a world needing all the help it can get?

As I sat looking at the floral draped gray casket at the front of the auditorium, and the framed photo that sat atop it, I was suddenly overwhelmed with my own sense of mortality. I leaned forward to rest my forehead upon my arms folded on the pew. What kind of God gave us the intelligence to create the questions, but not the cognition to discover the answers?

"Margaret."

I sat up as Gary's hand rested on my shoulder.

"Are you all right?"

"Uh, yes." I searched for a tissue in my pocket. "Just asking myself a few questions."

It was clear that he didn't understand and it wasn't the time or place to explain, even if I'd wanted to. Glancing toward the front pews I saw that Gary's parents were already seated and a few other mourners were scattered in the pews just behind them.

"I'd like you to sit with the family, if you feel comfortable doing that."

I didn't want to intrude, but I didn't want to be alone just now either. I walked beside Gary down the aisle and sat beside him. I suddenly wanted to take his hand, wondering if I should or shouldn't. In the end, I didn't.

The soft organ music made me overly aware of myself, as

if being here like this made all my thoughts introspective. Shouldn't I be thinking about Susan, about her parents sitting so still and straight in front of me?

There is something about a funeral that brings home so painfully one's own mortality and I didn't want to have time to think about how quickly everything I'd worked toward could be rendered totally meaningless. I'd sensed it first in Susan's apartment. Without her there it was less than a shell; like the shell left behind after the chick has hatched and having served its purpose can only be kicked aside out of the way.

Dr. and Mrs. Brady sat without touching, their shoulders seeming to purposely remain carefully one inch apart as if they were so fragile that even the faintest brush would shatter them. By leaning forward just a little I could see that not even their hands touched. They were so totally wrapped in grief that they seemed incapable of reaching out to anyone, even one another, in a time of loss that almost demanded by its enormity the touch of another human being.

The organ music swelled, played by someone out of sight. I didn't recognize the music and thought it a little strange in mood. Its sound was the other world sort that I associated with certain segments of futuristic movies. The piece seemed to be some sort of fugue, with its counterpoints almost jarring as they interspersed. I was glad when it ended and the pastor stepped to the stand.

"We are here today to mourn a life too soon taken from us; the life of Susan Brady. I would like to read—"

The monotone voice faded as I was once again caught up in the memory of the Susan I'd known. The shy young girl who was trying to decide who and what she should be, who fought the same demons of identity in the Brady family that I'd suffered.

Though I had been reluctant to lay upon the quiet girl my own doubts and questions, I'd shared in her own struggle for identity, the pushing against the rules and restrictions of a family in which she'd felt she didn't quite fit. Naturally, Susan had never said outright that she had those kinds of feelings, but it had been woven through her statements each time she'd been at odds with her parents over something.

But had there ever lived a teenager who didn't have those same feelings? I had suffered them, though my situation had been a little different. Being raised by parents who were intent on seeming larger by making the other seem smaller and ineffectual created obstacles that weren't there in the usual parent-child relationship. Though I now understood and accepted the emotional hungers of both my parents, knowledge could never totally erase the problems they had created. I'd purposely chosen a number of psychology classes in college in order to be armed for allaying my own demons, but I still occasionally stumbled across the carcasses.

Somehow, listening to Susan had helped me work through a few residuals from that relationship, finding myself repeating many of the same things my school counselor, who had been a great help to me, had said.

At the time, of course, I had rejected them as being totally cliché, but in talking to Susan I realized how right they had been. As a result, I'd repeated them to Susan and received the same response I'd given a few years earlier, "you don't understand."

I stared at the blanket of pink carnations covering Susan's casket. Tears blurred the edges of the blossoms, fading the darker pink of the ribbon into the paler tone of the flowers. The gold letters on the ribbon melted and disappeared. *Beloved Daughter.*

I wondered at the depth of meaning in the words. Was it there because it was truly meant, or had the words been expected? Somehow, Pauline Brady had not seemed the kind of person who would hold to anything so closely that it could be called beloved. But she was a great believer in supposedly doing what was right.

Edward was just as stiff and seemingly incapable of

warmth, certainly not a flexible person. He was almost militaristic in bearing and attitude toward life.

I chewed my lower lip. Perhaps that's why we never got along, Pauline and I, Edward and I. Gary's mother reminded me so much of mine. Perhaps that was why I'd known instinctively that no matter what I did, no matter how I tried to change, Pauline Brady would never accept me as Gary's wife, as a daughter.

A part of me had always mourned that which could never be. Face it, Maggie Rome, you're still 'mother's little girl' wanting someone to kiss your boo-boos.

Suddenly everyone stood and I managed to get to my feet awkwardly just as the minister began a closing prayer. I wished I could be anywhere else as the few students passed by the closed coffin. There were two older people, a man and a woman, who might have been professors. They had the look. Then, before I was ready, Gary urged me out of the pew ahead of him.

Sometimes, when I had to do something that everything in me rebelled against, like asking a victim how it felt to experience the tragedy of the story I was covering, or asking someone to catalogue his thoughts in the aftermath of some life-changing experience, I managed somehow to turn off my feeling senses. At those moments I forced myself to somehow operate mechanically, saying the words without feeling them, refusing to recognize the pain and hurt they caused.

Whether I convinced myself of the public's right to know, or that I was simply doing a job, I never came away from that type of experience without knowing I'd left some small part of myself behind.

Now, standing by Susan's casket, touching the petals of the pungent carnations, I'd never felt more sensitive to being alive in the face of feeling some injustice. Who was I to be standing here, and Susan unable to? What great fate had decreed that? And why? Was there, as some believed, some great purpose to everything that happened? Or were both of us, Susan and me, simply victim of some erratic circumstance?

I whispered the question to the smiling face I remembered so well. "Will we ever know?"

Yes, I vowed inside. I will find out. Not for Susan, who was past being affected by it all, and not for Gary, or his parents, but for myself. Because I needed to know what had happened to Susan, and why, and perhaps in some way to justify it.

But then, perhaps it was for a more selfish reason. Perhaps it was something like crossing your heart and hoping to die, stick a needle in your eye, over some promise. Perhaps knowing would be like a charm or talisman for my own life, keeping me just a step or two out of the reach of a meaningless death. That, I knew, would be the worst tragedy of all. To die and have it all mean nothing.

The graveside service was mercifully short. We stood in the snow, the bitter north wind dragging away the words of the minister before they reached even those standing in the front of the casket, which was suspended over a ragged hole in the frozen earth. Dr. and Mrs. Brady sat stiffly in metal folding chairs, two isolated persons who seemed so separated from the rest of us and from what was happening that a great wash of despair moved over me.

"Excuse me," I whispered to Gary. "I don't feel well."

Before he could ask any questions, I strode as quickly as I could over the uneven ground in heels that I was unaccustomed to wearing, toward the private car provided by the funeral home.

I huddled in a corner of the seat, staring at the small clump of people under the green funeral canopy. What a horrible day to say goodbye to someone. A movement behind the group caught my attention. A black limousine rolled slowly past. We were not the only ones saying goodbye to someone.

Then I allowed the sobs to come and let the tears flow down my cheeks. Why do people have to die?

Chapter Six

"Maggie? Mark. I've got some interesting stuff on that group you called about."

"Tell me."

I reached for a pad and pen, pushing my tangled hair away from my face. The funeral had left me drained and I'd been laying on the bed, just staring at the ceiling, when the phone rang.

I'd ridden back to the funeral home with the Bradys after the grave-side services, each immersed in our own thoughts, each anxious to be alone with them. When Gary suggested we go somewhere for a drink, I refused, suggesting that he go home with his parents for a while instead. I didn't quite understand his reluctance, but in the end he'd gone.

"Seems the Belgrades didn't leave California because they wanted to."

"Something about fraud and parents claiming their kids were kidnapped and held prisoner?"

"Right. The fine couple was ridden out on a rail, you might say. A friend gave me the names of a couple of people who are trying to kidnap their kids back from The Glorious Church and some others who have been successful."

"Was it really a case of kidnapping?"

"The Glorious Church is not some little vanilla wafer type of organization, Mag. The kids who have left tell some pretty bizarre stories about the group's activities. Stories about some strange music and dancing and rituals involving snake handling."

I shivered. I'd never been able to abide snakes. "What else?"

"The Belgrades left California after charges of child abuse were brought against Tony."

This was new. "Who brought the charges?"

"Investigations were spurred by the interview of a child removed from a Belgrade compound by order of the Orange County Superior Court."

"What kind of abuse are we talking about?"

"Uh, nasty stuff. Beatings, starvation, sleep deprivation, forced marches, sexual control, withholding of privileges, even to the point of not allowing the students to go to the bathroom at will; no showers, speaking only when spoken to, long hours of standing outside in the rain for minor infractions . . . it goes on and on.

"There's even one report by a young man whose testimony the authorities feel is unquestionable, that charges were brought by the group against one of their own for such infractions as . . . let me read this to you directly from the report.

"Maria B. was sitting outside number seven kitchen, alone, at five P.M. waiting for the van to take her and the others to church. I told Maria twice to come inside, reminding her it was a rule not to be outside after dark. But she did not receive my advice.

"The report is signed by a Larry D. Then, one of the kids who got out, brought a list of offenses that the students are taught to avoid. Listen to this little sample. Are you writing this down?"

"So far so good." I was scribbling furiously in a combination shorthand and my own version of speed writing.

I could almost see Mark skimming the information.

"There's entering the kitchen without permission, sliding furniture over any floor, talking too loud after evening service, interrupting a group unnecessarily while they are reading," he recited. "And bringing a vehicle back with less than a quarter tank of gas, stepping on flowers, entering the tract room without permission, hanging clothes to dry on fireplace screens—that indicates the laundry facilities were pretty crude. Then there's being late for choir practice without good excuse—emphasis on 'good' there—and to be motionless one minute or more while in the prayer room."

Mark hesitated. "Oh, here's something. Not getting up within five minutes after wake-up call, nodding during services, turning in donation cards not filled out properly, damaging tracts. Those are for the more advanced students."

"Wow," I breathed, still writing furiously.

"Yeah, wow. But there's more. Apparently there are some additional ones for the so-called 'baby Christians,' which includes sleeping during service, night watch or prayer hour, picking up cigarette butts off the street while witnessing—that's a no-no—and refusing night watch without a good excuse. I'm not sure what night watch is."

"Sounds like some kind of military basic training camp for survivalists rather than a school."

"That's what I thought, until I heard more about the punishments."

"Oh?"

"Talk of big paddles with holes drilled. The kind that create a great deal of bruising, breaking the skin. And then there's the sexual control."

"What kind of control are we talking about here?"

"Servant and master kind of stuff, group participation demanded for certain infractions of the rules. Real sick, and your good friend Tony's the controller."

My skin crawled.

"What about Sophia's participation?"

"None that I can find in that, though from what I understand it all went on with her blessing. Probably keeps Tony happy and out of her hair. She's twenty years older than him, and apparently totally devoted to the 'ministry'."

"How do they get away with this kind of thing? Hasn't there been a follow-up on the complaints?"

"As much as could be done, but the complainant either takes back what he's claimed, or just isn't around any more."

A chill went down my spine. "What do you mean?"

"Just that. Look, most of the punishments are the normal stuff for cult groups. If you break a group offense, then you're assigned special duties, like K.P., for anywhere from a week to a month. From what one of the guys said, this group then spends all day, every day, in the kitchen washing dishes, sorting out food.

"And that's another thing. Food. Apparently in order to keep down costs, certain teams were sent out to go through the garbage of grocery stores and pull out produce that had been tossed because of wilting and so forth, and dairy products that had passed the shelf date. They hauled this stuff home, cut off the rotten parts, and fed it to the group at large. This is what the kitchen help did."

I was still scribbling furiously while questions tumbled over one another in my mind. All this might not have anything at all to do with Susan's death, but I still felt there had to be some connection. It was just too coincidental that The Glorious Church moved here, the Bradys moved here, and now Susan was dead. Was it a stretch? Perhaps. But even if I didn't prove a connection, I still might have a story from the cult angle.

"What kept them from getting food poisoning?"

"Nothing. There were several cases. Also malnutrition. But it was all a part of making the grade, school wise. Plus, there's testimony about marathon Bible reading sessions or prayer sessions where the students spent literally hours on their knees. Then there's claims of sleep deprivation. When

I read this I thought it sounded like some kind of brain-washing technique. The Jim Jones kind of thing."

"This isn't your typical cult group, is it?"

"Well, there's more than a couple like that," he reminded me, "but it isn't like Satanists, which is what you automatically think of."

"I've never done any investigation into this kind of thing and I don't want to ask too many questions here, yet. Keep digging for me, will you? See if any charges were actually brought against the Belgrades that stuck."

"What are you looking for?"

"I don't know. I'm just swimming around trying to find something to hold onto."

"Okay. I'll keep in touch."

After saying goodbye to Mark, I spent the next couple of hours transcribing my hastily scribbled notes into something more readable. When I was finished, I rested my head against the back of the chair and thought about The Glorious Church. On the outside the organization could seem so normal, but underneath—what was going on there?

I glanced at the clock. The afternoon was gone and it was growing dark outside. I hadn't seen or heard from Gary since the funeral. I hoped he was spending time with his parents. The family needed each other now, whether they realized it or not.

I walked to the Parakeet for something to eat. As I pulled off my gloves and blew on my fingers, I glanced around the room. Neal Conrad was in a booth, finishing a plate of fries. How he kept trim on that diet was beyond me.

Taking his nod as an invitation, I waved at Ida Belle, mimicked a cup of coffee, and slid into the booth opposite the sheriff.

"Funeral over?"

I stole a french fry. "Umhum. A couple of hours ago."

"Then you'll be leaving in a day or so."

"Is that a question, or a suggestion?" I chose another fry.

"Neither," he shrugged.

"I'm here to do a story—"

"You're here to find out if Susan Brady was murdered."

Ida brought my coffee which gave me a moment to think. "You're right."

"Brady called here the day after his sister was found and made a lot of noise. Wasn't happy when no one sat up and saluted."

I had to smile. "Just knowing she's dead is horrible, but to know someone may have killed her, for no apparent reason, it wasn't even an accident, makes me need to know what happened."

"You should leave that up to me."

I met his gaze evenly. "I can't. I have to know for myself what happened to her."

"What happened to a reporter's objectivity?"

"I've already fought that battle with myself and come to a draw. Haven't you ever just had to do something, no matter what logic said?"

"It's sometimes hard to separate logic and emotion."

"I guess you'd know about that. I heard you left New York with a few problems following you."

Yes, his eyes could turn frosty. "Who told you about that?"

"No one told me *about* anything. I just know there was a shooting and it probably prompted your leaving the force. I've wondered, are you a New Yorker who bailed out? Or a country boy who came home?"

I thought he wasn't going to answer; he turned his coffee mug around and around, the sound of the crockery scraping on the table top seeming louder than natural.

"Bailed out."

"Do you miss it?"

"Miss the city? Nope."

"What do you miss?"

There was a closed look on his face and I hated that I'd caused it. Seems I'm always putting my foot in something.

"There were people, like Charlie, who stood with me."

I read between the lines. "Why wouldn't the others?"

"I shot a boy. A twelve-year-old boy."

I felt so sorry for having opened this can of worms. This might be more than I wanted to know.

"Under what circumstances?"

His eyes narrowed as they stared at me over his coffee mug. "Wouldn't you make some assumptions after a statement like that?"

"Not me. There's a number of scenarios that occur to me where it could be called a 'good' shoot, no matter the age of the victim."

He hesitated again, seeming to measure the value of telling me something that was not going to be pretty.

"The scene is a call about a robbery and assault, a dark alley, me chasing someone, jumping a fence at the end of an alley, having a shadow step out from behind a crate, a figure with an arm extended. I landed hard, went to my knees, ducked, drew my gun . . . and fired when he stepped forward."

"Did he have a gun?"

Again he concentrated on turning the cup in a precise circle.

"He did, but he was a kid. A front for the guy who took the goods when they made entry into a residence or store."

"You announced who you were," I guessed. "He could see your uniform, your badge—"

"That doesn't matter. Twelve years old. Not even shaving yet—"

"What happened then?"

"He . . . fell, I realized what I'd done, radioed for an ambulance. He died on the way to the hospital."

"And you blamed yourself for something out of your control."

"Was it?"

He told the story in shorthand, but it was clear that he'd

replayed that scene in his mind in infinite detail a thousand times, maybe a hundred thousand times. I knew he'd laid awake at night, second guessing himself, testing whether things would have been different if he'd done one little thing differently.

"If you'd waited to find out if the guy was twelve or twenty, you'd be the one who ended up dead at the end of an alley. Neal, I've seen some pretty tough twelve-year-olds. Some that I wouldn't trust any further than I could toss a Sherman Tank."

"Sounds good when you say it."

"But you haven't resolved that within yourself."

He sipped his coffee. "Guess you'd know something about resolution."

"Umhum. That's why I've got to do everything I can to find out what happened to Susan. Something like you coming here to hide while you heal."

His broad shoulders moved in a near shrug that I took as acceptance simply because there was no way to refute what I'd said.

"You sure I'm hiding?"

"Aren't you?"

He chewed at the inside corner of his mouth. Why was it I'd never thought about a man's mouth being a sensual part of him? Sensuality and this big cop didn't seem to fit, but there was something about him that drew me. Every time I saw Neal I grew more curious about him, about who he had been in New York, and who he was here.

"I'm from Little Rock," he said. "A hundred years ago."

"Went to the big city to see what it was like?"

"In a way. But coming here was a conscious choice, not choice by default."

"Did you come back to run for sheriff?"

"No, but the job was open so I put my name on the ballot. Won by a hundred fifty votes." A corner of his mouth twitched, "The first time."

I was surprised. "This is your second term?"

"Umhum."

"Bigger margin this time?"

"Let's just say . . . significant."

I liked this man. I really liked his cautious sense of humor, his conservative way of doing things. He might have been a good cop, but he might be an even better sheriff. I liked sitting with him, talking to him. I liked the way he looked at me, the way he smiled, the way his deep voice rolled out vowels in that slow way that was so much a part of his character. I really liked him.

"Then you're good at your job."

"Yeah, I am." His gaze held mine. "You're not going to accept that the case is as good as closed."

"I hope it isn't. You don't know who killed Susan."

"We might never know."

"I need to do what I can." I sipped my coffee. "Are you going to close doors, or help me?"

"I wouldn't say I'm going to help. I'm paid to keep the law, to be objective. But as long as you stick to our original agreement, let me know what you're doing and not stir in police business, then I guess you can say I'll help."

I relaxed. At least he wouldn't try to stop me. "Thanks. Now, can I ask you some questions?"

"Suppose so."

"What do you know about The Glorious Church?"

"They keep to themselves. Curious group, but there's never been any trouble. What's your interest in them?"

"Just let me ask a couple of questions before I make a fool of myself."

His smile changed the contours of his face, making him less intimidating.

"Shoot."

"Have any parents of the students there ever come to you, asking for help in getting their kids out?"

"No." His eyes grew sharp. "Why should they?"

"I've been doing a little digging into the group. Um, were you aware that they were forced to leave California?"

"No, but like I said, they've caused no trouble here so there's been no reason to ask questions."

"What do you know about The Glorious Church?"

"Here you go," sang out Ida Belle as she slid my hamburger and fries across the table.

She flipped the lid on the coffee carafe and peered inside, then refilled both my cup and Neal's.

"You talking about that church group again?"

"Umhum," I mumbled around a bite of burger.

"I saw that Sophia woman the other day. Looks like she's been saved again."

"Saved?" I glanced at Neal then back to Ida Belle.

"Sure. From what I hear, she had terminal cancer." Her voice lowered on the last word as if speaking it aloud would attract the disease. "Some of the kids come in here, ya know, asking for donations, leftover food and such. I heard one of 'em say that this Sophia was sick and they had to get back and pray for her. The way they said it was like they'd get Brownie points for it or something.

"Anyway, when I asked about her it was like I'd asked if God had bunions or something. They hurried out of here like their tails was on fire," she laughed. "I've never been to that place they run, have you?" she asked Neal.

"Can't say as I have."

"Guess I ought to go and check out the competition," Ida laughed, as if there was any. Maybe I should put candles on my tables and charge higher prices. That's the only difference I see."

The bell over the door announced a new patron and Ida Belle bustled behind the counter again.

"Why are you digging up stuff on The Glorious Church?"

"There's just something about it that fascinates me, and

now that I've heard some of the things going on, or at least, went on, inside the group it makes me even more curious. There's something about—"

"What about finding out what happened to Susan Brady?"

"I'm going to do some more digging," I said, whether it was a warning or merely an announcement, I wasn't sure, but I wanted Conrad to understand that I wasn't going to quit.

"I was afraid you would. What's next?"

"I think I'll go back out to the compound and see what I can find out."

"You've been out there?"

"Umhum. Unannounced. They let me in, finally, then Tony met me in one of those barracks buildings. Really strange. Have there been any rumors of drug use out there?"

"No. From what I've heard, they preach against drugs and alcohol."

"Well, that's to their credit, but from what I saw, those kids are either drugged or brainwashed somehow. They're like zombies."

I told him about what I'd seen and felt when I'd been out at the compound, then added my experience at the television station.

"Isn't that some kind of abuse that should be investigated?"

"No one's made any complaints, and the students them-selves would have to do it. They're adults, there because they want to be, from what I hear. Kind of survivalists, with-out the military connection. We've had enough of those groups down here to be wary."

"Yeah, I remember. Weren't a couple of highway patrol-men shot?"

"Not a direct connection, but enough to cause suspicion. Unfortunately, nothing was proved. Besides, what's all this got to do with Susan Brady?"

"I'm not sure, but I've run onto some of my most

interesting stories while pursuing another. I'm just letting my curiosity run wild, following trails to see where they go."

"Watch yourself."

His tone of voice made my antennae come alive. "Meaning?"

"Nothing more, nothing less." He grinned. "I'd hate to have to report to Charlie that I let you get into trouble."

I shoved my plate aside and drained my cup of coffee.

"Ready to go?"

"Umhum."

"Mind an escort?"

"Not at all."

I left the money to cover my bill plus tip on the table, as did Neal. Ida Belle waved as we walked out together.

The night air was crisp and cold, our breath making a fog, the frost on the sidewalk crunching beneath our feet.

"When does it get spring?"

"Earlier than in New York."

"You like it here?"

"Don't you?"

"Haven't been here long enough to know."

"I do like it. Job's good. No sirens all night long, just a yappy dog now and then, teenagers getting a little wild at graduation or after a football game. It's different."

"Mmmm, sounds like my home town."

"Yeah? Where's that?"

"Couple hundred miles from here. Mountain Grove, Missouri." I glanced up at him, newly aware of how much taller he was than I, and saw his surprise. "No, I wasn't hatched on the downtown subway, and I'm on assignment so much I hardly have time to experience New York at all. But, it works for me."

"Planning on staying with it then?"

"For now."

We walked beside one another and I watched him glance

inside store windows, try the handle of a door or two to check that they were locked, and wave to a couple of cars that honked when they passed. Neal Conrad, Sheriff, on the job, making sure his town was safe.

Neal might not like my digging around but I felt I had a kind of half blessing from him. At least he wouldn't keep me from asking questions and was willing to act as a sounding board should I need one.

Just as we stepped inside The Holiday, my cell phone rang.

"Sorry," I said, checking the caller ID. "It's my boss."

Neal nodded and turned his head to greet Sam Patrick, but the hotel receptionist beat him to it.

"Hullo, Sheriff."

"Sam."

I stepped away from the two men. "Hello, Ben."

"When are you coming back, Mag? I need a story from you."

"Soon, Ben. I've just about got everything I need."

Neal caught my eye and shook his head with amusement curving his mouth.

"Soon, Mag," Ben said.

As soon as Ben hung up, my phone rang again. The call was from Mark, perhaps with more information for me, but I didn't want to take it with Neal and Mr. Patrick standing there.

"I, uh, there's a little problem with the credit card you gave us," Mr. Patrick said softly.

"What kind of problem?" I pulled off my gloves and stuffed them in my pocket along with my cell phone.

"Um, you're over the limit, I'm afraid."

"That can't be! I turned in my expense forms before I left the office!"

Mr. Patrick was obviously embarrassed about the problem. A smile teased the corners of Neal's mouth and I glared at him.

"I'll call and get it straightened out in the morning."

"I'm, um, afraid that won't work, Miss Rome. You've been here two days already—"

"What's the problem, Margaret?"

Gary came up behind me.

"Oh, my card's over limit. Again. It happens all the time. Accounting delights in complicating my life. Why can't Connie just pay the damned—"

"You never did pay bills, Margaret. Let me take care of this."

He slid a gold card out of his wallet and tossed it on the counter.

"I'll take care of it myself."

I plucked the card out of Sam's fingers and handed the card back to Gary, wishing Neal wasn't witnessing this little scene.

"You can't. Your office is closed."

"Front Page never closes."

I was being stubborn, but I couldn't help it. Gary was enjoying the predicament and I hated being in the position where he could say 'I told you so', especially with Neal looking on.

"I'll phone Connie at home. I've done it before. Give me an hour, Mr. Patrick, and you'll have your authorization for charges."

"You could, uh, use this phone," he suggested, sliding the desk phone toward me. "I'll charge it to your room."

Trying to hide my exasperation, I drew my cell phone from my pocket again and dialed the familiar number. Connie answered on the fifth ring.

"Connie, Maggie Rome. I'm sure you expected my call."

"Perhaps," Connie returned, "but not at home. Can't this wait until the office opens?"

"You know it can't. You've let my card run out again and my hotel bill has to be paid."

Constantine 'Connie' Harold, was a thirtyish, bespeckled

bachelor who seemed older than his thirty-two years because he was, in my opinion, far too detail conscious. He 'grannied' everything to death, especially my expense reports.

"If you'd turn in expense sheets that anyone could read, you wouldn't have this trouble. And we haven't had the nerve to even look at what you turned in for your Afghanistan escapade."

I pecked the phone receiver on the desk, then returned it to my ear. "Is this a recording?"

I heard Neal chuckle and the creak of the belt that held his gun, cuffs and everything else a sheriff apparently needed to do his job.

"Maggie—"

I turned my back on the listening Gary, Neal, and S. Patrick.

"I turned in my sheet!"

"You turned in the form, but you've hit a new record in inaccuracy. Only half the receipts were there and those were virtually unreadable. There must be—"

"I was in Iraq for God's sake! You think they're going to give me receipts for everything? You're lucky you got the ones I could carry out with me. Give me a break, Connie. A bowl of beans, which, I remind you, was about the only thing I had to eat, besides MRE's, cost either half a Kuwaiti dinar, or five Iraqui dinars, or four Saudi riyals, or one U.S. dollar, depending on what the mood was. Besides, it's a little difficult," I assumed my most aggrieved tone, "racing across the desert in a lurching jeep, hoping no one will check in the springs of the seat for canisters of film when you're stopped and searched, to worry about keeping little slips of paper. Somehow worrying about receipts just didn't seem all that important."

"I see your point."

I heard the reluctance in his voice and knew I'd won.

"So, take care of it, will you? Meanwhile, tell Mr. Patrick here that I'm good for the hotel bill."

"Let me talk to him," Connie sighed, "but you're not off the hook yet, Maggie Rome."

"See you when I get back." I handed the phone to Mr. Patrick. "This is Connie Harold. He'll authorize charges on my card."

Leaving Mr. Patrick and Connie to hash out the details of my hotel bill, I turned to Neal.

"Who is Connie Harold?"

"Constantine Harold, Accounting Chief extraordinaire. World class bean counter—he calls it being an accurate accountant. If awards were given out for tedium, Connie would win hands down. If the least little thing is wrong on my expense sheet, he won't pay my credit card bill. I've been caught in Paris with no money and no credit, had my rental car repossessed in Canada, been thrown out of a hotel in England—in the rain."

"Sounds like you still don't know how to balance a checkbook," Gary inserted.

"Shut up, Gary. That's why we have an accounting department."

Some of our hottest arguments had been initiated by my inability to balance a checkbook. After some embarrassing repercussions, Gary had insisted upon having his own account separate from mine. Everything was fine, after I'd put five hundred dollars in my account but didn't enter it in the checkbook. The system had worked well, though Gary had made it clear he'd never understood the logic of it.

"You were really in Iraq?"

"Yes, Gary. And Iran, Saudi, Jordan."

"You could have been killed—"

I didn't want to get that discussion started again. I was tired of explaining what I did. Suddenly tired of a lot of things.

"Would you give me a few minutes please?"

His glance flicked from me to Neal, seeming to catch for the first time that we were together.

"Hello, I'm Gary Brady, Maggie's—"

"I know who you are, Mr. Brady. Neal Conrad, Sheriff."

"I see. Well, trust Maggie to get an in with the local authorities." He turned to me. "I'll see you upstairs."

We watched Gary stride briskly toward the stairs.

"Is he really an ex?"

"Didn't I make that clear?"

"Just checking. How about meeting me for breakfast in the morning? I don't get time off until the weekend."

"Business?"

"Nope, not unless you've got something to discuss."

"Not yet."

"Then I'll see you about eight. Ida Belle's."

I watched him stride out and disappear into the darkness, and then was suddenly aware that S. Patrick had heard every word.

"Hope everything has been handled to your satisfaction, Mr. Patrick."

He handed my cell phone back to me.

"No problems, Miss Rome."

Gary was waiting for me when I reached my room.

"What's between you and the sheriff?"

"Nothing, Gary. We just met at the café. How are your folks?"

I fished my room key out of my pocket along with the crumpled messages.

"All right, I guess. They retired to their respective dens so I waited around a while, then came back here. When I couldn't find you I drove around for a while. Found this restaurant that's not half bad. The Gold Road. They do a good steak."

"Gold Road? Where's that?"

"Oh, on the edge of town."

"I'll have to try it." I tossed my parka onto the bed and then glanced at my watch. "I'd like to talk to your parents."

"I'm sure they understand how you feel about Susan, but they're not very receptive right now."

I wasn't going to tell him that expressing my sympathy for the family's loss wasn't entirely the reason for my wanting to see his parents.

"Don't they know you asked me to come?"

"I told them I asked you to come, but I didn't say why. They're not up for interrogation."

"I don't plan to interrogate them." I dialed Mark's phone number. "But I do have a few questions about Susan during the days before she . . . um, died."

Gary drew a deep breath. "I suppose you're right."

"Mark? Maggie."

"Ran across a bit of information that I think you'll find interesting."

From his tone of voice I was sure I would. "What is it?"

"You said you were investigating some of those co-ed murders?"

"Yes."

"Well, were you aware of the kidnappings?"

"Yes. That's what first got me onto this. What's your point?"

"Did you know your Susan Brady was one of the victims?"

I glanced at Gary. "No, I didn't. What happened?"

"It wasn't nice. Her name was kept out of the paper but I found out through a police contact. Apparently she was picked up by some guys in a tan van one night when she was walking back to her dorm from the library.

"Uh, they drove for a while, she fought, she was struck, didn't know how many there were, didn't remember what they said. Didn't really remember being dumped out. She was found two hours later, wandering along a deserted road in the foothills, bruised, scratched, incoherent, and her hair had been shaved off."

I sank into a chair and closed my eyes, aware of Gary's frowning scrutiny.

"When did this happen?"

The date was six months before the Brady's move to Arkansas. That explained Susan dropping out of school and the move. It also explained something of her reclusiveness.

"Susan was taken to a hospital and her parents were called. She'd been assaulted. Apparently when she fought, they cut her hair. Some sort of punishment for that, I guess."

"I see. Anyone charged? Even suspected?"

"There were several theories. The most accepted explanation was some sort of fraternity prank that got out of hand, but nothing came of that. There was a suggestion about it being some kind of cult ritual, because of the hair thing, but, again, nothing concrete.

"Anyway, Susan was in pretty bad shape. Visited a shrink for a while, kept in hiding until her hair grew out, never went back to school."

"Thanks, Mark. That explains a few things."

We talked a few minutes more then I hung up the phone slowly, still stunned at what Mark had told me.

"What is it? You're pale as a ghost."

"Um, nothing. Just some bad news. It's all right."

I paced the floor a bit, then phoned down to room service for coffee.

Gary had settled himself in front of the television to watch the news, flicking it off when a commercial came on.

"No real news here," he said, tossing the remote control onto my bed.

"Uh, look, Gary. I need to ask you a couple of questions."

"Sure. What about?"

"You said Susan dropped out of school for a while before your parents moved here. Why?"

"Needed some time to decide what she wanted to do, I guess."

"I don't think so."

His eyes narrowed. "You've learned something."

"Did you know that Susan was kidnapped about eighteen months ago?"

"What?"

"One of my contacts discovered it. Susan was kidnapped from the U.C. campus, held for a few hours, assaulted, her head shaved, then she was released on a deserted road.

"My God," he breathed, obviously stunned.

"Apparently she wasn't the only one that happened to. Six in all. Three of them committed suicide within six months, two others are still under psychiatric care. And Susan."

He jumped up and began pacing the floor. "I can't believe it."

"How come you didn't know?"

"I was in Dallas for a couple of weeks," He chewed his lower lip thoughtfully, "and when I got back they told me they'd decided to move. I was stunned when they said Arkansas, but—they said Susan had taken a vacation. It was summer. I didn't think much about it, except that I thought it was a pretty sudden decision. I should have thought—I should have asked—my God! Mother must have been devastated!"

"I'd like to talk to your parents about it."

"Why?"

"It might have something to do with what happened to Susan. Perhaps it was suicide, as a result of what happened then."

"I didn't think of that." He pushed his fingers through his hair in frustration. "I was going out there tomorrow—"

"How about tonight?"

He frowned. "A little pushy, aren't you? What else did your contact tell you?"

"I don't mean to be insensitive, but time is running out. The police have exhausted their leads. There's little more they can do. I have to either come up with something solid enough for them to get involved again or get back to New York."

Digging around in Susan's life wasn't something I looked forward to doing, but Mark's comment about a 'cult thing' made my curiosity about The Glorious Church grow stronger. It was a broad jump, but if there was even a slim chance that there was a connection I wanted to find it. The group had once been based in southern California and Susan was exactly the type of person to whom a strong cult group would appeal. Had Susan fallen in with The Glorious Church or some other group because her need had been so great? That made me feel more guilty for my part in not responding to her. It was a thin premise but I had to know. Only Edward and Pauline could tell me, but would they talk? Probably not to me.

"I suppose we could drive out there. I don't know if they'll talk to you. Mom's very upset, and Dad's just brooding. Besides, I don't think bringing up something like this, something that was already over before—well, would it prove anything?"

"It would if it had something to do with her death."

"What kind of connection could there be? That was over a year ago and a thousand miles away."

"I don't know. Yet. I'll be very gentle," I promised, shrugging on my coat before he could change his mind.

I didn't look forward to questioning the Bradys, but I had to know if someone or something from Susan's past had followed her to Arkansas and killed her.

Chapter Seven

The Bradys' home sat in a heavily wooded area a little more than five miles southwest of Fayetteville. The travel atlas I'd found in the trunk of the rental car indicated that the road angled toward the edge of the Ozark National Forest, a beautiful, rugged, but isolated place.

From what I'd seen during my survey of the countryside, this area was as rough and wild, and just as compelling, as that around the home where I grew up. Huge maple and oak trees of several varieties grew tall and straight, the circumference of the trunks evidence that many were at least a hundred years old.

In the spring the rough Ozark Mountain range would be dotted with white and pink Dogwood trees along with Redbud and a variety of wild flowers. New calves with snow-white faces would look out through the fences at passersby then run stiff-legged to their mothers with a flick of a tail.

In the fall, crimson and gold would guild the hills and local folk and tourist alike would travel for miles to view the colors. Craft festivals and other entertainment would be abundant, inviting thousands of tourists to quaint towns dotting the hills. Old timers would cut a persimmon to see

117

whether there was the pattern of a knife and fork inside or a spoon to judge the weather for the coming winter. Others relied on the thickness of the 'fur' on black caterpillars. At night the hills would resound with the call of fox and coon hounds as they sought their prey; the hunters would be sitting in their pick-up trucks drinking a thermos of hot coffee, some laced with whiskey, listening to their dogs and bragging.

Winter brought everything to a near standstill, depending on how much snow fell. Winter was a time of renewal here, evenings by the fireplace, nights snuggled beneath quilts that might have been handmade, the cutting of a fragrant cedar for Christmas. The quiet in the woods would be almost eerie, broken only by the crack of an ice-ladened limb, or the swish of an owl flying low to catch an unwary field mouse. Sledding, snowballs, hoping school would be dismissed, hot chocolate. I remembered the rituals well.

It was a rough country, limestone cliffs rising above scenic highways and abutments pushing out between brambles and trees, but it was also wild and free and beautiful in its own way. For a moment I felt a twinge of homesickness, but I didn't let it linger.

Gary slowed the car and turned into a narrow lane from which the snow had been partially cleared by traffic. I was surprised when he stopped the car in front of a wrought iron gate. He went to a black box mounted on one of the brick posts and, hunched against the cold, talked into it.

The Bradys had been very social people when I'd known them, with a multitude of business acquaintances and a few close friends. There had been a security system in the house, but nothing this complex. Conrad hadn't been wrong when he called the Brady place a fortress.

A tall chain link fence ran as far as I could see. Like the fence at the complex of The Glorious Church, a strand of barbed wire ran along the top.

A burst of icy wind came into the car when Gary opened the door and slid inside.

"They're not happy about you being here."

"Nothing new." His hands tightened around the steering wheel. "Sorry."

"I shouldn't have brought you out here."

"Believe me, if I didn't feel it's important I wouldn't have insisted."

"I don't want you to ask them about what's happened. It will be too painful, especially now."

"You said you wanted to know what happened to Susan. And so do I. Even more than before. The assault may have some connection to her death. It might have been a reason for suicide, but there might be more to it."

"Maybe it would be better to just let it go. She's dead. Nothing can bring her back."

"If she was murdered then someone needs to pay for it."

His knuckles tightened on the steering wheel.

He drove carefully up a narrow drive that was closely lined with trees. With the snow and darkness I could see little beyond the beam of the car lights, but there seemed to be a lot of shrubs and trees in what had to have been at least five acres of yard space.

"I'm curious. Why do your parents feel its necessary to have a locked gate and a fence with barbed wire on top surrounding the place? Have there been threats against their lives or something?"

The dash lights made his face a mask as he peered intently through the fogged windshield.

"Not that I know of. Probably just a precautionary measure. They didn't know the area all that well, and it is remote."

It was that. From the city limits to the Brady house we hadn't passed a single house or vehicle.

"Do you suppose they moved here because of Susan? And

if protection was the idea, why was she living in her own apartment?"

His hands worked on the steering wheel.

"They told me they'd vacationed near here several times in the past few years and liked it. Dad wanted a life entirely different from the one they'd had in California. I'd think you'd agree with that, especially now. You never liked the socializing. Superficial, I think you called it."

I swallowed a retort. The barb was his angry reaction to not being told about Susan's trouble in California as well as to her death.

We drove in silence until the Brady house came into sight. I peered out the windshield and smiled. The Bradys might have moved to the wilderness, but they'd carried their pretentiousness with them.

The house, a two-story Colonial brick with white columns lining the wide front porch, sat on a knoll with a circle drive in front. Floodlights situated around the house left not one dark area, even though the landscaping included quite a lot of shrubbery, now banked with drifted snow.

"Just your parents live here?"

"Yes. Why?"

"It's just that it's a very large place for only two people."

"You expected them to live in a log cabin?"

At first it appeared the house was dark, but then I detected a faint light in a downstairs corner window. I followed Gary to the front door and waited while he rang the bell, my shoulders hunched to bring the coat collar up around my ears.

Finally the door opened and we were greeted by a familiar solemn face. I smothered a smile. Malcolm, the butler extraordinare. No wonder the community thought the Bradys strange. Little could be stranger than a family in rural Arkansas having a very proper English butler, employed by a family that had made their home a fortress and, if the rumors were true, had turned into virtual recluses.

The interior of the Brady home seemed, if possible, even more opulent than their California residence. The light from a large, crystal and brass chandelier washed the walls of mellowed light oak, highlighting a collection of landscapes that had an English flavor. The fox and hounds kind of thing. A hall table held a crystal vase of fresh roses, their scent light on the air.

"Malcolm. My parents are expecting me."

Gary handed the smallish man his overcoat, then helped me out of my parka.

"They are in the den. Shall I direct you?"

"No, I remember the way."

I followed Gary through the foyer, our heels loud on the marble floor, and through the long living room towards closed double doors.

Gary opened the doors and we stepped into a room that should have been comfortable, but wasn't allowed to be. The walls were a cinnamon color that was reflected in the floral pattern of the two couches setting stiffly at attention on either side of the wide brown brick fireplace. The woodwork was extra wide and ornately carved. The dark brown carpet was thick beneath my feet. But the furniture was set at straight angles, in perfect little squares, and there were no personal touches. Not a newspaper, magazine. Not even a plant that might err in dropping a leaf on the carpet.

Pauline Brady sat in a straight backed chair without using the arms, her ankles carefully crossed, her hands clasping a lace handkerchief in her lap. She was perfectly groomed, as usual, every hair in place. She wore a navy dress that was unrelieved by any sort of decoration. Her face was pale, her eyes slightly swollen and pink.

Dr. Brady, still athletically slim, stood in front of the fireplace studying the empty glass he held. He still had on the charcoal gray suit he'd worn to the funeral, complete with vest and jacket, his tie carefully knotted. A couple perfectly posed in front of a fireplace by a photographer to show the world how wonderful the most recent charity event had been. They looked like something out of a home magazine, perfect but lifeless.

I hesitated at the door, then went directly to Pauline. Kneeling in front of her, I covered her hands with my own. They were icy cold. Damn. I never knew what to say in these circumstances, and never to Pauline.

"I'm sorry."

"Thank you."

The words were whispered with a glance toward her husband. I rose as Malcolm cleared his throat discreetly from the doorway.

"May I bring you something to drink? Something hot, perhaps."

"Margaret?"

Gary perched carefully on the edge of the couch at an angle to his father.

"Yes, thank you. Coffee, or tea, whichever is easiest."

"I have a very good tea. Lemon or milk?"

"Lemon, please. And, thank you."

I pulled a chair near Pauline and sat down, cataloging the changes in her. I'd last seen Gary's mother two months before the divorce. I had gone back to the apartment to get the rest of my things and Pauline had been there picking up his dry cleaning.

It had been awkward, but I remembered particularly well how Pauline had looked. She kept athletically trim by playing tennis at least twice a week. At fifty-one she'd looked at least ten years younger.

But now she looked every one of those ten years and more. I'd never seen her so fragile. Her skin was dry and thin, like old parchment ready to crumble at a touch, and she'd trembled when I touched her.

As the silence stretched, Pauline worked with her handkerchief while Edward glowered from his stance at the hearth. Maybe I shouldn't have insisted that Gary bring me, but time was short. If I was going to find out anything about Susan's death, I needed to know what had happened to Susan eighteen months earlier, and since. And it seemed Dr. and Mrs. Brady were the only ones who knew.

"You home is quite lovely."

I went to examine a painting that hung beside the fireplace. Then I saw a framed photo turned face down on the mantle behind Dr. Brady and picked it up.

The picture was of Susan, but it wasn't one I recognized. Her dark hair was much shorter, ragged as it curled around her face, her brown eyes sadder, wiser. There seemed to be tension around the mouth.

I studied the solemn face. Somehow Susan didn't look as young and innocent as I remembered, but then, perhaps now that I knew what had happened I was reading something into the photo that wasn't there. I traced the outline of Susan's face with my fingertips and felt suddenly very sad.

"Susan was a lovely young woman."

Mrs. Brady smothered a sob.

"One of the things I missed most was our talks. She was like the little sister I never had."

"Margaret," Gary began.

"I wasn't aware you and she talked that much," Edward said. His voice was as cultured, as cool, as it had ever been.

I glanced up at Edward, noting that he too had aged, but not nearly to the extent of his wife. Sorrow, I supposed, drained the very life out of a parent who'd lost a child.

"Sometimes, when I escaped—" They'd frequently complained about me leaving their parties at the earliest possible moment. "I'd go to her room." I studied the photo again, touching the glass with a fingertip as if I might make some physical connection.

"I remember one time she was looking at a family photo album. She was sitting in the middle of her bed, her hair falling into her face. Remember how she was always pushing it back behind her ears? Anyway, we went through the album. She pointed out her grandparents on both sides, then your wedding pictures." I smiled in memory. "I remember she commented that everyone was blonde, except her."

"Why would she be concerned about that?"

Dr. Brady filled his glass from a decanter with abrupt movements. The clink of glass against glass was loud in the room.

"I don't know. I guess it was one of those things a teen-ager notices. Especially a sensitive young girl. Being differ-ent in any way is a big thing. It was to me. I told her I was the only redhead in a family of brunettes.

"Once, when I was about fifteen, I spent a whole summer believing I was adopted. I imagined I'd been left on the fam-ily's doorstep by my poor, destitute mother. I fabricated a whole story, like Cinderella or something. I practically wal-lowed in the injustice.

"How disappointed I was when I discovered I looked exactly like my great-grandmother. Freckles and all. Susan laughed about that."

"Susan looked like my grandmother," Pauline inserted, wringing her hands.

When she realized what she was doing, she stopped, but within seconds she was pleating her handkerchief.

"I was always jealous of Susan. But in a nice way. I told her that once."

"Were you?"

Dr. Brady drank half his drink in one swallow and paced back to the fireplace.

"Umhum. The Cinderella complex again, I suppose. Your home was so beautiful, like something out of House & Garden. It must have been difficult to leave. I never asked, had you lived there long?"

Pauline smoothed her handkerchief against her thigh before folding it carefully.

"We moved there when Gary entered high school. We needed more room to entertain."

She kept glancing at her husband as if each word needed his approval. The good doctor had now finished his second drink since our arrival and was pouring a third. I'd never noticed before that he was a heavy drinker. But, they'd just buried a daughter. Perhaps even Edward Brady needed a way to escape the sorrow. And here I was being crass enough to insist upon talking about her.

But I couldn't stop. I might not have another opportunity to see them again.

"I'm sorry to intrude, but I cared about Susan and because Gary asked me to come. He thought I might help—"

"Help? With what?" Dr. Brady tossed down his drink. "Susan is dead. She took her life. Nothing can change that."

Hadn't Neal told them that her death might a homicide?

"I don't believe Susan committed suicide."

"She poisoned herself. The sheriff said so."

Neal was too cautious, too careful to have told them that without some qualification.

"According to the autopsy there was a massive amount of Strychnine in her system. More than twice the amount needed to—I don't know what happened to her, but I don't think Susan killed herself."

His eyes narrowed and his fingers tightened on the glass he held.

"What are you suggesting?"

"Nothing. At least not now. I'd just like to know how Susan died, and why. And if she was murdered, don't you want to see her killer brought to justice?"

"I just want to put this behind us," Pauline whispered, dabbing at the tears spilling from her eyes. "Nothing can bring her back. Nothing can bring my baby back—"

Edward gripped his glass tighter and tighter, his nails turning white, until I thought it would burst. Pauline's handkerchief was a sodden string.

"Can you really put it behind you until you know what happened to her? I can't."

"Can't you see you're upsetting my wife? Even you should have more compassion. Leave us alone."

I weighed my options. Good manners against the need to know what had happened to Susan. I was running out of time. The need to know won out.

"When Susan was attacked on campus eighteen months ago, to what hospital was she taken?"

"Margaret!" Gary nearly jumped off the couch.

Pauline's gasp pulled me around.

"Who treated her?"

"That is none of your business."

Edward's face was a deep shade of red and the veins stood out on his forehead.

"Did she talk to you about what happened?"

"Gary, you brought this woman here. Take her away."

Though I recognized that I appeared to be unsympathetic I had to have answers; for me, for Susan. I wasn't going to be brushed aside easily.

"Did she have any idea why she was assaulted, why her head was shaved?"

"Gary—"

He glanced from me to his father in indecision then, surprisingly, sided with me.

"She's right, Dad. Besides, I want to know why you didn't tell me when it happened."

"That was months ago." He waved a hand in the air in dismissal as he stepped to the drink cart again. "Some stupid fraternity prank."

"Why didn't you tell me?"

I could have cheered. For once Gary stood up to his father.

"Susan didn't want anyone to know. It was to be kept very confidential." Edward's eyes were accusing when his gaze turned on me. "How did you find out?"

"A friend was doing some research for me and found the records."

"Why are you doing this?"

"I'm working on several co-ed murders that have taken place during the past few years."

"Your work," he said with a sneer, taking a big swallow of his fourth drink. "Always your work. You put it first when you were married to Gary, embarrassing us—"

I ignored his attempt to shift the subject to me. "Susan wasn't the only girl attacked. After the fraternities were cleared, the police questioned some members of a cult. They were working the campuses then—"

"I won't discuss this! Leave this house, and don't you ever come back!"

He took a step toward me, his fists clenched at his side. I took an involuntary step backward and my hand brushed the fireplace tools in their stand on the hearth. I bent, managing to catch them before they fell, but the loud clatter was jarring.

"I'm sorry—"

"Get out!"

He took another step.

"Margaret, let's go."

Gary clasped my arm and hurried me from the room.

Malcolm was waiting with our coats draped over his arm. The speculative look on his face made it obvious he'd overheard everything. Gary snatched his coat and jerked open the front door, leaving me to follow as best I could.

We drove silently back toward Fayetteville, his face taut with concentration.

"Slow down, Gary, the temperature is dropping and there could be ice."

He eased off the accelerator but the tension in his face remained.

"I can't believe they didn't tell me."

"Maybe they thought they were being kind."

"Why didn't Susan tell me? We weren't close, but we did talk when I was home. I never guessed—"

"Not wanting to talk about that kind of thing is a very natural reaction. It's very personal, a very deep trauma."

"Who would do that to her? A frustrated boyfriend? Someone she refused to date?"

"Rape isn't the result of frustrated sexual desire, Gary. It's the result of anger. A need to control. The fact that her head was shaved underlines that. It strikes me as a very vindictive statement. A kind of mark."

"That cult thing. Is that the truth?"

"The police initially thought the attacks were fraternity pranks gone too far, but then there was some speculation about a cult being involved."

"What kind? A satanist group? I know there were several around Los Angeles. Still are."

"Well," I hesitated to tell him what I suspected, but he surprised me.

"Is that why you're interested in this Glorious Church group?"

"I don't know if they have anything to do with Susan or not, but some members of The Glorious Church were working in the areas where some of the assaults took place. The fact that they're here—well, it's something I have to check out."

His hands tightened on the wheel. "You suspected them all along! Damn it, Margaret, why didn't you tell me what was going on?"

"I didn't make any connection. Not until today. It may be, as the police stated, only a coincidence."

He concentrated on the road a moment. "Then we must find out if there's anything to your suspicions."

"I didn't say I suspected anything. I'm working an angle. That's the way it's done. Keep working at any and all possibilities until something works. Until the puzzle pieces fit."

He drove silently for several more minutes. "I can't believe they never told me."

That seemed to bother him more than anything else.

"Maybe they didn't want to admit even to themselves that it had happened. Maybe they just wanted to shove it under the rug with all the other imperfect things that have happened in their lives. I'm sure there's been more than one."

His glance was graphic. "They never accepted the divorce."

"Our divorce, Gary. Our. You can't insulate yourself from it by calling it *the* divorce."

"What difference does that make! There's never been a divorce in our family—"

I scooted down in the seat to stare out the window at the darkness, resting my head against the back of the seat.

"No, people just keep living together, tolerating one another, building separate lives. The women just become an appendage with never an original thought or personal ambition—"

"That's not so!"

"Isn't it? Has your mother ever done anything that wasn't directed toward advancing your father's career? Has she ever done anything for herself?"

"She has always believed in my father."

"I'm sure she does, but that doesn't mean she couldn't have something of her own."

"She didn't want anything else."

"How do you know that?"

"You don't understand."

"You're right. I don't. That's why we're divorced."

He fell silent, but his knuckles were white as he gripped the steering wheel.

I drew a deep breath and studied the reflection of his profile in the window. The Brady family had never been picture perfect. When I married Gary, I'd hoped for a warm relationship with his parents as well as Susan. But each, in their own way, had seemed afraid of being close. In what other household could the mother learn she was expecting a baby and not tell the only other child? Especially when that child was already a teenager?

From what Gary had said, he'd simply gotten a letter one day announcing he had a baby sister. Eighteen years later, his sister was assaulted and again he hadn't been made aware of something that had the potential of creating dramatic changes in the family. How many more secrets were there in the Brady family?

"I should have been there."

"You can *should* yourself to death, Gary, and nothing will change what happened. Susan didn't want anyone to know. The authorities probably called your parents only because of her age. She couldn't tell them not to."

"Maybe all this could have been avoided if I'd known. If I could have helped her maybe she wouldn't be dead now."

"We'll never know that. But if Susan didn't commit suicide, if someone killed her, then there has to be a reason. I want to know what it is."

When we arrived at the motel Gary went directly to his room. I thought briefly about following him, maybe just to listen and be supportive, but decided he needed time alone. When he'd asked me to come to Arkansas he'd opened a can of peas and spilled it. Now he had a lot of thinking to do about the mess. So did I.

Tossing my keys on the nightstand in my own room, I shrugged out of my parka and pulled off my boots. Flexing my toes, I picked up the phone and dialed Mark's number.

Mark was good at his job. The best. I trusted any information he gave me. So, when he said he found no birth records in California for Susan Brady I knew I had to go see Pauline again.

I walked to the Parakeet for breakfast the next morning, expecting to meet Neal, but he wasn't there. Something must have come up during the night that held him at the office.

I sat at on a stool, drinking coffee and waiting for my order, studying the room reflected in the mirror that ran the length of it above the counter.

A number of obvious regulars, mostly older men, joked comfortably with one another. Here and there someone read a newspaper while waiting for their meal. Ida Belle was working in the kitchen, leaving the counter work to a young woman who looked like a younger version of her.

As I was pulling on my gloves outside the restaurant thirty minutes later, I glanced up in time to see Edward Brady driving past in a big, dark Continental. I weighed my options, mentally tossing a coin. Twenty minutes later I was driving out of Fayetteville toward the Brady mansion.

"Who is this, please?"

Malcolm's voice sounded tinny coming out of the speaker.

"Maggie. I'd like to see Pauline."

"Mrs. Brady does not wish to be disturbed."

"Malcolm, please ask if she'll see me. I, uh, want to apologize for last night."

It wasn't a complete lie. I would apologize.

"One moment."

Five minutes later, just when I thought I would freeze in place, his voice came out of the speaker again.

"I will open the gate."

"Thanks."

I parked in front of the door, hoping my hunch that Edward would be in town for a while was correct. What I planned to do might be termed cruel by some, but I couldn't set Susan's death aside now. Besides, if Susan had been my daughter, I justified, I wouldn't stop until I knew what happened to her.

"Mrs. Brady is in the sitting room."

"I'll keep my coat."

I knocked on the door, then opened it.

"Pauline."

She looked little better than the night before. Fatigue grayed her skin and lined her face.

"Margaret. May I offer you some tea?"

I took a chair opposite her, a small table between us, and accepted, more to give Pauline something to do than because I wanted anything to drink.

"Malcolm said you wanted to apologize?"

I sipped tentatively at my tea. "In a way. I'm sorry if I upset you last night, but that won't keep me from going on with what I'm doing."

"And what are you doing?"

"Trying to find out what happened to Susan."

"My daughter is dead."

I studied Pauline a long moment. Did I really want to do this?

"Was she your daughter?"

Her cup rattled against the saucer. "What do you mean?"

"I mean, there are no birth records in California. I checked."

Her hand trembled just the least bit as she sipped her tea. "Perhaps you've made an error in the hospital name."

"Then where was she born?"

"At a small private clinic. I don't believe it exists any longer."

"An associate of Edward's?"

"Yes. I believe so."

"But the birth certificate would have to be registered. It isn't. At least, not in the name of Dr. and Mrs. Edward James Brady."

Pauline stared at me. "Why are you doing this to us?"

"Because Susan was murdered, and I want to find out who killed her, and why."

When the door opened, I automatically stiffened, expecting Edward to storm in.

"Margaret? I'm surprised to find you here."

Gary shut the door carefully.

"Your mother and I were just talking. How did you get out here?"

"I rented my own car." Sensing tension, he looked from me to his mother. "What are you talking about?"

"Nothing," Pauline said quickly, picking up the teapot. "Have some tea."

I ignored her attempt to avoid the subject. "I had a few more questions to ask your mother."

Gary refused his mother's offer. "What kind of questions?"

"I was just wondering why there's no record in California of Susan's birth."

He looked blank, then a frown made a crease between his eyebrows. "I don't understand."

"Pauline?" She continued to stare out the window. "Either Susan wasn't born on the date I've always known as her birthday, or she was born to someone else and never officially adopted."

"Adopted? You're crazy, Margaret!"

He paced to the fireplace and rested one arm along the mantle, his hand covering the lower part of his face. The stance was his father all over again.

"This is absurd."

The statement didn't have the strength it would have had two days earlier.

Tears began to slip down Pauline's pale face, dripping off her chin and dampening the front of her dark turquoise dress.

I leaned forward, elbows resting on my knees.

"Pauline, did you and Edward adopt Susan?"

"Yes," came the tortured response finally. "Yes."

Gary sank into a chair, his face white with this added surprise.

"I don't understand. You told me a whole story about going to the doctor. Told me you were stunned and embarrassed to learn you were pregnant. Why would you lie to me about something like that?"

She waved a hand near her face as if searching for the right words to pluck from the air.

"We—we didn't want anyone to know."

"But why? What was the point?"

"You had just left for college. The house was so empty. Edward knew an attorney who knew a young woman about to deliver her baby. Her parents had approached him because she wanted to give it up for adoption." She studied the ceiling a moment, her lips pinched together. "We didn't want anyone to know that Susan wasn't really our baby, so we built the story we told you. Everyone believed it. We—we planned to tell her. Some time."

"Who arranged the adoption?"

I wished I had my notebook, or a recorder.

"Robert Delmar. In Los Angeles."

"Is he still practicing there."

"No. He died in a car crash not long after we took Susan."

"What happened?"

"His car went off the Pacific Coast Highway late one night. It burned. It was awful. Awful. But then, there was no one but Edward and I to know that Susan wasn't really ours. So, there was no reason to tell her."

Pauline was trembling, her fingers tapping against her face in an erratic rhythm that seemed beyond her control.

Gary paced the room, obviously trying to come to terms with everything he'd learned in the past two days. I felt a little sorry for him. Everything he'd believed his parents to be, his very foundation, was shaken. The Bradys were pretentious, but I'd never expected they were liars.

Pauline's story was just too perfect. Adopting a baby after Gary left home, the attorney dying in a car crash, the adoption papers somehow never being filed.

"You're sure Susan never knew she was adopted?"

"Oh, no," Pauline gasped. "It would have destroyed her."

But I wondered if Susan hadn't suspected. My mind kept going back to the night we'd looked at the photo album. How betrayed Susan must have felt at being lied to.

"Could she have found out? Could she have been upset enough by learning she was adopted to have killed herself?"

"Oh, my God," Pauline whispered, covering her closed eyes with a trembling hand.

"I thought you said you didn't think she committed suicide," Gary burst out.

"I didn't, but I didn't know this then either. Anything is possible."

Anything was possible. Even an affirmative answer to her next question.

"Pauline, were you and Edward ever members of The Glorious Church?"

"Margaret!" Gary burst out. "My God! Have you lost your mind?"

Pauline's face paled even more, and she seemed to shrink like a deflating balloon. He blinked in surprise when she lifted her hand to stop his outburst.

"Mother?"

"It's all right. Yes, Margaret. We were active in the church, for a very short time. An associate of Edward's asked us to go to a service and he was intrigued by what he saw. But then, we drifted away."

"Why was Edward interested?"

"Oh, I don't know. There were influential people there, I suppose. But, from what I understood, the very precepts of the church were against doing anything unnatural to the body." She shrugged her thin shoulders. "Edward is, was, a well known plastic surgeon. His practice was not only reconstructive surgery, but enhancement as well. I suppose he and the church did not agree on those principles, so we left."

I considered that for a moment, then asked the question that had nagged at me all night.

"When the girls found Susan that night, dying, she whispered, 'I'm sorry', over and over. What do you think she meant?"

"I don't know. Maybe—" She smothered a sob and held a handkerchief to her lips a moment. "Maybe she knew she was dying."

"Mother—"

"Please, no more questions. Leave me alone."

"We should go, Margaret. Mother, I'm sorry to upset you like this, again."

"I have just one more question."

"No. We're going."

He gripped my arm and, snagging my coat from the couch, escorted me quickly from the house and out to the car.

"I'll follow you back to the motel."

I pulled my arm out of his grasp. "Afraid I won't go?"

"Yes, frankly, I am. I thought even you would have more empathy for how mother is feeling. I want you to leave my parents alone."

"You wanted me to find out what happened to Susan. To do that I have to ask questions."

"I think you're asking too many questions about things that have nothing to do with how or why she died."

"Things like whether or not she was adopted?"

A muscle jumped in his jaw.

"Yes. There's no reason for you to ask them more painful questions."

I studied him for a long moment.

"Not even if there's some kind of a connection between Susan and The Glorious Church? What if it's something that got her killed?"

"You don't seriously believe that."

"I don't know. It seems pretty farfetched, but your parents were members, they both left California about the same time . . . and moved here, a place that doesn't seem to fit either your parents or the group. It all brings up more questions. Questions I intend to ask."

"Leave it alone, Margaret."

"I'm not working for you, Gary. I'm working for myself. I'm going to do what I have to."

I got into my car and drove away. When I glanced in the rearview mirror, he was still standing by his car staring at the house.

As I drove, I mulled over everything I'd learned in the last twelve hours. Asking Pauline about The Glorious Church had been a blind stab in the dark. I'd been almost as surprised as Gary when she'd admitted to being a member of the group, however briefly.

Pushing a hand through my hair, combing it absently, I began to ask myself the what-if questions that helped me sort through convoluted facts to create a story framework. Questions like, what if Edward Brady's connection with The Glorious Church, or his leaving it, had created some kind of schism? What if the attack on Susan months ago had been some kind of punishment against Edward? If so, had he come back into line, or remained separated? The family's move to Arkansas seemed to answer that question. But then, following that line of thought, how did Susan's death fit into it all?

Chapter Eight

Instead of returning to the motel, I drove out to the compound of The Glorious Church. Gabriel was guarding the gate again and recognized me.

"Miss Rome."

"Hi. I don't have an appointment, but I was wondering if I could talk to Mrs. Belgrade."

"I will check for you."

After a few minutes, Gabriel returned. "Sophia will see you. Please park there in front of the church. She will meet you inside shortly."

"Thank you."

I parked where Gabriel directed. Getting out of the car, I glanced back to see the two guards watching me carefully. My boots crunched on the gravel path that led up to the double doors of the small chapel. The door swung open easily on well oiled hinges.

The door banged shut, echoing loudly in the empty chapel. My steps echoed on the wood floor and I had the urge to tiptoe. I walked carefully down the center aisle, dust tickling my nose as I inhaled the musty odor. I shivered as the chill of the room reached inside my parka, but perhaps it was only the quiet, eerie feeling of the place. If The

Glorious Church had ever held services here, it hadn't been recently.

It was a quaint chapel, reminiscent of a long ago time. The narrow windows let in little light, but recessed lights in the walls near the ceilings glowed softly. I let my fingers trail on the backs of the pews. There was no dust, but the building still had an unused feeling.

I sat on a front pew and studied the raised platform. The two short benches matched the light oak of the pews but were upholstered in a royal blue fabric that matched the draperies hanging behind the straight wooden chairs in the choir loft.

A sound at my right drew my attention to a door concealed in the paneling. Sophia entered, dressed in a long dress of some kind of soft purple fabric that whispered as it flowed around her. She came toward me on feet encased in fabric shoes that seemed to hiss against the floor making a shiver move down my spine. I'd always had a phobic fear of snakes—probably from my cousins teasing me with the garter variety when I was a little girl—and the sound reminded me of the sound of snakes rustling through grass. My stomach rolled and I swallowed twice, very hard.

"Miss Rome. I'm happy to see you again." Sophia sank onto the pew near me. "My husband told me you had come unexpectedly before and he was forced to greet you in the barracks. I apologize."

"No, I apologize." I recognized the veiled chastisement. No drop-in visits allowed. "I was sorry to have missed you, but it was interesting to see where the students live. Your husband said you were involved in a prayer group."

"Yes. Prayer and discipline are the framework of our lives. How may I help you now?"

"As I said, I'm working on a story about the variety of religious groups in America. The religious freedom and such. And, since The Glorious Church seems to be one of the larger and better organized groups, I wanted to ask you a few more questions."

Sophia seemed pleased by my comments and I relaxed a little.

"We have been very successful in spreading our message."

She settled back in the pew, but her black eyes were still very watchful.

Though she was a slight woman, there was a sense of cloaked strength about Sophia Belgrade. Perhaps it was the kind that was invariably a part of people who have lived through great adversity. I had interviewed people who had survived tragedies and each seemed to have tapped into some kind of hidden resource and gained a strength to keep them from shattering.

If the rumors about Sophia being healed of a terminal illness were true, perhaps this was the origin of that strength, but I wasn't certain. There was something almost crafty in the intensity of the woman's dark eyes that put a different definition on what I was seeing, something I couldn't identify at the moment.

Breaking eye contact, I dug into my bag and extracted a notebook and pen.

"Forgive me for not being familiar with the church. I know you've been, as I said, more successful than many other organizations. To what do you attribute your success?"

Sophia smiled slightly. "We have something to offer for which people are searching, reaching out for."

Sophia Belgrade was irritatingly obscure. Her watching eyes made me suspect I was being intentionally baited, that she was attempting in her own way to decide what kind of person I was—a believer or a skeptic.

Hoping to present the persona that would convince her to be more open with me, I asked more questions. I wanted to appear not too easily persuaded but willing to listen to something new and provocative.

"What is The Glorious Church trying to tell the world?"

"Our message is simple. Love. If we, as individuals, can only love one another and forget self, then all wars would cease, there would be no crime, no poverty, no homelessness, no drug and alcohol problems."

"Then your denomination preaches against the use of alcohol and drugs," I clarified, writing in my notebook.

"The Glorious Church is not a denomination or a religious sect, as those are normally defined. We are a Biblical research and teaching organization concerned with feeding men and women from the Word of God."

"I stand corrected. How large is your membership?"

When Sophia estimated membership between twenty and thirty thousand people, I was stunned. In Sophia's opinion, people were drawn to them because the world had failed them; organized religion had failed them.

"There is a scripture verse in Matthew," Sophia said. "And it asks if your son wants bread, will you give him a stone? Or if he asks for a fish, will you give him a serpent? As a nation we've given our children stone fish. Our children have asked for love and we've given them electronic toys. A commercial society breeds selfishness, Miss Rome."

"And The Glorious Church gives—"

"Time. Peace. Tranquility. We attend to the needs of the students, not their selfish desires."

Thus the reason for the bare living quarters and the lack of clothing. What, I wondered, was considered 'need' when the basic needs of any human being include food and warmth.

The focus of the church was prayer, Sophia said. Prayer with humbleness and meekness were strengths to be cultivated along with an attitude of servanthood.

"Servanthood?"

"Giving, sharing, humbling ourselves in order to support another."

Due to that, the living quarters were very sparse. Materialism, Sophia said, was the cause of moral decay in America. She added that their students did not take a vow of poverty, which I doubted.

"The acquisition of things supersedes everything in

America. There is no time left for the giving of ourselves, no time left for even the family. This, we feel, is a ploy of Satan; it is his way of eroding the core of America through breaking down the home. Therefore, we enjoy only the basic necessities of life—food, shelter, clothing. We devote our time to learning, serving, and worship."

"But you have to live. The students have to be fed, housed, books purchased. Teachers hired and paid. That takes money."

"Yes, it does. And the Lord has been good to provide for us."

"How much does The Glorious Church receive in gifts each year, through collected donations and from your television program?"

"To discuss amounts would draw undue attention to the very thing that is undermining the moral codes of our country."

I waited, but she didn't continue. "Then, what amount do you pay taxes on?"

"We hold tax exempt status as a non-profit organization."

I made a mental note to have Front Page check into that.

"Our way is not easy. It is very structured and requires sacrifice."

"Such as the leaving behind of unnecessary creature comforts," I clarified.

"Yes, but we do not dwell on what we do not have, but what we gain by the sacrifice. The greatest sacrifice of giving of ourselves, without thought of what we gain in return. Certainly not in a tangible way. The experience itself, the exhilaration of serving, of pleasing another person, is the reward."

"The walk of sacrifice."

Her hand rested on my arm, her fingers icy cold as if there was no blood in her veins to warm her body. I expected her to give me copies of her printed material, tracts or manuals. Instead, her fingers began a rhythmic movement on my arm, up and down, up and down, so softly I could hardly feel them. She began to talk again in a low, persuasive voice that was almost hypnotic. I could feel my body growing lethargic.

"You asked about the basic ethic of The Glorious Church. The one ethic that threads through everything we are, everything we believe in, is truth. We are searchers for truth. All else, all the trappings of society that restrict the full expression of ourselves, must be left behind.

"When that is achieved, we can discover the truth in ourselves, and the deceit that is planted and fertilized by society can be left behind. Then we are free to be everything we were meant to be."

In a pretense of pushing my hair back out of my face, I removed my arm from her touch. I didn't look at her, but she seemed to shift away from me almost without moving, while continuing her sales pitch.

"Through our ministry, insights that have remained hidden since the time of the Old Testament are being revealed. The Bible was written by prophets with special discernment and it says exactly what it means. There is no room for interpretation or discussion. The Word is spoken through the work of The Glorious Church. The listener's responsibility is to adjust his thinking to the integrity and accuracy of the scriptures."

"And the other writings? What are they?"

"Some are written by the prophets of the Bible, some by others who had vision."

"And these are what I saw your students studying when I last visited?"

I was writing and missed whatever might have been evident in her face. But when she spoke again there was a change in her tone of voice that was somehow different, but so subtle I first thought I was mistaken.

"Our students study the Bible. The other writings are not available for open study."

I glanced up then and saw a sharpness in her expression that warned me to tread lightly.

"I see. Then how—"

"It is a part of my personal calling to share these other scriptures on an individual basis. Now, I apologize, but I have a prayer hour to conduct."

I stood with her. "I'd like the opportunity to talk to you again. I'm intrigued by what you've told me today."

For just the barest moment I thought she might refuse, but then she nodded briefly.

"I welcome your questions. Perhaps you will phone and set a time when we can talk at length."

"I will. Thank you for seeing me."

She turned and strode, with a whisper, a hiss of movement, toward the concealed door. Once it had closed behind her, I drew a long breath, realizing only now how tense I'd become during the brief interview.

Stuffing the notebook and pen in my bag, I took one last look around the chapel and then strode quickly down the aisle and outside. A slight wind had risen to make the just below freezing temperatures seem frigid, but the shiver that went down my spine was caused more by a feeling inside me. I shivered and pulled the collar of my parka closer to my throat.

The guards were still at the gate, but when I started my car they both turned to watch me leave. I noted once again that there were no expressions on their faces. They were mechanical in speech and action. Remembering the things Mark had told me, I wondered how much brainwashing technique the Belgrades employed in their teaching groups, and how much serving and in what form, was demanded of their students.

Driving slowly, I studied the barracks that were just visible through a line of trees and the tightly knit chain link fence. I really wanted the opportunity to speak to one of the students without the intimidation of the Belgrades. But that was impossible. From what I'd observed, and from Mark and Brian, the Belgrades exerted strong control over the students at all times.

My stomach growled, complaining about missed lunch. Gary would be wondering where I'd disappeared to and was probably this moment working himself into a temper. Needing some quiet time to think about Sophia and the rhetoric she'd spouted, I pulled to the side of the road and left the motor running so the heater would warm the car. I opened my notebook and began to fill in the blanks between Sophia's answers to my questions.

My stomach growled again and I fished around inside my bag for a packet of peanut butter filled crackers and munched them slowly while studying the compound. I really wanted to get inside and do a little snooping around on my own, but there didn't seem to be any weak spots in the defense. The fence ran around all sides, the grounds surrounding the barracks were clear of any shrubbery, leaving no secluded spots, and only the buildings and scattered trees broke the barren landscape.

Squinting, I leaned forward to peer through the trees toward one corner of the compound. The woods encroached close there and even before late evening it would be dark enough to cover a break-out, or break in—

With a quick glance back down the road to make sure I was out of sight of the gate guards, I got out of the car. Darting swiftly across the road and running along the edge of the trees, I slowed as I approached the corner.

Crouching down behind some underbrush, I peered through to the compound. Maybe, if I was very careful, I could climb the fence, negotiate over the barbed wire, and get inside. I didn't know what I'd find; maybe there was nothing to find but—

I ducked down when the back door of the nearest building opened. A student, a young man, came out. Was he being as furtive as I imagined?

He strode with a measured sideways step toward the fence. When he reached it he stood for a long moment, just looking into the woods. Then he began to move along the fence in my direction and I held my breath. Had I been seen?

My legs began to ache from remaining in a crouched position, but I dared not move. The young man was just standing now, staring out into the woods, his fingers laced into the fence as he half hung there. Something in his body language conveyed a yearning to escape; then, just as I began to toy with the idea of approaching him, he shrugged in an attitude of defeat and turned back toward the barracks, his feet scuffling against the ground, his shoulders rounded and head bent.

I waited for several minutes after he went inside to make certain no one else was coming out. Only when I could wait no longer did I hurry back to my car. I began to breathe again when I was halfway back to town and the questions were tumbling over and over in my mind. Who was that young man, and what was he doing?

By the time I reached the motel, I was starving. I checked my cell phone, deleting three from Ben before deciding I really should phone him.

"Ben? Maggie."

"Where have you been? I expected a report before now."

"Well, there's not a lot to report, yet."

I began combing tangles out of my hair with my fingers while I paced the middle of the room.

"Mag—"

"I know, I need to get something in to justify being here. But right now all I have is a lot of loose ends. There's something here though. Have you ever heard of The Glorious Church?"

"No. What is it? Some sort of religious group?"

"A cult, from what I can determine. On the surface it looks like a legitimate organization, but I'm not sure. Something about it just doesn't click. And, Susan's parents were once members."

"You're thinking there's some connection to her death?"

"I hope not, but the little voice inside my head says there might be."

"Take it easy, Maggie. Be careful."

"Always."

Chapter Nine

After telling myself a million times I was crazy for even thinking that the appearance of the young man at the fence the night before meant anything, I still drove back to the compound at twilight. Parking beside the road, in the shadows of overhanging limbs, I waited. Thirty minutes passed and darkness had fallen before the barracks door opened and someone shuffled out.

Watching him carefully, I got out of the car and walked quickly in a line parallel to the fence, keeping to the shadows. He went to the same corner, threaded his fingers into the fence links, and hung there, staring out into the dark woods.

Knowing the odds of him being receptive to my approach were slim, I still took the chance. I waited a few minutes, then stepped to the edge of the shadows.

"Hello," I said softly.

He jumped in surprise and jerked away from the fence, his pale eyes searching the shadows.

I moved forward a half step. "Please, I just want to talk to you."

"I can't."

"Please? I'll stay right here."

147

I knew I'd won a small victory when his shoulders relaxed. If a young man could be called beautiful, he was. Sculptured features, perfect mouth, compelling eyes rimmed with dark lashes. The starkness of his shaved head and hungry-lean cheeks gave him an other-world look that was both appealing and disturbing.

"I remember you. You came the other evening."

"Yes, I did." I was surprised that he'd seen me.

"I saw you go into the barracks. You met Tony there."

Even in the twilight I could see tension in his thin face.

"Why are you here? You're from the world, and the world doesn't understand our mission."

"I want to know about the church. I'm a journalist and Tony and Sophia have been willing to talk to me about The Glorious Church. I spent some time with Sophia yesterday."

I wondered how much I should tell him. Knowing I was a journalist didn't seem to concern him, but perhaps it was only because he knew Tony and Sophia had already spoken with me.

"As I was leaving last night I saw you. I thought you looked like you needed a friend."

He studied me for a long moment, his gaze level. "I have the brothers and sisters."

"I know, and I'd like to know more about them. My name is Maggie."

"I am called Michael."

I wished I could use my recorder, or at least my notebook, but I was afraid doing so would frighten him away. For now I needed to pose as someone just curious about the church.

"Is that your real name?"

"I am called Michael. I am the servant."

I recognized the unemotional tone of a rote response.

"Can you tell me your real name? Perhaps I could get in touch with your parents—"

"No! They are of the world."

Alarm transformed his face, making his eyes widen and his jaw clench with tension.

"Okay." I shrugged my shoulders as if it wasn't important. "I just wanted to talk to you for a moment anyway."

"What about?"

"Are you a student here?"

"Yes."

"How long have you been with the church?"

"Four years."

I was surprised. "Do students usually stay for a long time? I thought that at some point a student graduated, to establish a church elsewhere?"

"I . . . won't be leaving."

"But students do leave."

I couldn't imagine them making a lifetime commitment to the church and living in the barracks forever.

"Not many."

"What do you do here? Study?"

"They . . . we . . . carry on the work."

"And what is that work?"

"Spreading the good word." His hands clenched on the wire.

"Do you help spread the word?"

Talking with him was like walking a child through thorny brambles, slow and careful.

"No." Again the hands worked on the wire. "My duties are here."

Something was bothering him but I had to lead him to it gently.

"But others that you know work in the airports and on the streets."

"Yes. They bring in the contributions to support the work."

"And where does that money go? You live in pretty grim surroundings."

"Tony and Sophia are the stewards of God's money."

"Tony and Sophia. They're the only ones who determine what the money is used for?"

"It is used for the ministry. And to feed and clothe us so we can go out and spread the word."

Michael had learned the rote well.

"What did you do before you came here?"

His eyes flicked to me, then away. It seemed he had to concentrate very hard to answer the question.

"I was a musician."

"Oh? What did you play?"

"Guitar." He hesitated, then whispered. "Classical and rock."

"Did you work as a musician?"

"Yes."

"Were you successful?"

"I was good."

In other words, he was a working musician but hadn't made it yet.

"Why did you join The Glorious Church?"

He drew a deep breath and let it out slowly. Then he moved back to the fence and hung there on it as if his legs would no longer hold him. His hauntingly pale eyes looked into the distance and the longing in his face was so potent that it was painful.

"I was searching."

"Searching for what?"

"Truth. I wanted to find someone who could show me the right way to live. I read the Bible, but it was too . . . simple. Love God. Do right. Love one another. There had to be something more. Some kind of . . . price. Some kind of work. Some way, some plan, to be . . . perfect."

"How did you meet the Belgrades?"

"I was just walking around. Looking. And some people, some students, were handing out tracts. I took one and read it, but it didn't make sense. It wasn't what I thought it should be. But the students seemed so . . . certain. So . . . focused. I began to ask questions and they invited me to a meeting. To a church service."

"You went?"

"Yes."

"Tell me about it."

His gaze was measuring, as if he wanted to make sure I was genuine.

"I'd like to know."

"It was Friday night and I didn't feel like getting drunk and passing out again, so I thought, 'Why not?' They'd told me a bus would pick up anyone who wanted to go to the service, so I went to the corner they'd named and waited. Pretty soon I saw this big bus coming down the street. It had 'Heaven' written on both sides in big letters, and everyone inside was singing and laughing. I wanted to be that happy, so I got on."

"Then what happened?"

"We went to church."

"Tell me about that."

"Why?" Suspicion lit his eyes.

"I want to learn everything I can about The Glorious Church."

"Are you a seeker?"

"I'm not sure. Maybe I am, like you were."

He seemed hesitant. I hoped the wouldn't be frightened off now. Though he seemed to be totally plugged into the church ethic, there seemed to be a few doubts. Doubts that I might be able to use to learn what I needed by carefully persuading him to talk about the church and his contribution to it.

"It wasn't like anything I'd experienced. I'd been really turned off by church before," he said, the words beginning to tumble out as if they'd waited a long time to be said.

"I thought it was a lot of hypocritical pabulum. But this was different. The building was a converted restaurant and long tables had been placed in a large room. The students were sitting around the tables reading their Bibles, and there was a kind of noise, like lots of voices talking at once, coming from another room. I found out later that it was a prayer room where everyone was praying aloud. It was crazy."

"What was the service like? Was it like their television program?"

"You've seen it?"

"I saw it being taped the other night. I met Sophia there."

A near smile tweaked the corners of his mouth. "That's something, isn't it? The choir is very good."

"I thought it was interesting."

"Interesting. That's a good word. The whole thing is interesting."

He seemed to slip first one way then the other. One moment giving the ethic of The Glorious Church, the next exhibiting a faint questioning of what he'd been taught; a questioning that was evidenced in a tone of skepticism that lightly colored his words.

I hesitated, weighing my next words. "You sound a little disenchanted."

He chewed his lower lip for a minute.

"Maybe. I'm not sure. I'm not sure this is what I thought it was."

"How do you mean?"

He threw his head back and looked up into the sky as if searching for the answers there. I was keeping one eye on the barracks grounds for fear some guard would discover us, but the buildings seemed devoid of life. I wondered if some big meeting was taking place elsewhere, and if so, why wasn't Michael there?

"That first night there was a lot of music, a kind of gospel rock sound that appealed to me. I thought perhaps I could be of some service, contribute, and find what I was looking for at the same time. I knew I couldn't keep drinking the way I was, but nothing else seemed to help."

"It isn't what you expected?"

"I thought it was. That first night. The service was going on, Sophia was preaching that hellfire-and-brimstone message. You know, you're going to hell unless you love God and love one another kind of stuff.

"Afterward a number of people went to the front and gave their testimony, about how they'd been saved and brought to The Glorious Church through its wonderful ministry. Then, at the end of the service, an altar call was given for everyone who was unsaved to come forward and repeat the sinners' prayer, make a commitment to The Glorious Church, and work for it.

"I remember feeling . . . overpowered. Compelled. My feet moved like I was controlled by something outside myself. I went down front, they laid hands on me, warned me that if I didn't repent right now, God might turn his back on me and would never recognize me again. I might never have another chance.

"I remember it was so . . . emotional. I didn't want to be lost forever. I didn't want God turning his back on me.

"Then, when it was over, a bunch of them told me I was saved, but there was more. I had to be baptized by the Holy Spirit. They took me into a prayer room and a half dozen of them formed a circle around me and began to chant. After a while—it must have been hours—I lost track of time and I couldn't even think. All I could hear were the words, 'Praise you, Jesus, thank you, Jesus, praise you—'" His words faded out.

"Then what happened?" I prompted him softly.

He drew a deep breath. "It went on for what seemed like hours. Pretty soon I didn't even know where I was any more. The words became just sound that rose and fell, rose and fell, like a kind of monotonous tone that went into my brain and wiped it clean.

"I couldn't talk. My tongue was thick and dry and when I tried, the words were unrecognizable, even to me.

"Then they started shouting that I was speaking in tongues and they just went . . . wild. Shouting hallelujah and praising God. I was so . . . fuzzy. I didn't know what was happening. It was like being in a whirlwind and I was spinning and spinning and spinning out of control."

"What happened when you went home?"

Michael stared at the ground, his forehead resting against the fence.

"I didn't go home. I never went home again."

"Never?"

"No. From that minute on I was never alone. One of the brothers was always with me. Usually three or four. They asked questions all the time, quoted scriptures all the time, prayed all the time. Day and night. I don't remember ever getting an hour's sleep a night for what must have been weeks. They were always there."

"Didn't you want to leave?"

"I don't know. Maybe at first. But they told me God had chosen me. And when he chose me he wanted me there all the time. To protect me from the arrows of Satan. I couldn't go back into the Old World until I was thoroughly protected from Satan's demons. I was 'called' to The Glorious Church, and once there I was not supposed to go back into the world. I've not . . . I've not been out since."

He was quiet and I wondered what I could say to him. He seemed perplexed by what had happened to him and his response to it. One minute talking as if the life he lived was what he'd chosen, the next talking about The Glorious Church as if it had invaded his life.

"What about your parents? Your family. Did you let them know what you were doing? Do they know where you are?"

"No."

It seemed difficult for him to remember.

"I wanted to, but the brothers told me that my parents were my worst enemy. They quoted that scripture about the division between father and son and mother and daughter.

And it seemed right. My dad and I had never gotten along. Nothing I ever did seemed good enough. Mom went along with him." He shrugged. "She didn't like conflict and it was easier not to cause waves, I guess. The Glorious Church became my family. They are my brothers and sisters."

"Do you think about your parents?"

His forehead creased momentarily. "Yes. I wonder how they are."

"Don't you think they might be worried about you? Time has a way of changing the way we feel about a lot of things."

"Yes, it does," he said softly. "I don't know." Then again, "I don't know."

There was another lengthy pause before he spoke again, softly, as if to himself.

"It seemed so right. The answers seemed to be there."

"And now?"

We spoke in near whispers, the sound almost lost in the breeze.

"I don't know. I just don't know."

"Have you talked to Sophia about how you feel?"

He blinked as if I'd said something startling.

"No. We do not question. The brothers have the answers and we must share them with those who are lost."

"They have all the answers? I didn't think anyone but God had *all* the answers."

"Doubts are discouraged."

The way he said 'discouraged' alerted the little voice inside my head that was the infallible signal of something a little askew. Ben often teased me about it, but every time I ignored it, I got into trouble.

"How are they discouraged?"

He shrugged. "When you slip, you must be retrained."

"How is that done?"

"The brothers take you to a room and turn your thoughts back to the right way."

"How?"

The moonlight was strong, illuminating his thin face. His head sank back and his eyes drifted closed. His body hung loosely on the fence as if he was some bit of flotsam that had blown against it, held by some errant wind.

"Count it all joy—crucify the flesh," he intoned. "Thank you Jesus. Praise you Jesus. Oh, Lord, help me to be thankful for this."

I recognized his tone as that of another chant and knew I'd lost him, at least for the moment.

"Count it all joy—crucify the flesh. Thank you, Jesus. Praise you, Jesus. Thank you, Jesus. Praise you, Jesus. Thank you, Jesus. Praise you, Jesus. Thank you—"

I wondered how long the litany would continue if I didn't interrupt. "Michael. I'd like to talk to you again."

"We must not speak to the world. Satan's powers will come and pierce our shield—"

"I don't want to persuade you to do anything, Michael. I just want to know more about The Glorious Church. After all, Tony and Sophia talked to me."

His chin dipped and he looked at me. "All right."

"Tomorrow evening?"

"No, I have duties tomorrow."

"Then the next night. I'll come right here."

"I might have duties."

"I'll be here, and I'll wait for you."

With a nod he turned and hurried back to the barracks, furtiveness evident in every movement.

After he'd gone inside, I made my way back to the car. I sat for a few minutes before starting the car, thinking about what Michael had told me.

When I reached the motel, Gary was sitting in the lobby pretending to read a local newspaper. The way he snapped the paper shut and threw it into a chair, warned me that he was in a foul temper and I was apparently the cause of it.

"Where have you been?

"Working."

"On what? Your other story?"

"I'm hungry." I veered toward the dining room.

"I'm not."

"Sorry." I caught the attention of the hostess.

"Two?"

"One."

"Two," Gary said.

"Two," I agreed reluctantly, then followed the hostess to a corner table.

I picked up the menu but suddenly I was too tired to even think about food. "Coffee for me, please."

"Uh, scotch."

When the hostess left, I laid down the menu and looked at Gary. "I can see you're just champing at the bit to tell me what's on your mind, but before you do, just remember that I came here at your request. I told you at the beginning that I work on my own. You're too close to this case to be helpful."

"Of course I'm close. Susan was my sister—" The air seemed to go out of him. "At least I thought she was."

His fingers threaded through his hair in frustration and I could almost see him gathering his composure.

"God, I don't understand any of this. I'm sorry I jumped you. I guess I just needed to talk to someone, to sort through all this. You're the only one," he shrugged. "And you were gone."

The idea that I was the only one he could talk to seemed to not fall easy on his shoulders. It made me realize again how much we'd both lost in not being able to hold a marriage together. But maybe, for the time being, we could be friends.

"I'm sorry. I'm just so used to doing things my own way that I forgot how much of a jolt this has been for you." I drew a deep breath to clear my thoughts. "Look, Susan was your sister. An accident of birth doesn't change that. We both still care what happened to her and I intend to find out."

He ran his hand down his face as if he was washing it. For

the first time I noticed how tired he looked. His hand was laying on the table and I placed mine over it.

"Are you all right?"

"Of course. No. I don't know. I didn't expect all this."

The waitress brought his drink, poured my coffee, then took our dinner order. When we were alone again, I leaned forward.

"You really never suspected Susan was adopted? There was never a hint?"

"No. Never." He took a large swallow of his drink. "I know I'm not the most aware man. You accused me of that enough, and I've thought about it since, but there was never any doubt. Not once." He took another swallow.

I ran my fingertip around the rim of my coffee cup. "We're going to find out what happened to Susan."

The picture of Michael hanging onto the chain link fence, his face taut with strain, flickered across my mind.

"And I think I know who can help us, if he will."

Chapter Ten

I walked to The Parakeet for breakfast and chanced to find the sheriff just finishing a stack of pancakes. Neal laid aside the newspaper and waved me over. I grimaced at the newspaper as I slid into the booth and accepted a cup of coffee from Ida Belle with a grateful smile. Neal grinned at my stubborn opinion of his town's newspaper.

We'd had breakfast together the day before and had left business alone. We'd just talked about general things, about the area, and I was even more impressed with him as a man than as a lawman.

"Um, just cinnamon toast."

"No wonder you're so skinny," was Ida Belle's comment before hurrying off to the kitchen.

"For the record, I don't think you're skinny," he drawled, leaning forward a little with humor dancing in his eyes.

I couldn't help smiling back.

"You okay? You look a little pale."

"I'm fine. I think I'm catching a cold. Room service is getting tired of bringing orange juice to my room but—" I shrugged.

His look made it clear he didn't believe me. I was surprised that his doubt bothered me.

"How's things going on your story?"

"Slow. Anything new on your part?"

"Nope. As far as we're concerned officially, the case on Susan Brady is still open but on the back burner."

"I know." I sipped my coffee tentatively. It didn't taste very good. "Our agreement still stands, doesn't it?"

"Umhum. What's on your mind?"

"Any idea where the poison that Susan ingested came from?"

"Not a clue. Nothing in her place, nothing at the stables."

"She was found in the living room?"

"Sprawled on the floor, as if she was going toward the door."

"So she might have been trying to leave the apartment. Go for help?"

He shrugged. "We can speculate a lot of things."

"What about those around her? Any of them purchase Strychnine or have it available to them?"

Neal frowned thoughtfully. "Her parents? Friends? Pretty open field. But, officially, I did talk to the parents. And that butler. Straight out of the forties."

I grinned. Malcolm had always had a strict view of what his responsibilities and appearances should be.

"Anything?"

"Not a clue."

"What did you think of the Bradys?"

His mouth curved at one corner. "Not the Brady Bunch."

I answered his grin. When he smiled his face was transformed. "Never were."

"Lot of stress between the two."

"They've lost a daughter."

"Yeah," he agreed. "Can't imagine how painful that must be. What were those two like when you were part of the family?"

"Uptight. Always. Edward had high expectations of everyone and I never measured up. Pauline struggled. Gary seemed to . . . fit the proscribed mold. Susan . . . was quiet, impressionable. I wish I'd known her better, kept in touch."

"Edward Brady was a doctor?"

"Yes." I shrugged. "In fact, a pretty well known plastic surgeon. I thought he was at the top of his profession. I had no idea he planned to retire, but then it's been five years since I've been around them, so what could I know of his plans?"

"But still, it surprised you that he retired."

"Yes. It seemed . . . against his nature. But then, Pauline always wanted him to be home more. Perhaps she finally got through to him."

I fiddled with the cup again. "I learned something by accident that surprised me a great deal."

"Oh?"

"Susan was adopted shortly after birth. The Bradys never told her, or anyone. Not even Gary."

His gaze didn't flicker, but I knew the wheels were turning. Neal was a thinking law officer, the kind that mulled things over carefully, the kind that people too often mistook for being ineffectual.

"That's interesting."

"No other comment?"

"What can I say?"

"Well, I also learned that they were once members of The Glorious Church."

His response had a slightly different tone this time. "Crap."

"They say their interest was short lived. They were invited to a meeting by a business associate, attended for a while, but became disenchanted by the church teaching against physical enhancement. Edward being a plastic surgeon wasn't acceptable. They've not been involved since."

"Believe that?"

"Can't disbelieve it, or at least I don't have a reason to disbelieve it. I do think it's a pretty big coincidence. And

I've always wondered why they retired here. Nothing against your fine community, but—"

"They don't belong here," he finished for me. "Are you going to pursue that angle?"

"You're not?"

"No official reason, which limits my ability to ask many more questions."

"The limits of the law. Well, I don't have those restraints."

His gaze was measuring. "You wouldn't tell me if you were going to do something . . . let's say, pushing the limits, would you?"

"Why worry you?"

"Be careful," he warned. "Please?"

I liked the way he said that last word, because I knew it was one he seldom used.

"This ain't my first rodeo, cowboy."

"It might be a little rougher horse than you're used to. We don't know what's in the chute." His gaze caught mine. "I don't want you to take chances."

"I'll watch myself." I sipped my coffee, thinking.

I was attracted to this man, but there were a lot of reasons why I shouldn't be. I was here for only a few days at best. New York was my home and his was here. This story was growing and I still didn't know who was involved in Susan's death.

"Well, I do have a bit of news. Heard it this morning. Sophia is a bit under the weather. Apparently they're going to have a healing session."

"Oh? What's the matter with her?"

"You know she's had these episodes before."

"A recurring terminal illness, I've been told. But she's been prayed back to health by the students and their television audience."

"Umhum. I don't know how you feel about that kind of thing, but they've made it a support column of whatever it is they believe."

"I spoke to Sophia just a couple of days ago," I admitted.

"How did she look?"

"Fine. A very . . . careful woman. Graceful surface, spine of steel. Totally in control of herself and what goes on around her. I should have her confidence."

"Have you eaten at The Gold Road?"

"The restaurant The Glorious Church runs? No. What's it like?"

"Nice. Good food. Good service."

I wondered if there was something more in the suggestion, but didn't ask. The less Neal knew about what I was doing, the less responsible he'd feel.

"Well, I plan to be here for a couple more days. Maybe I will."

"Good. Let me know how you like it." He shoved aside his plate. "You think you'll have your answers in a couple of days?"

"I hope so."

"And then what?"

A week earlier I'd have had a quick answer for that. "New York is my home base."

His head tilted to one side. "You didn't say it was home."

"I've got an apartment, but I'm seldom there. I travel a lot."

"Ever think about settling somewhere permanently?"

"I've tried not to think in those terms."

At least not in the past.

"Running away from something?"

I rubbed the tabletop with my fingertip, avoiding looking at Neal. "I didn't think so, but I've thought more about it the last few days. Maybe I was, without realizing it."

"And now?"

"Now . . . I'm not running. I like my work, it satisfies me, and it fills my life."

"Totally?"

"No," I looked up finally. "Not totally."

"When you think it through," He picked up his check. "Keep me updated on what you find. If there's anything I can do, legally, I will." The backs of his fingers caressed my cheek and my toes curled. "And, don't take any chances."

I watched him walk out with that rolling walk of a man secure in himself, cowboy boots thudding against the tile floor, the strong handclasp with a couple of men who reached out to him as he reached the door. I liked Neal Conrad. He was the kind of man who was an anchor, an oak, and yet there was a gentleness to him too. It was a lethal combination.

I pushed Neal out of my mind and spent the day rethinking and organizing everything I'd learned thus far, then, shortly after dusk I drove out to The Gold Road restaurant. If the number of cars in the parking lot were any indication, it was a popular dining spot.

A tall young man in a dark suit, white shirt, dark tie, greeted me from behind a counter.

"One for dinner?"

"Yes."

"One moment please."

I shrugged off my parka and waited. Golden maple furniture sitting on a lightly patterned plush carpet matched the woodwork. Subdued lighting against mellow painted walls on which hung what looked like good original paintings—both oil and watercolor—lent an elegance to the cement block building that was not apparent outside.

A second young man entered from a door marked 'Office' and stepped behind the counter.

"Have you been helped?"

"Yes, thank you."

The name Michael was imprinted on the plastic chip pinned to his pocket. How many of the students, and I was certain everyone working at the restaurant was a student of The Glorious Church, were named Michael and Gabriel?

"Excuse me. Could you tell me—I heard this morning

that Sophia wasn't feeling well. Do you have word on how she is? I mean, it isn't anything critical, is it?"

His gaze was measuring. "You're speaking of Sophia Belgrade?"

"Of course. I saw her just two days ago and she looked in very good health," I continued, hoping my questions sounded like warm concern. "I was concerned—"

"If you'll give me your name, I'll be sure to let her know you were asking after her health."

"Maggie. Maggie Rome. We were going to talk again, but—"

"I'm sorry," he interrupted. "I need to take care of something immediately."

"Well," I blinked at his abruptness. "Certainly."

He disappeared into the office and I continued my perusal of the restaurant. I stepped to the entrance of the dining room and quickly surveyed the diners. The room would hold perhaps fifty patrons and was surprisingly full.

Crystal and flowers decorated the tables, strikingly elegant in contrast to the outward appearance of the building. Someone had put quite a lot of money into this endeavor and it appeared, at least at first glance, to be a successful venture. Perhaps another money-maker for the Belgrades.

I wondered again just how much money The Glorious Church really brought in and whether they were legally allowed the non-profit status they claimed.

"Miss Rome?"

I turned. Michael was framed in the office doorway. "Yes?"

"There's a call for you."

"Oh?" That was strange. No one knew I was there. Not even Gary.

"You may take it in the office."

I wondered what was afoot, but followed him. The receiver was off the hook and I picked it up slowly. Michael waited just outside the door, appearing to give me privacy but, I noticed, within listening distance.

"Hello?"

"Miss Rome?"

I recognized Sophia's husky tones.

"Sophia. I'm glad to hear your voice. I'd heard this morning that you weren't feeling well and I was concerned. But I didn't expect Michael to phone you."

"Michael is very conscientious. I'm sure you understand that we have to be careful about people who ask questions."

"Oh, have you had problems?"

"No, not at all. But one must be careful."

"How are you feeling, Sophia? I was looking forward to talking with you again about the church and its programs."

"I'm not entirely well, but this too shall pass. Perhaps we could talk this evening."

"I would like that, if you're up to it."

"I'm feeling very well today. After you have eaten, perhaps you'd allow a driver to bring you to our home where we can talk comfortably."

"I would like that."

"I will arrange it. Let me talk to Michael again, please."

I handed the receiver to Michael. He took it, but didn't immediately put it to his ear. It took a moment, but I finally realized that he did not intend to speak with his employer until I'd left the room.

With a small wave, I stepped out and closed the door behind me. When I found I could not hear his end of the conversation, I stepped soundlessly away from the door and returned to the foyer where I was immediately escorted to a table.

After ordering a salad and quiche, I sipped hot tea, into which I'd stirred a spoonful of honey, and studied my surroundings. The diners appeared to be upper middle class clientele and the service seemed to be impeccably gracious. I stirred my tea thoughtfully. Why had Michael immediately phoned Sophia when I'd asked about her? Was it in response to some kind of former harassment? And if so, were there threats against Sophia, or against the church as a whole?

Then, as it was sometimes want to do, my mind took another great leap. What if Susan's death had some connection to some kind of threat leveled against the church? Something that had some connection with the Bradys' former relationship with the church? What if they had lied about leaving the church and what if their membership had caused some problems between Edward and Pauline and Susan? Would that account for the added stress I had sensed in the Bradys? Did Susan have her own apartment because they'd had a big disagreement, and was it possible that disagreement was over the church? But what did all of that have to do with her death, except that if she'd been living at home she'd still be alive?

I worried over these questions while I ate the quiche, wishing my stomach didn't feel quite so queasy. Maybe the pharmacy in town would have something for a cold. As soon as I pushed my plate aside, Michael Number Two, as I'd tagged the second host, approached the table.

"Miss Rome?"

"Yes."

"If you're finished, a car is waiting to take you to the Belgrade home."

"Um, yes, I'm finished. If I could have—"

"Your check is taken care of. Please, Sophia is anxious to talk with you."

"Uh, thank you," I stammered, wishing Sophia had allowed me to drive myself, as it would have given me time to do a bit more thinking about this meeting. Michael handed me my parka and escorted me outside.

A tan van waited outside the building and for the briefest moment, an image of Susan being taken captive in such a vehicle flashed across my mind.

Michael opened the door and helped me inside, slamming the door behind me. The driver, obviously a student, kept his face turned forward. As soon as the door closed, he put the van in gear.

Twenty minutes later, we were approaching the compound, but instead of going to the gate as I'd expected, the van went past and slowed at a road a short distance further on. I sat forward slightly and peered out the window into the darkness.

"Where are we going?"

"To the mansion."

"Mansion? Where is it?"

"We will be there in a moment."

Obviously he was not going to answer any questions so I had to content myself with observing what I could by the lights of the van. The road was not paved, but was lined by chain link fencing. The trees were thicker here and the darkness was intensified where the limbs laced together over the road.

The van approached a gate that opened automatically, then closed smoothly behind us. As we drove along a meandering drive, I searched the darkness, frustrated at being able to see nothing but darkness and trees. Then the drive made a sharp turn and I suddenly had an answer to my questions about money and The Glorious Church. The Belgrades brought in plenty of dollars, through the television program and the soliciting of their students, which they spent on themselves. The vow of poverty preached to their converts had obviously not been included in their own calling.

The house that appeared in front of us was aptly named The Mansion. It was like something out of a Cinderella dream, constructed of some kind of stone that glowed beneath floodlights, all pink and purple against a dark sky. A full moon was visible just to the right of the highest spire and I had the insane impression that all the scene needed was the silhouette of a witch on a broom to make the bizarre scene complete.

The van stopped in the circle drive and the driver got out.

He slid the door back and offered his hand to assist me out. After indicating I should climb the stairs to the ornate front door, the driver climbed back into the van and drove away.

Swallowing dryly, I wondered what I'd gotten myself into now, and then began to climb the steps. Just as I reached the top step, the door opened and Sophia, dressed in a long, flowing royal purple dress, greeted me effusively.

"Maggie. I'm so glad you could come."

"Thank you for inviting me."

I followed Sophia into an opulent foyer. The floor was black marble, the walls a glowing pink stone. A gray marble slab created a table that sat beneath a gilt framed painting of Tony and Sophia.

My gaze followed up the wall until I was staring at a vaulted ceiling that had been painted with a cloud motif broken only by wide gold strips leading to a gold and crystal chandelier. The whole appearance was that of a fantasy land castle that gave me an eerie feeling of having fallen into some kind of time warp.

"Tony, Maggie has arrived."

"She certainly has."

The aging lothario's dark eyes measured me from head to toe. Remembering some of the things Mark had told me about Tony's disciplines, I suppressed a shiver.

"Tony." I clasped his warm, damp hand briefly.

"I'm so glad you've come," Sophia said to her husband. "I must take care of something unexpected. Perhaps you could give Maggie a little tour of the house."

Curiosity overcame the strong apprehension that had settled on my shoulders the moment I'd stepped into the mansion. I pushed aside the reluctance to spend any time alone with Tony in the hope of being able to learn something more about the Belgrades and having my curiosity about the house satisfied.

"I'd like that."

"So would I," Tony said, taking my arm. "We'll meet you in the den."

Sophia disappeared down a hallway.

"This is the main hall," Tony said, guiding me into a large room that matched the foyer, except that it was ten times larger.

"Quite impressive."

"Yes," he intoned, his hand sliding to the back of my neck to turn me toward a large mural that dominated the back wall. "Sophia had an artist from New York come to do that for us. It is his interpretation of what heaven will be like."

The mural was a swirl of white and blue and gold with writing, wisplike figures hovering on the fringes. Whoever the artist had been, he'd been quite adept at creating illusion without substantive form. The feeling of the painting was one of space and richness and made me feel drawn toward the vortex of the painting which was created by a tunnel-like feeling without a defined focus point. If I'd had time, I would have liked to examine the painting more closely, but Tony was already urging me toward another arched doorway.

The pink and purple ostentatiousness of the house made it seem a setting for a play—a somewhat bizarre but expensive setting for its eccentric owners.

Tony took me through rooms that unfolded one on the other like a deck of cards, naming them and their purpose with obvious pride. The floors and columns were all marble, from Europe, Tony explained proudly. The paintings and furnishings were expensive and larger than life. Oil paintings of Tony and Sophia, rendered in a doubtful style, dominated every room.

"And this is the master bedroom."

He opened a heavy door that was carved with scenes that looked like those from Dante's hell, but Tony whisked me through too quickly for me to examine it.

"We spend a great deal of time in here," Tony said, his voice low and suggestive.

I fought the urge to put distance between myself and the Elvis clone who had a firm grip on my arm.

"We had the bed specially made. The carvings are Italian, as are the drapings."

I swallowed dryly. The room looked like someone's conception of the harem of some eastern prince. The furnishings were heavy, with brocade drapings and wall hangings. The room was overly warm and the aroma of incense made me sleepy.

"You may touch, if you'd like. Come, I'll show you."

He was standing very close, too close, and his hand slid down my arm in an attempt to clasp my hand.

"Sophia will be . . . detained for a while. We have plenty of time."

His attempt at seduction was clumsy, but his interest in me was painfully clear. Too clear. Was he following Sophia's orders? Had she decided I was asking too many questions and devised this method of discovering exactly what my interest was, or was Tony acting entirely on his own? The man did have an inflated opinion of his personal attractiveness.

"This is quite lovely, but I am looking forward to talking with Sophia, and you, about The Glorious Church program and school. I have a deadline on my story."

"She was particularly pleased by your interest. We can go to the den for coffee, or tea, if you prefer. Sophia will join us shortly."

I hoped my involuntary reaction to his touch, to the low, oily, way he spoke in double meanings wasn't too obvious. I wanted to keep this door of opportunity open.

"I'd like that."

Tony opened a door and indicated I should precede him from the bedroom. The furnishings and decor of the den were as heavy and ornate as the rest of the house. The cheery fire in the overly large fireplace failed to warm anything beyond the hearth. I sat gingerly on the edge of an upholstered chair to avoid being swallowed by it and hoped Sophia would return soon.

She entered right on cue, followed by a student wheeling a cart on which sat a richly elegant silver serving set. Coffee was served by the student who exhibited an obviously adoring attitude toward Sophia. Obviously, Michael had been right. No one connected with The Glorious Church minded the dual standard of living—one for the leaders and an entirely different one for the students and employees. I'd have to ask Michael more about that.

"Thank you." I accepted a cup of coffee.

"Now," Sophia settled herself in a chair at an angle to me. "What more can I tell you about our work?"

I thought I saw her glance briefly at Tony with an almost imperceptive narrowing of her eyes, but it could have been my imagination. After the strange way I had been brought to the manor, it would only be natural that I became a little paranoid and began to see things that weren't there.

I forced myself to ignore the dark corners of the room and concentrate on the couple flanking me.

"May I take notes?"

"Certainly." Sophia sipped at her coffee.

I pulled the well-worn notebook from my bag and flipped it open, clearing my mind of everything except the questions I'd formulated during the afternoon.

"The work of the church seems to be quite successful—your investment in The Gold Road, the property holding the compound, investments. All this must take quite a lot of your time." I glanced up at Sophia. "Your family life must suffer from your dedication to the work."

"The students are our family. The work is our life."

"You've never had children?"

"To have borne children," Tony inserted, "would have diluted Sophia's devotion to The Glorious Church, and the people who believe in our principles."

"Tell me, what made you begin the work?"

"Need," Sophia said softly. "Their need to belong. Ours to serve. Our ministry is so successful because we make a place for those who have no one, no place to belong. The people no one cares about."

I wondered if providing that 'place to belong' found rewards in the wills of the wealthy, as often happened in other con games, if this was a con.

"Some of our students are former drug addicts, the result of broken homes, of unsupportive lifestyles. We make a place for them, create a supportive atmosphere that allows them to clean up their life and focus on something productive, something outside themselves."

"Do you have special programs for addicts?"

"Yes. Our own program with a very bold approach that has been very successful. Our efforts meet increasing opposition, however, which increases our need for financial support. Fortunately, we have been blessed with loyal supporters."

"What kind of opposition have you encountered?"

"Satan is on the offensive and his troublemakers are everywhere. There have been lies spread about our work, our methods, by outside agitators. But we will fight for our religious freedoms. There will come a day, and very soon, when we will be made martyrs for truth, when we will be persecuted for our faith.

"We embrace that persecution for God. We observe a course of action to withstand the slings and arrows of Satan and his forces."

Such a lot of rhetoric, very little substance, no facts.

"Well, I have to admit I've been doing quite a lot of reading about other groups and compared to them, The Glorious Church has been quite successful. As a result, some charges have been leveled against the church."

"Ah, yes, you would not be a good journalist if you did not do your research. And what did you learn?"

"There have been accusations concerning alleged mind control, poor living conditions, and slave labor, made by parents of some of your students."

"Made by people who do not understand that much of the

world's problems are brought about by its dependence upon material things rather than the spiritual. We, on the other hand, provide all the physical needs for our children. Without all the material trappings which society convinces us are 'needs', our students are able to focus upon God's word and upon the work he has commanded us to do."

While Sophia talked in her calm, quiet voice, I sensed her intense black eyes were closely observing my reactions, my acceptance of the rhetoric. Again I wondered what the purpose was behind their invitation. There had to be one. They did not like publicity.

"Perhaps you would like to come to one of our services. Observing the faithfulness of our people would convince you, I'm sure, that we are not holding our students against their will, as some have accused; nor is there any coercion. Perhaps then, the persecutors would be satisfied."

So that was the reason I had been accepted. I was a journalist, one that might be persuaded, they thought, to present their side of the story to the public.

"I'd like that."

Sophia stood, signaling the end of the interview. "Then I will be in touch so we can make arrangements. Thank you for coming."

I shoved my notebook back into my bag. "Thank you for inviting me."

"Tony, would you escort our new friend to the door? The van has been called."

Sophia disappeared down the hallway as Tony directed me in the opposite direction. For just the briefest moment I thought I heard music and voices, but almost before the impression was made, it was gone.

Tony opened the front door and I saw the van waiting at the bottom of the stairs.

"I have enjoyed spending some time with you," he said, clasping my hand between both of his. "Intelligence and beauty, a charming and provocative combination. I have always been fascinated by women with . . . discernment."

"I, um, look forward to talking with you again soon," I managed, extricating my hand.

I hurried down the steps, refusing to look back to see if he was watching me. As the van left the circle drive, I chanced a look back at the manor. Tony had gone back inside, but unless it was my imagination, someone profiled by a dim lamp watched from a window on the main floor.

Chapter Eleven

After the van left me at The Gold Road, I drove back to the compound, hoping I hadn't missed Michael. Parking at the side of the road some distance from the fence where I'd talked with Michael before, I peered through the darkness in hopes of seeing him waiting for me. Though I didn't see him, I made my way through the shadows toward the fence corner, hoping that if he was on duty he might have left me some kind of message.

I was surprised to find him crouching in the corner near the fence.

"Michael?" I approached him cautiously and whispered his name.

At first I thought he hadn't heard me, then he lifted his head.

"I thought you'd forgotten."

"I wouldn't forget. Here."

Pulling open a loose piece of fence, I handed him a large Styrofoam cup of hot chocolate I'd bought at a drive-through restaurant on the way out of town. He accepted it with restrained eagerness, holding it between his hands first before taking the lid off and sipping at it.

I crouched on the other side of the fence, careful to stay in the shadows.

"I had an unexpected meeting with Tony and Sophia—at the mansion."

"The mansion."

He whispered the words, making me wonder what kind of emotion was behind them.

"Have you ever been there?"

"Oh, yes."

"What do you think about it?"

He stared into the darkness, holding the cup between his hands. "Render unto Caesar—"

I didn't understand, but when he didn't continue I decided to try getting more information about life in The Glorious Church.

"Michael, how do you spend your day? What do you do here?"

"Study. Learn."

"You said you couldn't come last night because you had duty."

"We each have duties. Each one has a responsibility."

"What are your responsibilities?"

"We serve and observe."

"What do you mean?"

His thin shoulders moved slightly beneath the loose thin cotton shirt that was part of the uniform of The Glorious Church students.

"There are rules. Life has rules."

Oh, yes. The Rules.

"And if someone breaks the rules?"

"We are obligated to report them."

"What kind of rules are we talking about?"

I sipped my coffee and grimaced at its acrid taste.

"Maria didn't turn in her contributions. I told her. But she did not receive my advice."

"What happened to her?"

"She went to the mansion—for discipline."

The coffee turned bitter in my mouth. "What kind of discipline?"

"I did not see her again. Perhaps she was expelled."

A chill went down my spine. And perhaps she wasn't. The little warning bell inside my head was clanging like Big Ben.

"What other kinds of rules are there?"

"Many. Many. There are group offenses, for all of us. Individual offenses. They're judged according to our individual calling."

I remembered the long list of rules Mark had read to me.

"What happens if you break a group offense rule?"

"We are placed in a special group, or isolated for two days, perhaps a month, depending on the greatness of the offense."

"What is the special group?"

Again I longed for a notebook or a cassette recorder. Perhaps the next time I would try hiding one in my pocket to record what Michael said.

"The group might work in the kitchen washing dishes, sorting good food from bad. Perhaps staying with one of the older brothers in Bible study and prayer. We are not allowed to sleep. We must learn to live without sin, without thought of self."

Again there was the haze of brainwashing technique over everything Michael said about the practices of The Glorious Church. His passionless reciting of the rules and punishments supported that consideration. And if brainwashing was taking place, I wondered just how many of the 'students' of The Glorious Church were remaining within the compound at their own will.

"Who determines what is sin?"

His body jerked slightly as if he was coming out of some kind of trance. When he turned toward me I could see a slight frown puckering his brows during the fleeting moment his face was illuminated by pale moonlight.

"God has given us the power of the Spirit. If we are in the Spirit we will not sin. Sin is going outside the Spirit. Satan is outside the Spirit. We are in danger of being overcome. Vengeance is mine. An eye for an eye."

I recognized the passages from the Bible, taken out of context and twisted.

"Is that the basic rule? What about love?"

"Everything is done in love. Discipline is love."

"And Sophia has set up the code of discipline?"

"She is our teacher."

"I understand that Sophia is not well. What happens when she dies?"

"If Satan should prevail, the Chosen One will carry on the work. The Chosen One will take Sophia's place in interpreting God's plan for the church. Through the Chosen One the work of The Glorious Church will continue without interruption."

This was the first time I'd heard this term. "Who is that?"

"When the time is right, The Chosen One will be revealed."

My mind was moving quickly. "Is The Chosen One a student?"

"Sophia has prepared The Chosen One and The Guardian's task is to make certain the training is completed."

"Who is The Guardian?"

"I don't know."

"Who would know?"

"No one has ever seen him."

No one?

"Then how do you know he really exists?"

"I serve The Guardian."

I swallowed a fountain of questions, forcing myself to remain calm so Michael wouldn't be alarmed or frightened away by my eagerness.

"How do you serve him?"

"I follow his directions."

I recognized his evasions for what they were, a way to avoid any real connection with whatever The Guardian was involved in. For me, the implications of that were frightening.

I tried another approach. "How do you communicate with The Guardian?"

"Through messages," he shrugged, "or Sophia tells me what he wants done."

Sophia again. The spider in the middle of a growing web of suspicion.

"Only Sophia knows who The Guardian is, and who is The Chosen One?"

"When the time is right, The Chosen One will be revealed."

"What kinds of things do you do for The Guardian?"

"I keep his robes. I keep his case—"

"Case? What kind of case?"

"A leather case."

"What's in it?" Talk to me, I begged mentally. Talk to me.

"I have never seen inside it."

"Never? You just keep it?"

"The punishment will be extreme if I should lose it, open it, or if it should be out of my care at any time."

"Where is it now?"

"It is with The Guardian."

"Then he is doing something now? Handling some duty assigned by Sophia?"

"Perhaps, though he can exact justice at the instant it is required."

A shiver moved down my spine. "What kind of 'justice' does he exact?"

"It is not for me to know."

There seemed to be a number of things kept secret. Too many things, in my opinion.

"Michael, do you like your duties?"

"Like them?"

He seemed to think about that a moment, as if he'd never considered the question before.

"I don't know."

"Are you happy? Would you like to leave The Glorious Church?"

He sat very still for a long time, cradling the empty cup between his hands. Then one lone tear slipped down his thin cheek. My heart ached for him, for the despair that must be trapped inside him.

"I need—"

"What do you need?"

"I don't know."

"I will help you, Michael. I promise."

"No one," he whispered, "can help me."

Setting aside the empty cup, he got to his feet and strode back toward the barracks without a backward glance. I remained in the shadows, watching until Michael disappeared inside the building, wishing I could help him in some way.

I drove back to the hotel, mulling over everything Michael had told me. The organization of The Glorious Church had the overtones of an organization that was like an iceberg—the church program and school being the twenty percent visible portion, the Chosen One and The Guardian being the eighty percent hidden and strictly protected and possibly dangerous portion.

Was it possible that Susan had been a victim of this hidden portion of the organization in which her parents had held membership so long ago, or was I stretching the realm of reality for answers?

I strode directly through the hotel lobby and took the stairs to my room two at a time. I must have hurried too fast because I had to stop at the top and wait for a momentary dizziness to pass. Inside my room I dialed Ben's home number while shrugging off my parka and heeling off my boots.

While waiting for Ben to answer, I poured myself another glass of orange juice. Darn, I'd been so involved in thinking about Michael that I'd forgotten to get cold medicine.

"Ben? Maggie. I've got something!"

"Talk to me."

"The Glorious Church has a very interesting internal structure, including some strange rules, punishments, someone called The Guardian who apparently administers punishment for infractions of rules. I met a young man, Michael, who serves The Guardian. And," I emphasized the word, "there is this person, also unnamed, called the Chosen One, who will take the leader's place in the event of her death, which, I am told, has been close to happening a number of times."

"Who is Michael?"

"He's a student at the compound. I feel so sorry for him. Part of him wants out of the church, but he's so confused, so tangled up in the training that he can't seem to sort out what he really wants."

"Mag, don't get personally involved," Ben warned. "It gets you in trouble and gets in the way of the story."

"I know," I combed my tangled hair with my fingers as I paced the room. "But I wish you could see him. I was shivering in my parka and he was standing there in this thin cotton shirt and pants and had only thongs on his feet. He drank the hot chocolate I brought him like it was ambrosia. He's got to be hungry."

"He's helping you?"

"Everything I'd learned, he is substantiated, and given me even more. But it's like the game Operation, picking out tiny pieces with tweezers very, very carefully so as not to set off any buzzers or bells. He's very fragile. I just want to storm the gates and take him out of there."

"Mag—"

"I know. Let things work themselves out. But if I can break open the Glorious Church I can find out what happened to Susan."

"That's a big leap."

"Yes, but my 'little voice' is working overtime on this one. Somehow the Bradys' connection with the church is the key. And it's something that may have gotten Susan murdered."

"You're still convinced it's murder?"

"I've never been more certain. I just need a few more days to sort things out."

"Give me a date, Maggie."

I paced. "I can't—"

"A date."

"Three days. If I don't have something in three days—"

"Two. At least something I can see."

"Okay. Two days, and I'll fax something or dictate something—"

"I'll hold you to it. And Maggie?"

"What?"

"Be careful. Sometimes these things get out of control—"

"I know."

Just as I put down the receiver there was a knock at the door.

"Gary. I was wondering where you were."

"I'll just bet you were." He stepped past me. "Where have you been?"

"Doing a little digging. Ben's given me a deadline for a story, if I can come up with one, so I've got to get down to hard nails."

"I always loved your homey mid-western colloquialisms."

I recognized the tension in his voice. "What's wrong?"

He threw himself onto the bed and, lacing his fingers behind his head, stared at the ceiling. The bed squeaked loudly and I winced, but for once Gary didn't make a snide comment about the accommodations. Honeymooners must love it.

"I spent the day with Mom."

The little voice inside my head set up a clamor. "Oh? How is she doing?"

"About the same, I guess. I tried to talk to her about Susan, about . . . about when we were all at home. Just, memories. But she didn't want to talk. In fact, she got a little angry with me. Accused me of being cruel." He sat up suddenly. "I just want to know about her. I want to know why they lied to me."

I paced, thinking about the things I'd put into my laptop computer this afternoon. I thought better when I was typing facts, putting them in some sort of sequence, adding my what-if questions and listing possible answers, sorting through all the extraneous info until something began to make sense. So far, all I had was a little information, the possible connection between the Bradys and The Glorious Church, and a lot of questions.

"It was probably guilt."

"Guilt? What about? I wouldn't have cared any less for Susan if I'd known she was adopted. I probably would have understood more. It just seems to me that they were embarrassed about something. This afternoon I even wondered if the adoption thing was a lie. What if—what if Mom had an affair or something? What if Susan was her baby and Dad just went along with it—"

I laughed in spite of myself and he sat up, anger clear in his face.

"Gary, listen to yourself. Even if I could imagine your mother having an affair, can you imagine your father being that sensitive?"

He shrugged his shoulders, obviously unwilling to agree openly with my statement.

"I even began to wonder if I'd been adopted."

"Gary. You look exactly like your father did at thirty-five. I've seen pictures."

"You're right. I was just wanting some kind of logical explanation."

"As far as I can see, there's nothing logical about this whole situation. Maybe that's what bothers me most about all this. Nothing fits together. And until I make it all fit, I won't be able to put her to rest." I went to the window and stared out into the night, feeling a little of Gary's discontent. "She had such promise. Did you know she wanted to be a teacher? At least, when she was fifteen that's what she wanted."

"Yeah. She was good with kids, and older people. Did you know that she'd worked with an organization that provided meals to homebound people?"

"No. I didn't. But that sounds like her. But I wouldn't have thought your father would have allowed her to do something like that."

"He didn't like it. But," he shrugged, "he wasn't home much . . . then. Mom wasn't as . . . strict. I mean, Susan wasn't a goody-goody. She had her days. And Mom was totally against her being a teacher—"

That caught my attention and I turned around. "Oh? Why?"

"I don't know. Maybe it was just something I picked up, like, whenever Susan talked about it Mom, and Dad, too, always said something like 'you'll change your mind', or, 'there are a lot of options'. Mom kept trying to steer Susan in another direction, introducing her to her social friends."

"They never said what they wanted her to do?"

"No."

"Did you and she ever talk about her future, what major she should declare?"

"No. Like I said, for the last couple of years we didn't talk about much of anything. Just general conversation the few times we were together. You know the kind of thing—how's school, how's work, are you dating anyone?"

"Was she?"

"Hum?"

"Was she dating anyone?"

I poured the last of the orange juice into my glass and wished again that I had some aspirin. Maybe the front desk would have something.

"No. And I always thought that was strange, when I

bothered to think about it. One of those thoughts that comes and goes but you don't dwell on it, you know? Now I wonder if she had fun in college or if she was a book drudge."

I'd wondered that myself. Now, looking at Gary, I decided he was doing a lot of thinking about himself, and his relationship with his sister, and his parents, for probably the first time. He'd always just taken things in stride, accepting good things as his just due, shouldering off the bad as the fault of someone else, much like his father.

"Margaret, why didn't we have any fun?"

I blinked. "Fun? I thought we did."

"I don't remember. All I remember are the fights."

"I thought divorced people tended to remember the good times." I wished he hadn't brought up the divorce again. I really didn't feel very well; certainly not well enough to get into something as emotional as that again.

"What happened with us?"

"We were the wrong combination, Gary. That's all. Just the wrong combination."

"I guess you're right. It never would have worked, would it?"

"No. We both wanted it to work, but it just couldn't. Neither of us could change, and we shouldn't have tried."

"Maybe you're right. But I wanted someone to blame, someone besides myself."

I smiled, recognizing myself in what he said. "Me too. But I hope we can be friends now."

"I'd like that. I'm glad I called you about Susan. It was an impulse, you know. I just thought—"

"You thought I had the right connections. I have to admit that irritated me a little."

I sat on the edge of the bed beside Gary. "But I'm glad you did call. I would have been angry if you hadn't, especially under the circumstances. I never want to miss the opportunity of getting a good story," I smiled to take the edge off the words, "and if my instincts are right, this is going to be a doozy when I get it all sorted out. Now, you look like you haven't had a good night's sleep in days, and I—I don't feel very well."

"I noticed you looked a little pale, are you all right?"

"I don't know. I haven't felt well today and—"

The last sound I heard was Gary calling my name.

"Maggie. Can you hear me?"

I forced my eyes open but squinted them shut at the bright light. A man in a white coat was bending over me, speaking very carefully.

"Move your fingers, Maggie."

I obeyed the command.

"Very good. Now move your feet."

I tried.

"Good. Good. Do you have any pain?"

"No." I winced against the sound. "My head rings. Like I'm inside a barrel."

"Sound sensitivity. That's normal. You're very lucky."

I managed to open my eyes. "Lucky?"

"I think the sheriff would like to talk to you."

"Neal?"

The doctor left and Neal came in. His face was tense and a muscle worked in his jaw. He leaned over and brushed a kiss against my cheek and, even as bad as I felt, I wished his aim had been a bit better.

He pulled a chair close to the bed, picked up my hand, and sat with his elbows on knees to lean close. His roughened fingers caressed the back of my hand, the backs of my fingers. I could smell the remnant of his aftershave and see the gray flecks in his eyes. I was glad to see him.

"You gave us a scare."

"What happened?"

"You passed out. Brady called Sam at the desk, and yelled

he wanted an ambulance. Sam called me when they couldn't wake you up."

"I've never fainted before in my life."

"You've never been poisoned before, either."

I stared at him uncomprehendingly. "Poison?"

"In the orange juice, unless I miss my guess. Someone's been adding a bit to it. Any ideas?"

"No. Why would anyone do that?"

My stomach lurched and I was afraid I was about to embarrass myself by upchucking on the sheriff.

"Maybe you're getting a little too close."

"Susan?" I swallowed. Hard.

"Guess I don't have to deliberate any more whether it was murder or not."

I closed my eyes, wishing I could just curl up into a little ball and sleep.

"No. I guess not." I opened my eyes a crack. "Sam Patrick didn't see anybody?"

"Nope. Of course, he said people come and go all the time, and he's not at the desk all the time either."

"I just . . . I just never thought anyone would do—"

"Fortunately, you didn't ingest enough to—well, you just got sick. Perhaps it was more of a warning than anyone—"

"Trying to kill me? You can't ignore the fact that . . . that it's entirely possible someone did try and just failed." I didn't want to think about that. I felt so ill I didn't want to think at all.

"Maggie, I want you to stop."

I held his gaze. "I can't. This just makes it more important. Someone is threatening people. They've killed people."

He released a long breath of resignation, his head bowed, then looked up at me. "I was scared—I don't want anything to happen to you."

"I'm sorry," I whispered.

Finally he laid my hand back on the bed, stood, then bent and kissed my cheek again.

"Can't you do better than that?"

With a faint smile, his lips caressed mine briefly. "Get better," he whispered. "Then we'll see what we can do about that."

The hospital kept me twenty-four hours for observation. I was feeling pretty foolish when Gary came to pick me up.

He waited while I signed the release papers, and then we walked out to the car in silence. Only when we were sitting in the car did he turn to me.

"I made plane reservations. We leave in the morning."

"I'd thought about that since Neal had told me the juice I'd kept in my room was laced with Strychnine.

"No, I'm staying."

"But—"

"Susan was murdered, Gary. And whoever killed her, tried to scare me—"

"They tried to kill you!"

"Neal said the lab report shows there wasn't enough in the juice to kill me, just enough to make me really sick. A warning. The reason it hit me so hard was because I was drinking so much to knock out my cold. It won't happen again."

"You're right. We're going home."

"You can take that flight, Gary, but I'm staying. Now I've got my story."

Finally accepting that I wasn't going back to New York, he drove me to the hotel. Mr. Patrick was at the desk and became very solicitous of me, until I convinced him I wasn't going to sue the hotel for not having better security. I thanked him for calling Neal so quickly. If he hadn't, valuable evidence might have been destroyed by accident or by plan.

Gary unlocked the door to my room.

"Can I get you anything?"

"No, I want to do a little work."

"You need to rest."

"I will." I hated to say it but I had to. "Thanks, Gary, for taking such good care of me. I'm not used to that, but it was nice."

"I . . . I wish—"

"I know. Sometimes I do too."

After Gary left, I stood at the window and indulged in a little self-pity, a little wishing that things could have been different and the dream Gary and I had tried to build had come true. But, the past was past, and I wasn't about to repeat my mistake.

Turning my mind back to Michael and the things he'd told me, I spread out my notes, opened my laptop computer, and began putting the bare bones of a story together. It was four o'clock before I finally fell asleep, but even then the Belgrade mansion haunted my dreams.

Chapter Twelve

I met Neal Conrad at The Parakeet for breakfast.

"How are you feeling?"

"A little foolish, but almost back to normal."

"I talked to Sam. He says no one saw anybody strange about the place. It wouldn't be hard though for somebody to get upstairs."

"I know. I just never expected anyone to make a move against me, especially in that way."

"You must be stirring up somebody for them to go to the trouble of putting small doses of Strychnine in your juice."

"Yeah. Now if I just knew who. And what would they have done if I hadn't been drinking juice?"

"Maybe that wasn't their first reason for being in your room."

"You may be right. Perhaps they just wanted to read my notes, find out what I knew, and the juice was handy."

"Gary said you and he were going back to New York."

"I know. I'm not going . . . yet."

"I wish you would."

"Trying to get rid of me?"

He was slow to answer. "No. But I don't want you to

191

become a statistic either. You're determined to stick with this?"

"I have to. Especially now that there's no doubt I've hit a nerve. There's something definitely now nice going on here and I want to know what it is."

"You wouldn't consider just letting me do my job?"

"You said yourself that there wasn't enough evidence to allow you to do anything. I won't get in your way."

"I'll take that as a promise, along with one to take better care of yourself."

"You've got it."

Though I was quick to make the promise, I wasn't as unconcerned about the warning I'd received as I tried to appear. I'd never had anyone make a serious attempt on my life before, and even though Neal had told me the poison was administered in a light dose in an obvious attempt to only make me sick, I couldn't stop remembering that the same poison had killed Susan. If someone wanted me to stop digging for information, and I didn't, what would be their next move?

I poured myself a cup of coffee from the carafe Ida Belle had left on the table.

"Have you heard about Sophia?"

"What about her?"

He looked at me over his coffee cup. "She died last night."

"What?" I blurted out the word, then lowered my voice. "I saw her just two days ago and she seemed just fine."

"You saw her? When?"

"The night I collapsed. Between seven and eight. I went to The Gold Road for an early dinner and had a very interesting evening."

"Tell me."

There was an edge to his voice that made me even more curious. "I went to the restaurant and while I was waiting, I asked about Sophia's health. Apparently the host called her immediately, because before I was seated I was called to the phone. She invited me out to the compound. Anyway, I thought I was going to the compound. A van picked me up outside the restaurant and I was taken to the mansion."

"Damn, Maggie. You shouldn't have gone."

All I could do was shrug. Hindsight was always twenty-twenty.

"I hear it's quite a place."

"You've never been there?"

"It's quite well-protected, in case you didn't notice."

"I did. Anyway, the thing looks like something out of a garish fairy tale. The whole visit had a strange feel to it. I was met by Sophia, who left me with Tony for the grand tour. Then she met us in the den and we had coffee. The whole time I felt like I was being tested somehow. It was very strange. I asked some questions, got more rhetoric about how Satan is trying to make inroads into The Glorious Church, that kind of thing. Then I was put back in the van and returned to the restaurant. What happened to Sophia?"

"I got a phone call about four this morning. Sophia apparently died last night. An ambulance was called and they tried to revive her, and then to transport the body to a funeral home, but Tony stopped that."

"Why?"

"He says he wants her body left untouched. It was only because he was rattled by the failure of a special prayer group to heal Sophia that he called an ambulance. They were delayed at the gate, because they got confused about where to enter the compound."

"The compound? She wasn't at the mansion?"

"From what I understand she was at the church."

"At four in the morning? That doesn't make sense."

"Nothing that group does makes sense. Anyway, he's already contacted an attorney who's petitioning the court to have the body released to The Glorious Church immediately. I don't think he's going to get it done, but it won't keep him from trying."

"Do you think he'll be allowed to bury her on the property?"

"Not the way he wants it done."

"What do you mean?"

"You haven't heard about the crystal casket?"

I almost laughed. The bizarre stories seemed pile one on top of the other. "No, I haven't."

"Well, Tony claims Sophia isn't really dead. She's only sleeping. Something like Snow White, I suppose. He says she'll fulfill the prophecy by rising once each month to bless the work."

"Rise each month—"

"I know. But that's no more bizarre than some of the other stuff. Old Tony was a bit hysterical this morning. Warned me I was standing in the way of God's work, that Sophia's body and soul are regenerating so she can return to lead The Glorious Church on to greater glory. And there was some other rhetoric that I couldn't possibly remember and certainly not repeat. Course, when the County Court turns him down he'll appeal. Could take some time."

"Do you know much about their work?"

"Only what I've heard on the street and what I've seen on their television program."

"You've watched the program?"

"Now and again."

"Have you ever noticed the choir, how spacey they appeared?"

"I've always thought they were a little shy of good sense, but if that was a crime, three-quarters of the county would be in jail. Anything specific?"

"Do you know anything about brainwashing?"

He frowned. "Only what I've read, but generally in connection with war activities. Why?"

"I've been talking to a student, and from the things he tells me, the teaching tactics of The Glorious Church very closely parallel those of brainwashing techniques—sleep deprivation, punishment, isolation, repetition of rhetoric, fear, poor food, poor housing. Hasn't anyone complained to you about the conditions out there?"

"No, Maggie, they haven't. And until they do, until one of their students comes in and files a complaint, there's nothing I can do. They're on private property and the students are there of their own free will. Will your contact file a complaint?"

"I don't know. Not yet anyway. Right now he's trying to figure out what to do."

"Care to tell me who he is?"

"He's given me the name Michael, but I've noticed that most of the men, the ones guarding the gate and those working at The Gold Road, have the names of angels. Names seem to mean little and the use of only a few seems to be a part of the process of erasing the individual identity."

"Making a wide assumption there."

"I know, but I think I have to make another."

"Like what?"

"Like, something or someone connected with The Glorious Church being involved somehow in Susan Brady's death."

"Got any proof?"

"No. Just that I've been asking a lot of questions about them, and the same poison was used on her that made me sick. Plus a lot of pieces that don't fit together."

I wasn't certain I was doing the right thing, but I wanted to know Neal's opinion of what Michael had told me.

"Have you ever heard anything about someone called The Guardian, or The Chosen One?"

Neal frowned. "Connected with The Glorious Church?"

"Umhum."

"No. Your student tell you about these individuals?"

"Yeah, and it scares me a little. Not only the way he talked about what they do, but the way he looked when he said it."

"I'm listening."

I outlined briefly what Michael had told me and the crease between Neal's brows deepened as I talked.

"You're right. It does sound like some form of brainwashing."

"Exactly. Jim Jones used six generally accepted brainwashing techniques." I ticked them off on my fingers. "Isolation, rigid schedules involving total obedience, study groups to drill followers in his philosophy, punishment for infractions of the rules, which involved torture and reward for those who won approval, and interrogation sessions to elicit confessions. He led them to a kind of promised land where those outside were evil, those inside good. He also told his followers that they were the chosen. Sound familiar?"

"Very. And didn't he use poison on his followers? What are you going to do with this?"

"Keep digging." I reached for my bag. "Just keep digging."

"I wish you wouldn't."

"It's what I do."

He studied me for a long moment and I realized how comfortable we had become with one another in such a short time. At another time, in a different place, under different circumstances . . .

"Maggie, don't go out there alone again."

"Thanks for caring, but it's even more of a personal thing now. Not only for Susan, but for me. I won't be intimidated, but I will be more careful."

"This is personal. Be careful."

I liked what I saw in his eyes, but it scared me too. I wasn't here to get involved with anyone, but Neal could seriously threaten that resolve.

Wanting to avoid running into Gary at the hotel, I decided the library was the most peaceful place I could find to ruminate for a while. I chose a quiet corner where a large table allowed me to set up my laptop along with a couple of legal pads. I began reading all the articles again, in order, writing down any additional questions that occurred to me, answering them as I worked through the material. I wrote down what I knew of the Bradys' activities at the same time, creating ties between the two.

The initial ties were few. Then the what-if process began. Hypothetical questions and possible answers had brought me to some startling conclusions in the past, and I hoped it would help me work out the puzzle surrounding Susan Brady and The Glorious Church now. Ben had almost cut me off after the poisoning but relented once again when I put in a vacation request. But there was a limit to his patience and I was fast approaching it.

I clarified the notes of my first meetings with Edward and Pauline Brady. I reviewed my impressions after watching the taping of The Glorious Church television program, my first meeting with Tony, with Sophia, my discussions with the sheriff, and everything I could remember from my talks with Michael. Ninety minutes passed before I settled back in the hard wooden chair and stared out the window.

I could not ignore the connection between Susan's kidnapping and the others. Neither could I pretend that Mark's information that members of The Glorious Church had been operating in the area at the same time was merely coincidence. Not when the church had set up a major compound here and the Bradys had moved here not long after. So, what did that leave? A very big what-if question.

What if Edward and Pauline Brady had lied? What if their connection with The Glorious Church was not quite so long ago, and not quite so short lived? What if it was eighteen months ago? That would explain their moving to Arkansas, and it made more sense at this point than retirement.

It seemed certain that Susan had never lived in the compound. There weren't any time gaps large enough for that. I'd verified that Susan had been in college, a full-time student, when she'd been kidnapped and attacked. After that she'd lived at home. Gary had verified that. Since the Bradys moved to Arkansas, Susan had lived in the apartment where she'd died and she'd attended classes every day.

But if those questions tracked, the next question had to be, what did Susan have to do with all this? Had she been a member of The Glorious Church? If so, was it possible her attack had been punishment for the breaking of some rules? It would have been extreme, but after what Mark had told me I knew it was entirely possible.

And if that was possible, the next question had to be what if Susan's 'sin' had been great enough to require the ultimate punishment? Death.

I suppressed a shiver of apprehension. If the group had gone that far over the line, what would be next? And if they had, who had actually given the direction to kill her, and who had followed through?

Had The Guardian administered the poison to Susan Brady? If so, then he had to be someone she knew, someone she trusted enough to let into her apartment. That led to the question of whether The Guardian had also laced my orange juice, and had I already met him?

If The Guardian had administered the lethal dose of Strychnine to Susan, had Michael been a party to it? Was this the thing that had made him question his mission and who he served?

And if this wasn't too far off the mark, then what had been Susan's sin? What could have been great enough to warrant death?

When I glanced at my watch I was surprised to see I'd been at the library for hours and it was ready to close. Gathering up my things, I hurried out. I'd almost reached my car when I encountered two students from The Glorious Church who had taken up a vigil to hand out brochures. I accepted a pamphlet, hesitated, scanned it, then turned to one of the students.

"Could I ask you a couple of questions about this?"

The thin face lit with surprise and I hated to squelch the hope I saw there.

"Sure. How can I help you find the way?"

"I've spoken with your leaders, Tony and Sophia, on more than one occasion—"

"Then you are a believer?"

"I'm searching," I said, telling myself it was, in a way, the truth. "But I heard this morning that Sophia died. I'm confused. Why wasn't she healed again?"

"Our leader has been allowed to leave us for a time in order to strengthen our faith."

"But she has been healed before."

"She has been gloriously touched by the spirit of God through prayer and supplication for her healing. That same healing power can be yours if you embrace the faith."

"Please, help me understand what has happened." They were painfully eager to share their belief. I adjusted the strap of my bag and prepared to listen.

"Many are confused about our ways. But if you embrace the faith, you will begin to understand."

"Tell me how I can do that."

"First you must understand that our leaders have been especially chosen by God to carry his message. Our mission is to spread that message everywhere. We must fight against the forces of Satan and his attempts to sway us from the true path."

"How can I avoid sin? I thought we were all sinners?"

"That is a false teaching of the recognized churches of the world. The churches that Satan uses for his work. Sin is the result of straying from the path. Our bodies, our very mind, is of the devil. Any thought that comes into it that conflicts with the way God has taught us to live is the devil putting words in our minds. You must concentrate on the ways of God. Strive for perfection. By listening to his word and following his word, you will reach perfection."

"And Sophia interprets God's will."

"Yes. She is God's tool for good in an evil world. She teaches us the way to avoid evil."

"How can we hope to avoid evil? It's all around us."

"The way to make Satan flee is through prayer. Constant prayer. Sophia has taught us how to pray, how to keep our minds filled with God, keep our thoughts filled with the ways of The Glorious Church and our mission in the world."

"But what will happen now that Sophia is dead? Who will interpret God's word? How will the work go on?"

"The world sees only surface things. Sophia is not dead. She is immortal. She is only sleeping. Her body and soul are regenerating so she can return to lead the church on to greater glory."

I tried to be patient. Listening intently to the rhetoric, the merry-go-round of words that meant nothing was like enduring nails scraping on a chalk board. They grated against everything logical.

"But how will this happen? I don't understand."

"As Jesus, the prophet, was raised from the dead after three days, Sophia will return to us in due time."

"But, she will be buried—"

"No. A place has been prepared for her. Tony has petitioned for her to remain with us in the body while her spirit is away receiving a new mission. Like Jesus of Nazareth, our beloved teacher will return to us. Until that time her body, this outward shell, will be kept in the crystal casket until such time as her soul is returned to her body."

No wonder The Glorious Church preferred to avoid publicity. While I wasn't active in church I recognized blasphemy when I heard it. I barely kept myself from glancing at the sky in anticipation of a lightning strike.

"What is this crystal casket?"

"It is only a place, like the tomb, but it allows Sophia to return to us. It allows us who are human, who need to strengthen our faith, to see her. When the veil is torn away, and she can return, there will be a great celebration."

The students were obviously repeating the rhetoric they'd been fed by Sophia and Tony and could not recognize the fantasy.

"And until that time? Who will give guidance to The Glorious Church? Will Tony step in until—"

"Oh, no. A perfect way has been planned. The Chosen One is waiting. The Chosen One will be Sophia's voice is interpreting God's plan for the church. Once she returns to us, after her glorious revelation as to the future of the church and the believers, then she will go into seclusion where she will continue in prayer and supplication to God for us. The Chosen One will be the voice of our faithful leader, interpreting to us the will of God."

"Who is the Chosen One?"

"He has not yet been revealed. At the proper time the Chosen One will be anointed by our leaders and by God."

"No one knows who this is?"

"Only Sophia and God."

"And you don't know when this person will be revealed?"

"No. Several learners who were especially chosen by Sophia have been in training. At the right time, one will receive the special calling to be The Chosen One . . . he or she may have already received that calling."

"You don't know who the candidates are?"

"No. We all strive to reach that level of knowledge and empowerment, but few are able to achieve it. A special communication with God and with Sophia, with total concentration, is required over several years, awaiting this time of revelation."

"Well, this has been very enlightening to me."

"May God grant you wisdom as you search for the truth. The times of our services are on the back of the brochure. If you need personal guidance, shepherds are available for individual prayer and teaching."

"Thank you for your time. You've been very helpful."

I hurried back to my car, wishing I could erase the faces of the students from my mind. Like Michael, they were pale and thin, physical evidence of malnutrition. Their faint body odor and oily hair confirmed the charges of poor personal care conditions at the compound. That was, in my opinion, the reason most of the students had very short hair. It was easier to care for, and it made dealing with lice and other problems easier to treat. Gray smudges beneath their eyes were testimony of them not getting enough sleep, and the desperation in their voices had been pitiful evidence of their need to convince followers of their true way.

I spent the rest of the day reading and resting, with Gary's solicitous concern nearly driving me crazy. I left my room early the next morning and ate at The Parakeet, chatting a bit with Ida Belle.

The County Court hearing was scheduled for nine a.m. and I arrived just as court was being called to order. I slipped into a seat at the back of the room and quickly surveyed the crowd as Judge Carolyn Rafferty asked for a reading of the petition. I didn't see Neal and wondered why he wasn't in court, if not for professional reasons then for personal interests.

Judge Rafferty was a surprise to me. A tall woman about forty years old, her hair was blond and stylishly cut, her features strong and classical. In short, she was an impressive woman, one that would look good in an advertisement for law and order.

Tony Belgrade sat at a table with another man who looked like his attorney, and his bodyguards were directly behind him. A few students were seated in the front seats behind Tony, all dressed in their television suits, all staring straight ahead at Tony's back. Tony wore his usual costume of black pants, black shirt, and dark glasses, but without the cape.

The petition was read, accompanied by a great deal of murmuring among the spectators. The attorney for the county, also a woman, spoke first, stating that she had already been presented with a petition holding a number of signatures against allowing a burial.

"I believe, your honor, that allowing this type of bizarre burial would set a precedence we do not want in this county.

I believe we can all agree that we've had quite enough publicity, what with the death of a young woman hardly more than a week ago. Allowing such a circumstance is against everything moral and ethical and would create a circus atmosphere. Why, the media would have a field day. We would be the laughing stock—"

"I object, your honor."

Tony's attorney got slowly to his feet.

"The petitioner wants nothing but privacy. In fact, to avoid such a circus atmosphere is the reason Mr. Belgrade is making this request. The place where his wife will be interred is inside the compound, in a very well guarded area that is open only to the students."

"The court is aware that the compound is well guarded, Mr. Stanton. What I don't understand is," the judge leaned forward a little to peer at Tony, "why do you want Mrs. Belgrade enclosed in," she looked at her notes, "in a crystal casket?"

The buzz of conversation rose again in the court room and the judge administered the gavel to reclaim quiet.

"Your honor, the request is in line with the beliefs of the church."

"Because they believe Mrs. Belgrade is going to rise again?"

Again the buzz of conversation caused the judge to sound the gavel.

"This court room will be quiet, or it will be cleared. Continue, Mr. Stanton."

"Yes, they do."

"And is there anything that would cause this . . . resurrection to not happen?"

I saw Tony straighten just the slightest bit.

"No, your honor—"

"Then what difference does it make whether Mrs. Belgrade is placed in this crystal casket, or interred in a normal casket and placed underground? Petition denied."

The decision was made so quickly that I jumped when the judge's gavel smacked wood.

The sharp crack seemed to galvanize Tony into action. He jumped to his feet, knocking his chair over with a bang that made everyone in the room flinch.

"You hypocrites! You vipers! You have done your evil work—"

"Mr. Belgrade! You are out of order!"

The room had burst into a cacophony of sound, and every head was turned toward the red-faced religious leader.

"Satan is among us! But God will prevail! Our work will not be stopped!"

"Mr. Belgrade, the court—"

"There will be retribution for this thwarting of the work!" His arm swept in an arc and many of the spectators actually ducked, then flushed with embarrassment. "Each of you will pay!"

Several people on the back rows near me quietly left the room. My fingers itched to reach for my camera but they weren't allowed in the courtroom.

"Clerk, see that this man—"

"And you!" Tony roared, turning toward the judge. "You are a whore of Satan!"

The judge half stood, then sank back into her chair, pounding her gavel relentlessly.

"You have been directed by the devil himself to personally thwart a plan greater than any you can imagine! A plan that is the world's only salvation when the Great Tribulation comes. You, with your gold bangles, your trappings of the world—"

"Someone get him out of here!" The judge yelled from the bench.

"—have clouded the eyes of the truth seekers."

I watched, fascinated by the spectacle. Several were caught by the exhibition, wanting to move, but not wanting to draw attention to themselves by doing so. Tony, obviously out of control, ignored his attorney who kept patting his arm and the clerk who tried to calm him, and continued his tirade.

"But you will not overthrow the plan. The Glorious Church will endure! The Chosen One will step into place and direct the path of the church. Sophia will arise and be our great mediator with God, giving direction as the church spreads the gospel of truth."

Cameras started flashing as soon as Tony had started his rhetoric. Reporters were scrambling, documenting what would undoubtedly be front page news the next morning. Grabbing my own camera I began to shoot photos rapidly, catching the judge standing and pounding her gavel, Tony shoving aside his attorney, the clerk, and spectators.

"You will not prevail! The Lord will prevail! You have interfered. The Lord will reduce this town to rubble! A plague, such as Egypt suffered for their enslavement of Israel, will be visited on this town!"

With a dramatic whirl, Tony began moving through the crowd, a crowd that parted easily in front of him. The students followed in his wake.

At that moment, the courtroom door opened and Neal Conrad, followed by a handful of deputies, entered.

Though Tony tried to shoulder aside Neal and the deputies, he was taken into custody and escorted from the courtroom. The students, silent, marched in a row, following closely behind.

I stood on the seat, furiously snapping pictures as spectators scrambled to exit the room. Only when the courtroom was empty did I relax and sit down.

"Maggie."

I turned and looked up into Neal's concerned face.

"Quite a circus, Sheriff."

"Yeah. Well, it'll continue in a cell for a few hours. Are you all right?"

"I'm fine. You're holding him?"

"For a while." He glanced around the courtroom. "What went on here?"

I recapped for him and he sat shaking his head.

"Quite a performer, isn't he?"

"I don't know. Was he creating a publicity stunt, or does Tony believe everything he said?"

"What do you think?"

"I'm not sure, but I know I've got to talk to Michael again."

Chapter Thirteen

Neal phoned the next morning before I was awake.

"Got something you'll be interested in."

"Don't tell me Sophia rose again." I sat up, pulling the covers with me, and reached for my notebook.

"Well, she is gone."

"You're kidding!"

"Nope. Gone slick as a whistle, and nobody saw nothing."

"Of course. Wonder if she's in her crystal casket out by the pool?"

"Wouldn't doubt it. And if she is, I can't touch it. It's on private property."

"You can't find some loophole?"

"Nope. Not until somebody makes a mistake. Just thought you'd find that interesting."

"I do. I'll see what I can do."

"Maggie—"

I liked the sound of my name when he said it.

"I know. I'll be careful."

"Report in, okay?"

"I'll keep in touch."

After Neal hung up, I called Ben to report Tommy's

outburst in court, his arrest, and the disappearance of Sophia's body.

"Heard anything more about The Chosen One?"

"No, but I wish I had. Sure would clear up a lot of questions." I chewed the end of my pen. "Ben, what if The Chosen One was Susan?"

"Is that possible?"

"I don't know. But it might fit. Listen to this and tell me what you think. Susan was adopted. That happened in California near the time and place The Glorious Church was established. All records are sealed, the attorney who handled the adoption died suddenly and under somewhat questionable circumstances. The Bradys worked very hard at keeping the adoption a secret, even from their natural born son.

"Susan was then kidnapped, attacked, and marked by having her head shaved. Shortly after that, the Bradys moved here—a place totally at odds with their background and interests—suspiciously close to where the The Glorious Church headquarters was moving. Add to that, the Bradys were once members of the cult."

"And all that creates even more questions."

"Yep. But as The Chosen One, wouldn't Susan have to be especially trained? Wouldn't she have to learn all the inside secrets of The Glorious Church? But no one ever saw her and Sophia together.

"As far as anyone knows she was never on the compound, and certainly not a student. On the other hand, the attack she suffered fits in with what I've learned about the discipline aspect of the church. And if I'm reading between the lines right, I really believe her death could have been committed by the church for something she did."

"That's a pretty big jump."

"I know. But what if Susan was The Chosen One and she rejected the calling? What if she was chastised, then the Bradys moved here to keep Susan close to Sophia, close to the church?

"The only problem with that is, Susan was so quiet, so gentle. I can't even in my wildest imaginings see her adopting Sophia's flamboyance. Nor can I imagine her having the strength to keep an organization like The Glorious Church together, much less lead it into the big plans they obviously have for the future. I can more easily see her knuckling under. The bottom line is, who killed Susan and why?"

"What if Susan got some backbone and threatened to reveal the inner workings of the group. Michael did, why not her?"

"Maybe, but I don't know. I need a witness. Someone who knows who The Chosen One is, and I don't think anyone does, except The Guardian, and maybe Tommy. I hope to talk to Michael again tonight to see if he can add anything, otherwise I'm at the end of the leads."

"Do I need to say it?"

"No. I'll be careful."

"Keep me up on things. Tomorrow is your deadline."

"I know, I know."

Gary had left a note that he was spending the day with his mother, which pleased me. Perhaps the breach caused by the truth about Susan could be healed.

Darkness had just fallen when I parked my rental car at the side of the road to watch for Michael. An hour passed and then another thirty minutes. I fumed for another half hour. Time was running out. If I didn't have something concrete to support my suspicions about Susan's death within the next twenty-four hours, I had to return to New York without a story, and without knowing what happened to Susan.

Almost before the idea was fully formed, I was driving toward the Belgrades' mansion. Bypassing the gate, I drove further down the road until I found a narrow dirt road that ran parallel to the drive and up to the mansion. When I reached a point that I judged to be opposite the mansion, I parked. The wires of the barbed fence were close together, but by holding my breath and holding to a post, I managed to get through without snagging my parka or jeans. I ran through the pasture that lay between me and the woods surrounding the mansion, and in just a few minutes I was testing the flexibility of the chain link fence that edged the trees. Fortunately, there was no row of barbed wire at the top and I managed to climb over without mishap.

So far so good.

I began my trek through the woods hoping I was in the vicinity of the mansion. I reached it in short time, then crouched at the edge of the clearing to observe the house. Though there were cars parked on the circle drive, there seemed to be no activity inside the house. Perhaps some sort of memorial service was being held for Sophia. If so, perhaps I'd be lucky and the front door would be unlocked.

Well, in for a penny, in for a pound.

My heart pounding, I ran to the steps and, keeping to the shadows, made my way up them and flattened myself against the wall next to the front door. Drawing a deep breath and hoping I was lucky, I gently turned the knob. I nearly fainted with relief when the door opened.

The house was deathly quiet. If there were people in the house there was no sign of it in the foyer or main hall. In fact, I'd have sworn the place was deserted. I'd have liked it better if there had been some noise or conversation to cover any sound I might make.

Orienting myself, I made my way down the hall toward the den where I'd met with Sophia and Tommy. There had been a large desk in the room that had captured my curiosity. Perhaps there was a calendar or some files that would give me some clues. At this point, anything would help; anything that would persuade Ben to let me stay a few more days.

It was then that I heard something, perhaps voices, a kind of music maybe. It was too distant to tell.

Letting my curiosity push aside caution, I moved carefully down the hall to the door into which Sophia must have disappeared the day I'd talked with them. The sound was more distinguishable, and I pressed my ear to the crack to listen.

There was the rise and fall of voices. The words were a kind of chant, a litany of several voices. Then there was music. Music that was reminiscent of the old time gospel sounds I remembered from childhood, but with another overlaying sound that reminded me a little of the music at Susan's funeral. That was strange. I listened closer. The music wasn't moving from verse to chorus and back. It was repeating, almost hypnotic.

Almost without will, I turned the knob. The door opened on silent hinges into near darkness. Peering through the crack carefully, I determined there was a landing from which steps went down into the basement of the mansion. The music and voices were louder.

"Jesus, Jesus, Jesus. Your protection is our veil. Your strength our strength. You have proven yourself worthy of eternal life and hast lead us forward by your hand. You are the power! You are the protection! You are the way. Satan is cast down. The blood of Jesus against you, Satan! The blood of Jesus against you, Satan! The blood of Jesus—"

I crept forward, holding my breath, hoping the music and voices would cover any sound I might make. Letting the door close behind me, and making sure it didn't lock, I peered over a banister. I'd never seen anything like what was taking place below.

The basement room was windowless and held perhaps twenty people. The music ebbed and flowed, growing in intensity, the chords repetitious. The people moved in rhythm in the semi-darkness. Four or five had separated themselves from the main group and danced at the front of the room, their bodies moving to the rhythm, their hands held high, their faces turned upward with eyes tightly closed. The sweat of exertion glistened on their faces, the sounds and movement making them seem almost otherworldly.

One man played a guitar and a woman sat at the piano.

Over and over the chords were repeated and the group prayed louder and faster. Sound reverberated off the walls, creating a vibration that seemed to penetrate every pore of my body. It was so hypnotic I found myself almost moving with it.

As they danced, the four kept repeating 'Jesus, Jesus, Jesus, Jesus'. There was a kind of uneven buzzing sound I couldn't identify that underlaid everything that was happening. As I tried to pinpoint its location, one man began to dance separately, dipping low and waving his hands high when he straightened, moving ever closer to a wooden box that sat in the center of the stage area. Suddenly, he reached inside the box.

"Glory! Glory! Glory!" the rest shouted.

I smothered a gasp of horror when he lifted a large rattle snake over his head, never missing a beat.

One by one, each of the other three reached into the box and withdrew a live snake.

They caressed the slick, smooth bodies, wrapping the coils around their forearms. The music reverberated off the walls and the shouts of 'Glory! Glory! Glory!' joined the bedlam. My stomach rolled and I covered my mouth with both hands to stifle any sound. I had to get out, but the sight was mesmerizing.

I stared in a mixture of amazement and horror as they manipulated the snakes, bringing the fangs so close to their faces that the darting tongues seemed to lick the perspiration.

Then one who had been dancing separately, one who had not yet reached into the box, moved to the wooden speaker's stand. Once again, the others shouted 'Glory! Glory! Glory!' and lifted their hands toward the ceiling as if striving toward something just out of reach.

He picked up a glass container that looked like a fruit jar filled with water. He poured some into a glass and drank it, his throat moving rhythmically as the dancing grew more feverish. When he finished, the others shouted as if he'd done something spectacular. I understood none of it, but I knew I couldn't watch any more.

Moving very carefully, though I wanted to run like hell, I opened the door and slipped back into the hall. My heart was pounding like a trip–hammer and I leaned against the door to regain my senses.

Knowing I had to move quickly, I made my way back down the hallway to the door of the den. I listened carefully before testing the handle. My relief was overwhelming when it turned. For one brief moment I wondered if this could all be a trap; everything had been so easy, and Tommy was nowhere to be seen. I pushed that thought away and stepped into the den.

The room was dark and my eyes strained to see. Slipping the lock on the door behind me, I used a pinlight that I'd slipped into my pocket before leaving the car.

The top of the desk was clear except for a calendar that had no notations. Testing the drawers, I found the file drawer locked. Knowing I'd gone too far to turn back, I used a silver letter opener that I found on the desk to persuade the lock to open for me.

Inside were a dozen files, all unmarked. Holding the light between my teeth, I quickly scanned their contents. Finding nothing except copies of letters to suppliers, including the television station, and general correspondence to and from supporters of The Glorious Church, I impatiently shoved them back in place. I flinched as the metal rods grated and one of the file supporters fell into the drawer with a clatter.

Mentally cursing my impatience, I lifted the files out onto the floor to replace the rod. Suddenly something didn't seem right. The back of the drawer seemed slanted.

Almost afraid to hope, I removed the other rod and tested the panel. The drawer was indeed shorter than it should be, and when I pushed at the panel, it moved, then fell into my hand. Obviously someone had put the false panel back into place hastily, leaving the rod loose enough to fall when the files were disturbed.

Readjusting the pin light between my teeth, I lifted out the panel. I almost dropped the light when a large journal fell into the drawer.

With a glance at the door, hoping I still had time, I opened the journal. Spiral bound, the book had the appearance of a college notebook. The initial entries were dated almost twenty-five years earlier and were written in a spidery, back slanted script that had to be Sophia's. The beginning of The Glorious Church was documented in diary style, not on a daily basis but as particular events took place.

If this was only a journal of the beginning of the church, why was it hidden so carefully? There had to be some other reason.

The idea came like a voice out of the darkness. Susan. Sophia. The Belgrade connection to Gary's parents, Edward and Pauline. Susan's adoption.

I flipped the pages forward to the entries that had been written near the time that Susan would have been born, hoping against hope that this was indeed Sophia's private diary. As the pages shuffled, a manila envelope fell out.

Knowing that the longer I was in the house the greater chance I was taking, I opened the envelope and dumped the contents out onto the desk. I could hardly believe my luck. A birth certificate lay on top. I glanced at it quickly, my heart racing. A baby girl, born alive, to Sophia and Tommy Belgrade. The date was the same as Susan's, though this baby had been named Sophia Suzanne.

A second packet took my breath away. It held adoption papers, papers that made Edward and Pauline Brady the adopted parents of Sophia Suzanne at the age of four days.

Quickly shoving the papers back into their envelopes, I turned again to the journal. Beginning at the back, I noted that the entries had stopped only two days before Sophia's death. In fact, there was a notation of my own meeting with Sophia.

I fanned the pages again. When Sophia and Tommy were ejected from California, the writing became harder to read but the words were filled with hate and vows of revenge.

Then Gary's name caught my eye. I could hardly believe what I read. The vandalism of Gary's clothing store that had drawn us together when I was assigned to take pictures, had been an act of warning to the Bradys. Apparently, Susan had already shown some reluctance to fulfill her calling, not studying the ethic of the church, not being totally coopera- tive. Sophia had decided the Bradys must have a warning. I closed my eyes. Even then Sophia was exerting control over the Bradys, demanding they fulfill their duty to raise Susan in the doctrine of the church and see that she carry out her own mission.

I wondered if Gary had any idea of why his store had been defaced, his stock destroyed. I knew he'd been very upset, but at the time I'd thought it was because he had no idea why a bunch of young hoodlums would have demolished his store. Could he have known who had done the damage, and why? I'd never thought he was involved in any way before, but now I couldn't ignore that possibility.

Fast on that thought was the question of how much had I become involved in Sophia's plans? Had the attempt on my life been for a past or present sin? If for a past one, why had she waited until now? And . . . how much had Gary had to do with this?

No wonder Sophia had made herself somewhat available to me. She'd needed to learn how much I knew and my pur- pose for being in Arkansas. Had Gary's request for my help been genuine? Or part of Sophia plans? If part of her plan, for what reason?

The possible answers to all these questions were more frightening than I wanted to consider right now.

Wishing I could take the time to read the whole journal, or had the nerve to take it with me, I quickly flipped the pages to the date the Bradys had moved to Arkansas.

There were several notations about The Chosen One, how this one had violated the trust placed in her. This was the first time a sex had been given to The Chosen One and a shiver went down my spine. Sophia wrote of her disappointment in The Chosen One's unwillingness to accept *her* calling.

"Satan is at work. The Chosen One has betrayed a trust; she rejects her calling. This must not be allowed. The work must continue."

And, "The Guardian has been called. A punishment to fit the disobedience has been decided. There will be no doubt."

The date was about the time Susan had been kidnapped.

My heart ached for the Bradys. They must have been desperate to protect Susan. Surely they must have known that Sophia had directed it, and why. The guilt must have been overwhelming. No wonder they hadn't wanted to talk about it.

Susan, being Sophia's child, must have been designated from birth to be The Chosen One. The Bradys must have been much more deeply involved in The Glorious Church than they had admitted; otherwise, Sophia would not have chosen them to adopt her baby. There had to have been some promise, some dedication to raising her in the church. Then, when she rebelled, they punished her, expecting that to bring her back into the fold.

I let the journal rest in my lap as I tried to assimilate everything. How strong Susan must have been, how much stronger than I had ever imagined. It would have taken such great courage to go against everything that she'd been taught from birth, to go against her parents, that I could hardly imagine gentle Susan being up to the challenge.

Even after the kidnapping, she'd stuck to her decision. That was obvious now, looking back. Either that, or the Bradys had been swayed by her decision and tried to protect her. But, they moved to Arkansas afterward, nearer The Glorious Church, nearer Sophia, so that didn't follow. The Bradys were obviously still dedicated to trying to make Susan fulfill her 'calling'. But Susan must have not been persuaded, because she was dead.

Suddenly Susan's last words ran through my mind. "Tell them I'm sorry". Perhaps that was Susan's last apology to her parents. Was she sorry to have failed them, sorry for having brought them pain, and for having caused her own pain and death?

The entries near the date of Susan's death mentioned no names, only notations that The Guardian had been called in to 'exact punishment' for 'The Chosen One's great sin, for her blasphemy'. There was a gap of nearly a week. The next entry was about Sophia talking with me and a notation that 'this one is questioning'.

So, Sophia had decreed Susan's death. I felt sick. The woman had authorized the death of her own daughter. Only the question of who had carried it out was still unanswered.

Knowing that every second I remained in the house was stretching my luck, I quickly closed the journal and shoved it back into its secret place. Replacing the files, I closed the drawer carefully, hoping the faint scratches on the lock wouldn't be too obvious.

Moving carefully to the door, I slipped the pin light back into my pocket. The lock clicked as I opened the door and I caught my breath, then peered out into the hall. Hearing only quiet, I slipped out and began moving cautiously down the hall as quickly as I dared.

I reached the corner, praying for another few minutes of luck, and stepped into the foyer just as the front door opened.

Gabriel was nearly as surprised as I was, but he reacted quicker. Before I could move, my arms were caught in his tight grip.

He propelled me back down the hallway, stopping only when Tommy stepped out of the shadows.

"Miss Rome, you've been naughty."

The tip of his forefinger caressed my cheek, moving over my chin and down my throat to the vee of my shirt. I fought the urge to cringe away from his light, cool touch.

"You'll have to be punished."

Visions of the various methods Mark had described danced in my head.

"Take her downstairs," he directed Gabriel.

Where there had been a babble of sound before, now the dancers were slumped in various states of exhaustion, their bodies dripping with perspiration. When Gabriel forced me down the stairs, they watched silently, then rose and melted into the shadows.

Gabriel grabbed one of the wooden chairs with one hand and dragged it to the middle of the room.

"Sit."

I could do nothing but obey. My legs were like jelly and he was much stronger than he appeared.

The dancers slipped silently from the room, moving up the stairs with only a whisper of sound, their faces carefully averted.

Pulling my arms behind the chair, Gabriel bound my wrists then tied my ankles to the legs of the chair. I knew that protesting would be futile. He was totally under the control of Tommy Belgrade. All I could hope now was that Tommy wouldn't come and exact his form of punishment before I could find a way to get out of the mess I'd gotten myself into.

After he'd finished his job, Gabriel followed the last of the dancers up the stairs. The door closed with a solid thud, and then there was silence.

It was cold and damp in the room. The dirt floor was worn smooth by the dancer's feet but the stone walls were rough and turning green with a mossy film. Already my skin was clammy and chilled.

I tested the ropes and found them secure. Still I worked at them, rubbing my wrists raw without success. My mind raced. I'd thought that without Sophia, Tommy would be less effective. It was clear she was the driving force behind every decision, and Tommy was little more than a puppet. Still, there was something insidious about him and he'd made his interest in me clear from the beginning. Perhaps that interest would give me an avenue of escape.

It was then that I heard a sound that made my blood run cold. It was like a whisper, faint in the darkness. It reminded me of when Sophia had come into the chapel, her slippers sliding across the floor. Bile burned in my throat. The snakes!

Straining to see in the darkness, I located the wooden box. The top had been left off. A whimper escaped my throat as a long body oozed over the edge and thumped softly onto the floor. A second followed, and a third, their tongues testing the air, seeming to sense my fear, their obsidian eyes seeming to glitter in anticipation as their flat heads waved my direction.

They began to move toward me. In desperation I tried to work the chair backward, a gain of a mere inch preferable to sitting and waiting for them to reach me. The legs caught and I stopped trying to move for fear it would fall and pitch me onto the ground, where I would be even more accessible to the snakes.

Frozen with panic, I watched them come toward me. A soft keening sound filled my ears and I wondered where it came from before realizing it was inside my head. I whimpered in terror, afraid to do anything that would attract the snakes to me. My muscles jumped, quivering with tension. I couldn't breathe. Panic was a hand around my throat. This had to be some kind of nightmare.

Forcing myself to remain absolutely still, I watched the deadly reptilian army move across the floor, their bodies whispering against the hard floor. Perspiration beaded my face, a rivulet running between my breasts as they reached my feet and began to entwine their bodies around the legs of the chair, then around my own legs. A sound like that of a small animal in pain squeaked in the darkness, and it was me.

Chapter Fourteen

The darkness. The rock hardness of the chair. The chafing of the ropes. The snakes, their movement inaudible but so clear in my mind I was certain I heard their cold skin moving against the soft fabric of my jeans, the hot flesh of my legs. I was certain I could feel the lick of their tongues tasting my fear. The smothering silence. The absurdness of the situation; a nightmare, an aberration of some creative mind brought to the movie screen of my life. I almost giggled. Suddenly, in my inability to cope with the terror, I had grown poetic.

How had it come to this? Why had I thought I was somehow invincible? Why had I ignored the fact that something was very wrong with everything that touched The Glorious Church?

The muscles in my legs quivered with tension and I tried to make them relax for fear the snakes would be alarmed. They were still exploring around my feet, perhaps drawn by the warmth of my body.

There was the rattle of warning and I stiffened, anticipating the prick of fangs. Then, from the corner of my eye, I saw a movement on the stairs. Almost unable to comprehend, I watched a figure move through the shadows. There was a flash in a stray square of moonlight and I knew that whoever was coming toward me carried a knife. At that moment I almost preferred to die by the knife than snakebite, though why it made a difference I couldn't have said.

The thing that flashed through my mind then, in a ridiculous flight of whimsy, was that I was going to die without knowing what happened to Susan, and Gary would be proved right. My job did get me killed.

Then, almost unable to believe what I saw, I breathed a sigh of relief.

"Michael."

Without acknowledging my frantic whisper, he scooped the snakes up with a swift movement as if they were nothing, though they rattled in protest, dropping them back into the box and shoving the lid back in place. Then he slashed through the ropes holding me.

"Come," he whispered almost soundlessly.

Grabbing my arm, he pulled me toward the stairs. My muscles trembled from disuse and tension, and I stumbled awkwardly up the steps. Michael halted at the door and opened it, carefully peering out before motioning for me to follow.

The mansion was silent as we hurried down the hallway. Instead of turning toward the main entrance, Michael led me through the darkened living room and down another hall into what seemed to be a kitchen. Here he stopped to peer out another door before opening it carefully. My breath caught at a tiny squeak of the hinges.

Once more I blindly followed Michael down another series of steps that ended up at a landing and another door. This door opened to the outside. We raced across an open yard, keeping to the shadows as much as possible. By a circuitous route we reached the woods.

My heart pounded as we crashed through the underbrush. I had a sense of being followed, but when I looked back over my shoulder there was nothing. It was like when I was a child and had to go to bed. The light was across the room from my bed and every night, though I'd already checked a dozen times, I'd turn off the light and race for the bed, jumping for it a yard away because I was certain a hand was going to come out from the darkness underneath and grab my foot.

When we reached the farthest edge of the trees, near where I had entered earlier in the evening, Michael finally stopped.

I leaned against a tree to catch my breath while he crouched in the shadows.

"I don't know how you found me," I whispered, "but I'm sure glad you did."

"I heard Tommy say you had been discovered."

"Was I going to just disappear?"

His shoulders moved in a shrug.

"Who was he talking to?"

"You must leave quickly."

"Will you come with me?"

"No."

I knelt beside him. "Please, Michael. Come with me. Let me help—"

"I must return. The Guardian is coming."

"You're not going to—"

"You must go."

"Michael—"

"Take this with you."

From the underbrush he took what looked like a briefcase and shoved it into my hands.

"Go."

"What is this?"

"Go."

"Please—"

"Go."

In the blink of an eye he had melted into the shadows and only the faint rustling of old leaves marked his progress. I felt sad that he couldn't bring himself to totally break the hold of The Glorious Church, and I was afraid of what would happen to him if Tommy, or The Guardian, discovered he'd helped me. Tommy might seem unfocused without Sophia's guidance, but perhaps he was even more dangerous without guidelines. His erratic behavior made him totally unpredictable. He could be rendered ineffectual, withdrawing into his childishness, or he could become more venomous in his anger at his losses.

Knowing there was nothing I could do now but get away before my escape was discovered, I oriented myself and then crept along the edge of the trees until I was opposite my car. Obviously, Tommy had not paused to consider how I got to the mansion and I was grateful. It was difficult to make myself leave the trees and shadows. Even their small protection was preferable to being in the open and vulnerable. Again, the darkness under the bed.

Holding my breath, I held the case close to me and ran as fast as I could. Dipping through the fence, I cursed when my parka caught and I fell, mud wetting my jean knees, my hands skidding in wet grass. With a glance toward the mansion, I tore my coat loose and ran for the car.

Uncertain what I had in my possession, I placed the briefcase carefully on the seat beside me. Starting the car, I breathed a prayer that I could get back to the main road and past the compound gate without being seen.

When I reached the road I only hesitated before driving as fast as possible toward town. By the clock on my dashboard, I saw that it was only ten-thirty. It seemed I'd lived a lifetime since I'd been foolish enough to sneak into the mansion.

Stopping at the first service station that was open, I got directions to the sheriff's office. The attendant stared at me as he mumbled directions. I found it twenty minutes later.

"Can I help you?"

The officer at the front desk looked me over curiously. I

realized I must look like a hysterical woman, grass and leaves in hair that must be flying everywhere, my torn parka, muddy knees and hands. I was probably filthy from my stint in the basement room with the snakes, and I smelled slightly less than tempting.

"Is Neal Conrad here?"

"No. Can someone else help you?"

He eyed the black case.

"No. Please, this is an emergency. Will you call him and tell him Maggie Rome must see him."

"I'll call the sergeant—"

"You can, but I won't talk to him. I have to talk to Neal."

"Just a minute."

He left, presumably to go talk to his sergeant, then returned with an older man.

"Rob Thurman. You want to talk to the sheriff?"

"Yes." I had regained some composure and held out my hand. "Maggie Rome, Front Page Magazine, New York. I've been talking with Neal about a story I'm working on and I need to see him immediately."

"I don't know—"

"Please. If you don't call him, I'll find him myself."

Sergeant Thurman looked skeptical and studied me for several moments. I must have looked a little more sane, because he nodded at the other officer.

"Jack, give Neal a buzz."

"Thank you."

"You, ah, look like you could use a cup of coffee."

"I could. Thanks."

I sat in the chair he pulled toward me, balancing the briefcase on my lap, and accepted the Styrofoam cup he handed me.

His sharp gaze swept me from head to toe, cataloging all the symptoms of someone in trouble. "Are you all right?"

"I'm fine. Just had a little scare." I anticipated his next question. "But I need to talk to Neal about it."

Jack returned.

"He's on his way. Said for her not to move."

The lifted eyebrow indicated Rob's surprise.

"Okay. Should take him about fifteen minutes."

I nodded, sipping the hot coffee, grateful for its warmth and stimulation.

Fifteen minutes later, right on the dot, Neal walked through the door.

"Maggie? What the hell happened?"

The mix of worry and anger in his face nearly undid me. Reaction to everything set in and I began to tremble.

I had been so scared. It was hard to admit even now, but I couldn't deny it. Maybe it was because I didn't understand the kind of people that drew The Glorious Church, or how they could do such evil in the name of God. I didn't know. But that, and the snakes, had rocked what I'd thought unshakable. My belief that I could handle anything.

I swallowed hard. "I just—I need to—"

"In here."

He dragged me into his office and slammed the door, ignoring the surprised looks on the faces of his deputies.

I had the brief impression that his office was typical of law officers with its scarred desk, black phone, and well-used coffee mug. I clung to him, desperately needing his solid strength as delayed fear made my knees buckle.

He held me, his strong arms around me. I rested my head on his chest and listened to his heart beat.

"Okay, Maggie, tell me what happened."

"Well," I drew a deep breath and blurted it out. "I did a stupid thing."

He held me back from him and his gaze sharpened. "What?"

"I went to the Belgrade mansion. I, uh, broke in. Well, I didn't exactly 'break' in—"

"Damn, Maggie! I should haul your a—"

"I found some interesting things," I inserted quickly.

A muscle jumped in his jaw. "And?"

"I got caught."

He half sat on his desk, still holding my arms as if he thought I'd collapse. He was right. I might at any moment.

I told him briefly what happened, his face growing stonier with every revelation of how foolish I'd been. But when I got to the journal his look held interest as well. The journal was the proof we needed. All we had to do was figure out how to get hold of it legally.

"Michael found me and got me back to where I could reach my car."

He just stared at me, disbelief stamped on his face. I wished he'd yell at me . . . or something.

"My God, Maggie, I don't know whether to strangle you or lock that door."

Before I could respond, he dragged me into his arms and walked me backward until my back was against the wall. Hard lips met mine, fierce and demanding, then softened tantalizingly. This, I realized, was what I needed. The affirmation that I was alive, that everything was all right. Well, not all right. I hadn't expected this . . . but it was exactly what I wanted.

He tasted with little sips that were maddeningly soft and compelling. Lean, tanned hands framed my face, tilting my head back so he could deepen the kiss. I felt the roughness of his cheeks.

"We've got only about five minutes before one of those deputies knocks on the door."

Our whispers rasped in the room. Sounds of the office on the other side of the door faded.

"Not enough time."

"No, not enough—"

He pressed me against the wall and I felt his body from chest to knees. I slid my hands up his chest until my arms circled his neck, then I closed my eyes. I breathed in his scent, a tangy, musky scent that I would never forget.

I let my senses take control. He was solid, hard muscled, strong. He tasted male; he felt male. He kissed the way a woman dreamed a man would kiss. It was as if he knew exactly what I wanted, that he would rather taste my mouth than take his next breath.

And that's exactly the way I felt. As if I'd rather be kissed by him, kiss him, be held by him than take my next breath.

"I was so scared," I whispered against his neck. "I've been in wars and never been so scared."

"When Jack called, I was afraid you'd—I knew what happened to Susan and I didn't want to think what might have happened to you."

Here, in his arms, I felt safe. This wasn't supposed to happen. I wasn't supposed to be here . . . in Fayetteville, in Armen, in this man's arms. But somehow I was, and it felt right. Too right.

I pulled back. He held on to my upper arms and studied me lazily as if waiting for me to make the next move. When I tasted my own lips his gaze dropped to my mouth and I couldn't breathe.

I couldn't, shouldn't, the timing wasn't right; but I did. Tilting my face up, I pressed my lips to his then let my tongue slide along his bottom lip. When his breath caught, just the slightest little bit, I smiled. So, I wasn't alone in what I was feeling.

"I didn't come here for this," I whispered.

"I know. I didn't either," he replied softly. "But we're here. Question is, what are we going to do about it?"

"Wrong time. Wrong place."

He drew back. "Wrong man?"

"I've answered that question." I stepped out of his arms. "The timing—"

"Is lousy."

I rubbed my arms, suddenly cold again. "Yeah. It's lousy."

He turned and paced away a bit, his back to me, and I felt

awful. I didn't know what to do with this, but I knew I couldn't think about it now.

He reached for me again and held me close for a moment before setting me back from him.

"You were lucky."

"I tried to get Michael to come out with me. He wouldn't, but he gave me this."

I set the briefcase on his desk.

"Have you looked inside?"

"No. I wanted you to see it. I'm sure it's the case he keeps for The Guardian."

He looked like he didn't believe me, and I wasn't sure I believed it either. But, why else would Michael have given it to me?

"He said The Guardian was on the way to the mansion. If he is, he'll want the case. If Michael can't produce it, I don't know what will happen. I don't want him hurt, Neal. We need to do something."

"Well, let's look at what we've got here."

He examined the locks carefully, then with a shrug he snapped them open. We were both surprised it wasn't locked.

"Whooeee."

He turned the case around so I could look inside.

The case had been specially made. Lined with foam rubber, it held small vials, each corked and labeled, along with measuring spoons and cups.

"Looks like we know where the Strychnine came from that killed Susan Brady and made you sick."

"I wonder if Michael looked inside. He said before that he never had."

"Maybe he did."

"There must be a dozen different types of poison there."

"Whoever this Guardian is, he's not nice. This gives us enough for a warrant." Neal stepped to the door. "Jack!"

"Yeah."

"I need fingerprints off this. Rush. Handle it careful. It could be real important."

"Okay."

"And call the judge. I need a warrant to get into the Belgrade's mansion. We have a whole case of strychnine that came from the mansion, probably the same stuff that killed Susan Brady. Now. Alert all deputies. I want them here within thirty minutes. Full gear."

Jack disappeared and I sat down again, my knees suddenly going soft again. I'd been here a week trying to find out what had happened to Susan, and now everything was happening so fast I could hardly think.

"What are you going to do?"

"We're gonna pay the compound a visit."

Forty-five minutes later, Neal had his warrant, his men were organized, and they were ready to leave.

"I'm going."

"No, you're not."

"I'm either going in your car, or my own."

Looking resigned, he motioned for me to follow him.

Riding in Neal's front seat, I checked that my camera was ready and that I had extra film open and ready to pop in if I needed it. By the time we reached the compound, residual reaction and anticipation of what we might find had my nerves wound tight.

There were no guards at the gate. Two deputies jumped from a van and snapped the heavy chain with cutters, then held open the gate for the line of patrol cars and vans.

The mansion was almost dark, except for the outside floodlights. Deputies dressed in flack jackets, with weapons ready, converged on the mansion. Warning me to stay in the car, Neal approached the house carefully, flanked by deputies.

I slipped out of the car and moved forward in a crouch, snapping pictures. No one answered when Neal pounded on the door. Testing the door and finding it locked, he kicked it in and jumped aside in the same movement. They were met with silence.

Six deputies and Neal disappeared inside the mansion, leaving the rest crouched behind their patrol cars. I waited anxiously, fearful of what Neal might find. Tension was evident in the deputies who watched the front of the house intently.

Several minutes later, Tommy Belgrade appeared in the doorway, his hands on top of his head, but he was far from subdued. He stepped onto the wide porch, into the bright lights of the patrol car headlights that were trained on the front of the mansion. As soon as he saw the officers waiting for him, he began his tirade.

"The Revelation has come! It is the judgment."

I snapped pictures, emptying both cameras, as I ran up the steps. Tommy was so involved in his diatribe that he didn't even look at me as we passed. I shot photos, front and back, close-up. Two officers took him to a patrol car.

I met Neal coming out.

"Told you to stay in the car."

"I'm the press. Got to get my story."

"Come see this then."

I followed him through the living room to the right, to French doors that were standing open.

"Look out there."

Floodlights shone across the water in an Olympic size swimming pool that was surrounded by a tall privacy fence. To the left was a gazebo type structure with columns that held an ornately carved roof. I walked beside Neal toward the structure, snapping pictures as I went. Two deputies stood looking down at something encased in cement and I stepped up beside them.

"My God," I breathed.

Sophia Belgrade was indeed entombed in a crystal casket that was protected by cement, like an open crypt. And she looked exactly as she had the first time I saw her.

"Bizarre," I said in between breaths. Everything connected with The Glorious Church was shadowy, imponderable and ominous. I'd never felt it more than now.

My hands trembling, I took several shots.

"Bill, have this taken to the morgue."

I followed Neal back through the house. I took a couple of shots of Tommy sitting in the back of a patrol car and we returned to Neal's car. He was being held on the evidence of the case of poison, as well as having a body illegally on private property. They'd surely find more after going through the mansion. Tommy seemed stunned and I wondered if he'd even heard the rights read to him.

"You didn't find Michael?"

"No one else in the house."

"Did you look in the basement?"

"Very quickly. I found the chair, the ropes, the case of snakes. I also found the jar of stuff you saw them drink from."

He looked at the ground, then up at me.

"I think what we have here is some stuff taken from religious groups in the hills. Snake handling, that kind of stuff."

I studied his face a moment. "I'm originally from the Midwest, and I've heard of those kinds of stories. Windy Bagwell's albums. But I didn't think anyone did that kind of thing any more."

"Some do. Deep in the hills. Anyway, I think we'll find Strychnine in that jar."

I found it difficult to comprehend what he was telling me.

"You're saying that man actually drank Strychnine?"

"Umhum. The theory is that handling the snakes and drinking the poison without being hurt proves God has his hand on you, is giving you some sort of special blessing."

"But just a little of it made me sick."

"A couple hundred years ago women drank Arsenic to make their skin prettier or something. Sometimes they overdosed by accident, but a lot of them drank a small amount for a good many years for vanity's sake. It appears that a certain amount of immunity can be built up, in some cases." He shrugged. "But who can say that God doesn't protect some against their own foolishness."

"God takes care of fools and children?"

He smiled. "Umhum. Both, in this case, from the looks of things."

I couldn't suppress a shiver as the knowledge of what could have happened swept over me again.

"Let's go. Tommy's on his way to jail. Now we'll see about rounding up the students."

Neal had left half his force on the road to watch the front of the compound in case there was an escape attempt.

The students were being herded out of the barracks, covering their heads, blinking, in the bright floodlights from the police cars as they were directed toward vans and buses. It was an eerie scene. Young men and women dressed in wrinkled khaki, shuffling out, in total silence. No protest. No questions.

I almost forgot to take the pictures that would accompany my story, and, more importantly, remind me forever of this time in my life. A time of leaving behind the past, of asking myself questions about a time when I might have been as pliable, as easily molded to someone else's image as these young persons had been.

And there was Neal. I'd never met a man who drew me more, but I had to be in New York in just hours. It would take some time to think through it all.

"They're all loaded up."

I forced my mind back to the present.

"What happens now?"

"We're taking them to jail, because there's nowhere else to take them, then we'll start calling parents, if they want us to. We'll want statements and that could take days."

"Michael?"

"He might be here, but I don't know. You can check when we get them into town."

It had taken an hour to load the two hundred students into the vehicles. By the time we followed the entourage back to town, it was one o'clock in the morning and I was exhausted. But before I returned to the hotel, I had to know that Michael was all right. I was afraid for him, especially if The Guardian had discovered he was no longer in control of the black case.

Forty-five minutes later, the students were crowded into cells, milling about and still looking lost and confused by what was happening to them.

"Want to look for him?"

"Yeah."

I began walking through the cell block with Neal, growing more fearful for Michael. I almost missed him in the crowded cell. He was standing in a corner, his head down.

"Michael?"

I called his name twice before he lifted his head and looked at me. He looked incredibly sad and frightened.

"I was worried about you."

He came to the bars.

"Are you all right?"

His knuckles whitened as he gripped the bars.

"What will they do to us?"

"The police just want to talk to you, Michael."

"What's going to happen to us?"

"After they talk with you, you can call your parents."

"I don't know—"

"Don't you want to see your parents?"

"I don't know. They don't know about me. When they do—"

"Michael, please don't be afraid. Everything's going to be all right. You just need to tell the sheriff the truth."

His eyes shifted to Neal who was standing a little way behind me.

"Neal, this is Michael. My friend."

Michael's glance returned to me as if he didn't quite believe I thought of him as a friend.

"You saved my life, Michael. I'll never forget that. It took a lot of courage. All you need is a little more."

"I don't know."

"I trust him, Michael. You can talk to him, just like you talked to me. He'll help you."

He stood with his forehead against the bars, his fingers working on them. There was a lot going on inside him—right versus wrong, logic and morality pitted against the indoctrination of The Glorious Church. I knew he'd have to work things out for himself, and understand everything that had happened to him, and the things he'd done. I hoped his parents would understand and just love him, if he called them.

"I'll give Neal my phone number back in New York. I'd like you to call me whenever you want to. Will you do that?"

He nodded, then stepped back from the bars.

Knowing I'd done everything I could for him at the moment, I walked Neal back to his office.

"You all right?"

"I don't know. I'm tired. I feel sad. I'm glad this is about over. But it feels unfinished. I know The Guardian killed Susan, but we still don't know who he is."

"Maybe we will after talking to these kids. Man, this is a mess."

"Maybe if I stayed and talked—"

"Go back to the motel, get some sleep. You're beat."

"I—"

"Maggie, let me take care of Michael. You can't do anything for him now."

He was right, but it was hard to admit.

"Okay."

I started to leave, but Neal's hand on my arm stopped me.

"You take it easy. Whoever this Guardian fella is, he'll

know you had something to do with this. He could be very unhappy."

"I'll be all right."

His knuckles brushed my cheek. "I'll see you later."

The sleepy desk clerk only looked up when I entered the hotel and then went back to his nap. I walked up the stairs, looking forward to a hot shower and bed, but as soon as I got inside my room, there was a knock at the door. I had the chain on and peeked out cautiously, telling myself I was being smart, not fearful.

Gary. I wished I could put off talking about what had happened during the last few hours. It was all too fresh and I wanted to sort it out for myself first. But I slid off the chain and opened the door.

"Come in, Gary."

"I was waiting for you. It's almost three o'clock. Where have you been?"

"You wouldn't believe me if I told you."

I collapsed on the bed and closed my eyes a moment.

"Something's happened."

"Yeah. A lot of things."

I filled him in briefly on what had happened, leaving out what I'd read in Sophia's journal. He sat, staring at me like I was crazy.

"That's incredible! You could have been killed!"

"A rather large understatement." I sat up. "But I wasn't. Now, I'm exhausted. I just want to take a hot shower and crawl into bed."

"Okay. But I want to hear more about this tomorrow."

"Okay, okay." I waved him out the door, almost too tired to get undressed.

After a few minutes, I managed to get to the bathroom, turn on the shower, and strip off my grimy clothes. The hot water felt wonderful; it was so wonderful I almost fell asleep under the spray.

Leaving my hair damp, I pulled on a t-shirt and fell into

bed. But once there, my mind was whirling so fast I couldn't fall asleep.

So, we knew, or almost knew, that The Guardian administered the poison to Susan. That means she knew him. Evidence at the apartment indicated she'd let her killer in, and had drunk something that had the poison in it, so that meant they had at least a short social conversation. Or, was she intimidated enough by The Guardian to drink the poison because he told her to? She was, after all, The Chosen One and had already been punished for refusing her 'calling'. Perhaps that training was strong enough to make her drink the poison. It had worked for Jim Jones in Guyana. It had worked for that group in California. They'd bought expensive new sneakers and then laid down and died.

I rolled over. Who was The Guardian? Could it have been Tommy? He was controlled by Sophia, but somehow I didn't think he was the executioner. From the things Michael had said, I believed that he didn't know the identity of his master. That left a whole list of possibilities, and a lot I couldn't even put a name to. Almost anyone connected with the church could have been placed in the role. Too little was known about the inner workings of the group, and with Sophia gone, there was a lot that would never be known.

It all went round and round in my head, but there were no conclusions. I finally fell asleep, knowing I'd have to wait until Neal interrogated all the students, especially Michael, before anyone could begin sorting things out.

I didn't know how long I'd been asleep when I awoke with the sense that someone was in the room. My heart pounding, I made my muscles relax and tuned my ears to any sound of movement. I opened my eyes just a little and almost gave myself away. A shadow was moving toward the bed.

Galvanized into action, I rolled off the bed just as the figure lunged. Screaming as I hit the floor, I rolled again as the door exploded open and light flooded the room.

"Hold it!"

I'd never been so glad about anything as I was to hear Neal's voice at that moment.

I rolled to my knees and looked over the edge of the mattress. A long knife had ripped open my pillow and now lay in the middle of the bed. Feathers filtered across the bed and onto the floor. It had been so close I swayed momentarily.

Neal pulled me to my feet.

"You okay?"

"Um, yeah. Fine."

But when I saw the man Neal's deputies were handcuffing, I found myself wavering again.

Just then Gary burst into the room. He wore blue pajamas and his perfect hair was standing on end.

"Maggie?"

I glanced at Neal.

"What's going on!" Then he saw the prisoner. "Dad?"

Dr. Edward Brady was being escorted from the room, a burly deputy on each side of him.

"Dad? Wait a minute! Dad!"

When Gary turned to go after the deputies and his father, Neal caught his arm. "You Gary Brady?"

"Yes." His gaze shifted to me. "Maggie? What's happening here? Where—"

"Mr. Brady, your father is being read his rights. I'd get him a good attorney if I were you."

"Attorney?"

He seemed dazed. He wasn't a good enough actor to fake it. Any thoughts I might have had about Gary being involved in The Glorious Church and a part of the whole mess were totally wiped away in that moment.

"Your father is The Guardian."

"The Guardian? No, that's—Maggie?"

"I'm sorry, Gary."

He sank into a chair and buried his face in his hands.

"I don't believe it. He couldn't—"

Neal carefully slid the knife into a plastic evidence bag. "I'll let you handle this, if you're all right."

"I'm fine, Neal. Thanks. Say, how did you know—"

"Michael. I talked to him right after you left. He didn't know who The Guardian was, but he told me everything he could."

"When he handed me the case, he told me The Guardian was coming to the mansion."

"Yeah, and after you got away, I thought maybe they'd try to finish the job."

Some people I meet on a job are just important to the job. When it's finished you don't think of them any more. But Neal was one of those that you never forget. My granny used to call some people 'salt of the earth'. When I was little I didn't know what that meant. But I'd never been more aware of how people like Neal flavored life with their strength and quiet competence. Like salt, they are unobtrusive and seemingly unessential. But without them, there's a lot missing when you taste life.

"I'm glad you were here."

"Does this finish it for you?"

"Yeah, I think it does. I got my story. I know Susan didn't commit suicide."

"When are you leaving?"

"My boss says tomor—today."

He stood with one hand on the door jam, looking at the floor, then drew a deep breath and let it out slowly.

"Stop by before you leave town."

There should be more to say, but I couldn't think of the words.

"I will. And thanks again."

With a salute he closed the door behind him, leaving me and Gary alone. I folded onto the floor beside his chair.

"I wish I knew what to say."

"I don't understand. It's got to be some mistake."

"It's a very long story. Maybe you should—"

His face was haggard. "I have to know."

I understood that. I told him what I'd found in the diary and what Michael had told me.

"When your mother said they'd left The Glorious Church, she was telling the truth. As she knew it. You know how uninvolved your parents are with one another. Apparently, your father stayed with the church, grew with it. He proved his worth to Sophia. He grew to be trusted enough to be given the responsibility to raise Sophia's daughter.

"Sophia told me she was too involved with the church to raise a child, but she had terminal cancer. Sophia was an opportunist, but she was a realist, too. No matter how many times she was 'healed', she had to make sure the church continued. Someone had to be trained to take her place. What better person than her own daughter? That child was entrusted to Edward and Pauline, without your mother being aware of who Susan was."

"But how did he get involved in this? It's incredible—"

"The Glorious Church uses brainwashing, Gary. In order to make sure no one was allowed to make the church vulnerable, so their own standing was kept safe, Sophia developed this position of The Guardian to use as a control tool. The Guardian's identity was kept secret, and he became a sinister figure. Over the years, through Sophia's direction as The Guardian, Edward's purpose was to eliminate threats to the cult's activities."

"But he had nothing to do with Susan—"

"I'm afraid he did. He authorized the attack on Susan eighteen months ago as a stern warning. She had decided not to follow through on her calling. I don't know whether the attacks on the other girls or the other murders had any connection at all with what happened to Susan, but when she was kidnapped, she knew exactly why and who."

"My God," Gary breathed as he began to absorb the enormity of what his father had done.

"I can't imagine how she must have felt. Still, she had courage. Even after being trained in the doctrines of the church, she decided she didn't want it. I don't know what happened between Sophia and Edward; whether she threatened him, or if he did it willingly, but he followed his own 'calling' and murdered Susan, the child he'd raised as his own."

"Oh, God," Gary breathed. "Mother—"

He stood, uncertainly, seeming not to know what to do next.

"You'll need to help her."

"Yeah, yeah. I'd better go out there—"

He shuffled toward the door in a daze. "What are you going to do?"

"I'll be leaving in the morning. First flight. Anything you'd like me to do for you?"

"No, uh, I'll call the store. Get somebody to fill in. I'll have to check with Mother about an attorney for . . . for him. God, Maggie. How could he—?"

"We may never know, Gary. Many of us get caught up in things bigger than we are. Maybe that's what happened to him. Maybe he couldn't get out."

"Yeah. Maybe."

He finally went to his room and I closed the door. I didn't believe a word of what I'd said, but I didn't see any point in being cruel. We both had a lot of sorting through to do.

Chapter Fifteen

I hadn't gone by the sheriff's office that morning. I didn't want to see Neal. Those few moments in his office the night before had left me unsettled in more ways than I wanted to think about.

As I reached the door of the plane later that morning, I stopped and looked back for a moment. Most of the snow was gone, leaving small dirty piles in corners. Bare trees blended with the rough mountain landscape, dotted with clumps of gray-green cedars.

The sky was growing gray and heavy. It might snow again before night. Fresh white flakes would cover the slush and grit, the piles of dirty snow left from the pollution of every-day living, the residue of people tramping along oblivious of the trail of dirty footprints they were leaving behind.

The air was still biting cold, and would be until March when the thaw brought rain to wash everything clean. Clean. How long would it be before I felt entirely 'clean' again?

We'd been in Fayetteville for less than two weeks and it seemed almost a lifetime. For Gary it had been. He'd lost a sister, a fake history he'd thought was truth. Now he had to comfort his mother and try to cope with the repercussions of his father's treachery. I felt sad. For Susan. For the pain and unhappiness she must have suffered. And for Gary. Everything he'd believed in, his very foundations, were shattered. I wondered if anything would ever be right again for him and his mother.

The plane took off with a roar. I settled into the seat and stared out the window. After a sleepless night I'd phoned Ben and filled him in on everything that had happened. The story would work great, but I'd be leaving out some of it. I owed that much to Gary.

I'd spoken to him briefly this morning. He was pale, his eyes shadowed, shoulders slumped. He seemed to be functioning automatically. Pauline, he said, was devastated, still unbelieving.

He'd phoned an attorney in L.A. who was flying in to see what he could do. Dr. Brady was refusing to cooperate. There was a twenty-four hour guard at the door in case of any suicide attempts.

I still had difficulty comprehending that the man who had been my father-in-law had become so enmeshed in anything so sinister. Almost as unfathomable as Gary's unawareness of what his father had been involved in, and Pauline's insulation, was my own. I considered my self an 'aware' person. How could I have been that close and not been aware that something was wrong?

Then there was the guilt. Susan had been a victim of something so malignant it was incomprehensible, and I had been blind. I, who considered myself rather sensitive to things, had been totally unperceptive. When I'd known her, Susan had to have been searching already. Maybe if I'd been more open, more approachable—I should have seen something, anything. That was something with which I would have to come to terms.

But what about Edward Brady? Had he been searching for something, or had he, too, been caught up in something he couldn't control? What made anyone so ready to believe in something as bizarre as their doctrines? Why do we believe such abject lies in our search for the truth? Was Sophia right? Did our children ask for simple things like love and comfort, and we instead gave them the stone fish of 'things' so we could go in search of our own comforts?

I closed my eyes wearily. When I'd left Gary, I'd told him to come see me in New York before he went home to L.A. I wanted to satisfy myself that he would be all right.

If there had been anything good that came out of this trip, it was that the leftover emotion from the marriage, and divorce, had been resolved. I was no longer hiding from what I had considered a failure.

We'd both made mistakes. Now we could be friends. I felt good about that. And I'd done what I set out to do. I'd found out what happened to Susan. Maybe one day I'd feel good about that too.

Ben met me at the airport. I was surprised but glad he'd made the effort. I needed his sanity right now.

He put his arm around me. "Connie sent you a message."

"Dare I ask?"

"Here."

I took the folded papers.

"Expense reports?"

"By nine o'clock, he said, or the credit card is cut off."

I laughed. I would be okay. One day.

The weeks passed and I was busy in the office getting my story put together, sorting pictures, getting new short-term assignments. I didn't like being in the office for so long, but somehow things weren't working out for me to go on another long assignment. Ben seemed to be making sure I was all right about Susan's death, The Glorious Church and all it meant before sending me out again. Part of me was warmed by his concern, but another part was growing impatient. I needed to work, needed to fill the hours.

It was nearly eight-thirty before I left the office. I was tired, sick of paperwork, and wanting to get out of town again for a while. I'd lain awake too many nights asking myself questions that had no answers. Did I want to be with Front Page for the next ten years? Did I want to live out of suitcases and in musty motel rooms? That was what I knew, what had built my career, and if I didn't want that, what did I want?

No sleep, no answers. I was grouchy. Even Mrs. P was losing patience with me. She'd quit watering my plants for a week and they'd dropped leaves until I apologized. I needed to make some decisions. Soon.

I rounded the corner and smacked against a stranger. Automatically grabbing hold of him I stepped back, an apology on my lips when I looked up to see blue-gray eyes that crinkled at the corners and a wide mouth that I remembered so well.

"What are you doing here?"

"You didn't come by the office before you left."

I hadn't even called like I'd told myself I would.

"I had some thinking to do."

He studied me for a long moment.

"Brady stayed with his mother."

"He should have."

"You're all right with that?"

"I told him he needed to stay."

Neal drew me aside as another couple from the magazine passed.

"What are you doing here?"

He grinned that slow way of his. "Came up to see . . . Charlie."

"Yeah?"

"Umhum."

"Thinking of moving back to the big city?"

"Nope."

He wore jeans washed nearly white, a blue shirt with a bomber jacket over it, and his cowboy boots. And there was that scent I'd never forget. I breathed it in, making a new memory.

"I thought I'd see if this New York magazine journalist might be missing me as much as I'm missing her."

Something in me turned over. "Yeah," I managed. "She is."

Only then did I know it was the truth.

"And to tell you that Frank's got the Armen Reporter for sale. Know anybody who might be interested in owning a weekly rag?"

I laughed, a tension loosening in me that I hadn't realized was wound so tight. I rose on my tiptoes to kiss him. "Yeah, I just might."

His arm slid around my shoulders and we linked hands. "Let's talk about it over dinner, then see what happens."

"Oh, yeah, slow and easy."

"It's the best way," he said softly. "The very best way."